SILENCER

David Bishop

First published in 1994 by
Virgin Books
an imprint of Virgin Publishing Ltd
332 Ladbroke Grove
London W10 5AH

Typeset by CentraCet Ltd, Cambridge
Printed and bound by
Cox & Wyman Ltd, Reading, Berks

ISBN 0 352 32960 2

ACKNOWLEDGEMENTS

Like all the Judge Dredd novels, this story owes a great deal to the Judge Dredd comic strips published in the fortnightly *Judge Dredd Megazine* and its weekly parent title, *2000AD*. Without the writers, artists and editors who have contributed to the Dredd mythos, *Silencer* could never have been written. Special thanks go to: Carlos Ezquerra, Mark Harrison, John Freeman, Adrian Salmon, Chris Standley, Trevor Hairsine, Gordon Rennie, Frank Quitely, Peter Doherty, and – most of all – John Wagner.

For Rebecca, Andy and Peter,
who put up with many of the insecurities,
indecisions, and insanities;

For Steve,
who gave valuable and much needed
endorsement, enhancement and
encouragement;

But most of all for Alison,
who married me. Kia kaha!

PROLOGUE

Facial Alteration: So-called 'face change' technology has been widely available for more than 30 years, having evolved from old plastic surgery techniques. Any citizen with enough creds is able to go into a New You clinic and have their entire facial appearance altered to whatever they desire – assuming it's legal, of course.

When the technology was released to the public, fugitives used face-change machines to alter their looks and escape detection, some even having their fingerprints replaced with a new set. Now all New You clinics are required to cross-check their clients against a Department database for wanted felons. So perps began stealing face-change technology and altering their looks in private.

To close this loophole, the Department began recording the voice patterns of all perps for recognition purposes. This has proved highly effective. Few criminals were willing to have artificial voice-boxes fitted (and then replaced whenever they committed a new crime) to avoid detection by the Judges.

Extract from *Mega-City One Medical Dictionary*
J. Campion (editor)

'Scream again and I'll redecorate your ceiling with an exciting new paint colour – it's called your brains!'

The female fugitive held the Lawgiver against Nita Grant's head and tightened her trigger finger for emphasis. The New You beauty consultant clamped her mouth shut, her eyes bloodshot from crying, make-up streaked down her cheeks. Nita had been the last staff member left in the clinic after closing, doing some preparations for the

1

next day. She was just about to leave when the intruder burst in and began threatening her.

'Now, let's try again shall we?' asked the kidnapper patronisingly. 'I want you to give me a new face, but I don't want it showing up on the Justice Department computers. Can you do that, or shall I go ahead with my interior redecorating plan?'

Nita managed to nod, but it was barely perceptible with her body shaking so much from the fear and sobbing.

'Sorry, was that a yes or no?'

'Y-yes. I-I can disengage the cross-check,' stammered Nita.

'Good, I'm glad to hear it.'

'B-but the Judges will still register the face change taking place. When they realise it hasn't been officially sanctioned, they'll send someone to investigate,' explained Nita.

'That's all right,' smiled the fugitive, nudging the beauty consultant with her weapon. 'I'll be long gone and you won't tell them about me, will you? It would be very hazardous to your health . . .'

'N-no, I won't tell them anything.'

'Very good. Let's get started, shall we?' The fugitive lowered her gun and let Nita turn round to examine her face. It was covered in blood-soaked bandages, mostly centred on the nose.

'W-what happened?'

'Let's just say I had a little accident. I had something removed from my face and the operation was not a total success,' explained her captor.

'Y-you'll need to be unconscious for part of the operation, it can be quite painful – ' Nita tried to explain.

'What! Do you think I'm a fool?' The intruder jammed her weapon up Nita's nose. 'Knock me out so you can call the Judges? Perhaps I should be the one giving you the face change. How would you like to look like this?' she demanded and pulled off her bandages to reveal a bloody, horrific mess.

'N-no!' Nita cried out.

'Then get the machines warmed up. It's time to play Operation!' The intruder stepped back, allowing Nita access to the controls for the face change equipment.

As the beauty consultant began restarting all the systems, the intruder took a moment to glance around the room for security systems and possible points of entry. This was the consultancy area, where potential patients came to find out about the procedures involved in face change operations. A large, open chamber, it was gleamingly clean with the faintest hint of peach to the white walls, chairs and tables, giving what could easily be a forbidding place a friendly, warm aspect.

There were two doorways, one at each end of the room, and windows set into one wall, opening out onto the small skedway outside. The intruder could not see any obvious security scanners recording her image. No matter! Soon she would have a new face and then the Judges would never send her back to that hellhole in space.

Nita noticed her captor's attention was elsewhere and fumbled around with the equipment, taking as long as possible to get it started up. When her captor had first burst in, just a few moments before, Nita had just been setting the alarm system. With any luck, the intruder's sudden entrance had triggered it. Right now, a silent alarm should be alerting the Judges at the local sector house to the intruder's presence. If Nita could keep the fugitive here long enough, the Judges should arrive and save her – if she was still alive then . . .

Laverne Castillo stepped out of the cascading hot water and stood on the white tiled floor of the shower room, steam rising slowly from her trim, taut body as she towelled away the excess water. Next she walked through an Insti-Dry™ cabinet, warm jets of sterilised air blowing away any last, lingering droplets before striding into the locker room. None of the men in the room flinched, or grew embarrassed or leered at her, despite her nakedness and the well-filled curves of her young body. In fact, they completely ignored her as she strolled past them, utterly naked.

This was a Judges' locker room and all such areas were unisex for enhanced efficiency. Judges had no time for lust or love or sex, they only had time for the Law. In Mega-City One, where every one of the 400 million citizens in the sprawling futropolis was a potential criminal, the men and women in that locker room were part of an elite police force empowered with the role of dispensing instant justice – judge, jury and executioner in one, if need be. The Law came first, their sexual and emotional urges were never even a consideration for any good Judge.

Castillo pulled open her locker to reveal a fresh uniform, gleaming darkly inside. First she pulled on her u-front panties and a bra: sturdy standard issue Justice Department garments made of hard-wearing but comfortable synthetic stretch fabric. Silk, satin, lace – no such niceties had any place in the garb of a street Judge.

Next on was the body suit, a kevlar-reinforced blue-black garment encompassing leggings, a reinforced crotch and posterior (for riding motorcycles for hours on end), full body and sleeves. This had a full-length fastening running up the centre from the bottom of the crotch to the neck, which Castillo drew up over her breasts.

Then the waistbelt, a tough green leathereen utility belt ringed with pouches, each containing spare clips of ammunition, frag grenades, fuse wiring, lumps of hi-ex and remote control detonators, as well as sundry other useful devices, like the hand-held Birdie lie detector. Not one hundred per cent accurate in any circumstances, but immensely useful as a back-up indicator of a perp's guilt – or so the tutors at the Academy of Law had said. Indeed, not so much said as shouted, drumming the lessons into Castillo when she had been a cadet there, only a few weeks before. The young woman had spent 15 years there, training for this moment, this day – her first day out on patrol as a full Street Judge.

4

She shook herself out of her reverie and concentrated on her preparations. The utility belt was held together at the centre with a heavy metal buckle, cut in the stylised shape of an eagle – the symbol of the Justice Department, which controlled the Judges and, through them, the whole city. Incorporated in the centre of the buckle were the red, white and blue stars and stripes of the old flag of the United States of America. The USA had existed for nearly 300 years before the Atomic War of 2070, but the Judges had chosen to keep the stars and stripes motif as a reminder of their heritage of Justice for All.

Next Castillo slipped on her moulded rubbereen kneepads, an essential item for all motorcycle riders, yet one that had passed into common usage by nearly all Judges, and indeed many citizens. In fact, kneepads had recently become a designer item, some even impregnated with scents and bizarrely surreal colour schemes. There was nothing surreal about Castillo's kneepads, she reflected ruefully, just standard issue Department green. The Department favoured uniformity: it enhanced conformity and authority.

Boots next, with thick, inch-high airsole heels to give the wearer an extra inch of height from which to tower over perps, while still keeping Judges fleet of foot. Green again, to match most of the ancilliary items on the uniform.

Shoulder pads, gold of colour, a standard design for the left shoulder, a specially moulded eagle for the right, the head of the eagle jutting out at right angles from the shoulder. Then green elbow pads and gauntlets, the latter of reinforced kevlar again, but with a special webbing on the palms to enable better gripping. Also, the webbing meant the Judge's personal heat 'signature' could be read by the special device built into the handle of their Lawgiver pistol.

Next, the chain and badge of office. Castillo smiled, remembering her graduation from the Academy. She'd been so nervous, she had dropped the badge when the senior Judge presiding over the event had handed it to her. Throughout her years at the Academy, she had worn a simple cadet's badge, like all the others. Then, on the day of her Rookie test, she had been given a half-eagle badge to wear.

Now, Castillo ran her fingers over the six-sided badge with the ever present eagle symbol etched into its face just above her name. She attached it to the special clip on the left breast of her uniform, links of gold chain connecting it to her body suit fastener.

Finally, the helmet, blue-black with vibrant red trim and a polarised one-way mirrored surface for her to see through while disguising her own eyes. A respirator was moulded into the crown of the rounded helmet, ready to be pulled down over the nose and mouth in moments if necessary. Castillo slipped the helmet on and it instantly adjusted to fit the contours of her head, moulding snugly but firmly around her skull and black, curly hair.

The new Judge stood before a mirror, making sure everything was in its place. Finally, she looked up at herself and was genuinely surprised. She looked like a Judge! Somehow, after all those years of hard work and struggle and pain, she had done it. Her achievement didn't seem real yet. Sure, she had passed all the tests, met all the standards required of her. But now it was time for the real thing. Now she had to prove herself on the streets.

A guantleted hand clasped her on the shoulder pad.

'When you've finished admiring yourself,' chided Judge Nyman gently, 'we got a sector to patrol.'

Castillo snapped to attention. 'Yes, sir!'

'One person dies every twenty-seven minutes in Mega-City One, according to startling new statistics. It's midnight and you're watching tri-D 23, I'm Chip Blake – '

'And I'm Candy O'Hara. Welcome to our first bulletin of this bright new day, Mega-City One! It's time to wake up and smell the synthi-caff.' Across the city the beaming

6

faces of the two news presenters smiled out from three-dimensional television sets, bringing massive grins and newsbites galore to insomniac citizens.

'That's right, Candy! Top of the hour news, views and reviews. Our lead story – startling new statistics have just been released by the Justice Department's media liaison office. They show that crime is down in nearly all the city's 300-plus sectors, with rapes and sexual offences cut by a tenth following the threat of a new shoot-to-castrate policy being mooted by Chief Judge McGruder.' Chip smiled authoratively as file footage was projected behind him.

The leader of the Judges, a grizzled looking woman in her fifties with hard, flinty eyes and a line of white stubble about her chin, burst into life: 'Hell, if the creeps don't stop themselves, we'll have to order our Judges to shoot the cajoolies off them! That oughta persuade them.' She crunched her hands together on screen as an illustration of what effect the new policy could have on potential felons.

'Thanks Chip,' laughed Candy, stealing back the limelight from her co-host. 'Also in the news this morning . . .'

'Item! Intruder alarm at New You face change clinic in Sector 44, corner of Rogers and Astaire!'

'Nyman to Control! Castillo and I'll take it!'

'Roj that, Nyman.'

Judge Neil Nyman gunned the engine of his Lawmaster motorcycle and pulled away from the side of the skedway and into the flow of night-time traffic, followed closely by his new partner, Laverne Castillo. They had been thrown together just a few hours before and were still learning each other's ways. Nyman looked over at his new partner.

She was fresh out of the Academy, a real greenie, and still a little nervous on the streets. In the little time they'd been together she'd seemed competent enough, but fractionally hesitant about getting into the real rough and tumble of enforcing the Law on the skeds. In a place like Mega-City One, you had to be tougher than that to survive.

Now they were about to go into their first real combat situation, and there was just a flicker of doubt at the back of Nyman's mind about his new partner. He dismissed it completely, knowing any such doubts could be fatal for one or both of them. Nyman activated his helmet-com to speak to his partner.

'Castillo, you ready for some real action?'

'About time I saw some!' she replied.

Nyman smiled. She was going to be okay.

Nita pushed another control. 'How about this one? It's called the Pretty Woman. As you can see it's got a slightly wider jawline but the structuring of the nose and its size in proportion to the rest of the face is just perfect.' Nita was enjoying this, despite herself. She always got a kick out of going through the face charts with a customer and helping them select their new visage. It was like a vocation to her, a special calling.

Ever since she'd been a little girl, she knew she wanted to help people. Since starting at the clinic two years ago, she knew this was what she had always been destined to do – make people happy by giving them new faces. She'd learnt a lot in those two years; customer management and coping with stress were among the special skills she'd acquired. Now Nita was finding those skills especially useful, as her current 'customer' had a gun pointed at her. The beauty consultant flipped on to another face. 'Now this one is the Divorced Diana, it's very popular. It's got – '

'Cut the crud, just pick a face and let's get on with it! I ain't got all night to sit here listening to the sound of your voice,' grunted the intruder grumpily.

'No, sorry, of course you haven't,' Nita said soothingly. 'I think we'll go with the Divorced Diana, that should suit you nicely.' She activated the controls and the previous face reappeared on the three-dimensional projector with two words superimposed over it: *confirm choice?* 'Yes, definitely that one. Now, what colour hair do you think you would like?'

By now the intruder was getting suspicious. 'What's happening here? You stalling for time?'

'No! No, I'm not,' gasped Nita, just a little too quickly for comfort. The fugitive swung the weapon into the beauty consultant's face and shoved it into her open mouth.

'Somehow, I just don't believe you. All this looking at face charts and selecting the proper features – you've just been dragging things out until the Judges arrive. Well, when they get here, they're going to have a little mess to clean up – you!'

Then came chaos.

Nyman and Castillo rode through the night city at speed towards the crimescene. Around them towered hundreds of citi-blocks, hundred-storey-high buildings housing between ten and sixty thousand citizens.

Each block contained everything a person needed from birth to death: maternity services, schools, artifical parks, beaches, holiday resorts, entertainment and shopping centres, smokatoria if they suffered from nicotine addiction, funeral parlours. Many citizens never left their block in their entire lifetime, never once set foot outside the door. Of course, this built up incredible loyalty that sometimes led to conflict between buildings, better known as block war.

The two Judges drove down a quiet skedway and stopped just short of the clinic, letting their engines quieten as they rolled towards the building. 'If there is an intruder, no point letting them know we're coming,' explained Nyman.

'Standard procedure at the Academy,' replied Castillo dryly. The pair drew their Lawgiver pistols and began to advance towards the building. Nyman reached a window first and looked inside to see two women seated in the centre of a room. One had a face covered in blood, the other had a gun in her mouth – a Lawgiver. He turned to speak to Castillo behind him.

'We've got a hostage situation in the front consultancy area of the clinic. One perp, one hostage. The perp's got a Lawgiver in the hostage's mouth, has probably bluffed her way in there, trying to get her face changed without her identity being checked against the Department monitoring system,' he explained.

'The hostage obviously doesn't know that perps can't fire a stolen Lawgiver,' suggested Castillo, and Nyman nodded his agreement. To prevent Judges' guns being stolen and used against them, every Judge had his palm print heat signature set into his Lawgiver by the Quarter-Master when the weapon was issued from the Armoury. If anyone else tried to use it, the bullets in the cartridge of the weapon would explode, killing or disabling the user. This was common knowledge among seasoned perps, but not generally known by the citizens of Mega-City One.

'There's a door on the far side of the consultancy room that they're in,' noted Nyman. 'I want you to go round the other side of the building and get ready to come through that door in two minutes.'

'That's a Roj,' replied Castillo and scurried away to take up her position. Nyman checked his own weapon was locked and loaded before moving to the doorway, awaiting a helmet-com signal from Castillo that she was in position. When that came, he gave her a short countdown for them to burst in.

'On my mark – three, two, one . . .'

Suddenly doors on either side of the consultancy room burst open and a Judge stepped through each, both covering the fugitive with their guns.

'Freeze, creep!' shouted Nyman.

'Make me,' spat back the fugitive and pulled the trigger

10

on her weapon. Nita Grant's head exploded backwards over the tri-D screen behind her, blood and brains dripping down the face of Divorced Diana. The intruder kept firing, now aiming at Nyman while she used Nita's body as a shield. One round clipped him in the arm, another blew through his chest and out of his spinal column, disabling him instantly.

The fugitive swung round to cover the other Judge, but she was just standing there, frozen to the spot. The killer laughed and ran out the other door, past Nyman's convulsing body.

Castillo remained motionless for another few seconds before Nyman's cries for help brought her back to reality. She ran across the room while yelling into her helmet-com.

'Castillo to Control – Judge down! I repeat, Judge down, at the New You face change clinic in Sector 44, corner of Rogers and Astaire!'

'Roj that! Back-up and med-wagons on their way!'

Castillo crouched beside Nyman, who was coughing up blood. She pulled off a gauntlet and pressed it against his chest wound, trying to staunch the bleeding. 'Nyman, I'm sorry.'

'The Lawgiver – it didn't explode . . .?' coughed Nyman.

'I know. I saw the perp blow that woman's head off and I – I just froze . . .' muttered Castillo, shaking her head in shame and disbelief.

'The perp?'

Castillo looked at the floor. 'She got away.'

Twelve hours later, Castillo was forced to repeat the details of what happened yet again. By now she had replayed the events over and over in her mind so many times, she was beginning to believe she would never think of anything else.

'So you simply froze – no explanation, no reason why?' asked the sector chief for 44, Judge Blayne. Castillo nodded, not looking up, trying not to catch his eye. Instead he turned to a woman with flame-red hair standing in the corner. 'Karyn – any explanations you can offer?'

The Psi Judge stepped forward to offer her report. 'I've given Castillo a full Psi-probe, but it's revealed no abnormalities or aberrations, no reasons why she should have frozen.'

Blayne turned back to Castillo. 'So you just chickened out, is that it, Castillo? You saw some blood flying around and it was too much for your delicate sensitivities? Is that it, Castillo?'

'No,' she muttered.

'I said *is that it, Castillo*?!'

'*I said no!*' she shouted back, now looking up at him, eyes blazing, angry tears running down her cheeks. 'I just – froze.'

Blayne shook his head in disgust. 'Sweet Jovus, with the kids they're sending us from the Academy these days, it's a wonder we catch any perps at all! All right, Karyn, dismissed.'

The Psi Judge nodded and left the room, leaving Castillo to face her sector chief's wrath alone. Blayne got out of his chair and walked around his desk to stand next to Castillo.

'You know what, Castillo? I'm kicking you out of my sector house. If you're going to choke every time you see a little bit of action, you're just going to get more good Judges killed. Well, we don't want chokers here in Sector 44 – you got that?'

Castillo nodded sullenly.

'And you can wipe that look off your face: nobody's going to feel sorry for you here. So pack your bags and get back to Justice Central – maybe they can find you a nice, safe desk job where you can't hurt anybody else. Now get out of my sight – I never want to see you in my sector again!'

* * *

12

Castillo strode into the locker room and kicked the ever-living stomm out of her locker. Finally, by the time the door had fallen off and she'd had enough, she slumped down on a bench and had a bloody good cry.

'I know how you feel,' ventured a quiet voice behind her.

Castillo whirled round to see who had spoken. Psi Judge Karyn stepped out of the shadows and approached her, but this just infuriated Castillo further.

'Just drokk off, okay? Look, you're a Psi Judge, that means you can read my mind – so what. It doesn't help me one little bit. Can you turn back the clock? Can you give Nyman back his left lung? Can you save that woman's life, that woman whose head I saw splattered – ' Castillo burst into tears again and sunk her head in her hands. When the sobbing had subsided, Karyn spoke again.

'Look, you screwed up. Everybody screws up.'

'Not on their first day.'

'You were just unlucky. It could happen to any of us,' persisted Karyn. 'But you've got to get over it, otherwise you'll never become all that you can be. And you can be a Judge, a damn good one, if you're willing to try. But it won't be easy.'

'What? You can see the future as well as read minds?'

Karyn smiled. 'Actually, my telepathy isn't that good. My special talent is precognition – so, yes, I can see the future a little. And I can see a little of your future – it won't be easy, but if you survive the next few months, you'll make it.'

Castillo looked at her, not sure if she could believe this stranger or the hope being held out to her. 'Really?'

'Really. Look, I've got to go,' said Karyn. 'But here's an idea. Why don't you keep a journal? It's a great way to sort out your thoughts, analyse what's going on around you and inside you. It helps a lot.'

Castillo nodded, but the Psi Judge had already gone.

* * *

13

Neil Nyman opened his eyes and smiled at his visitor. 'Hey, Castillo, how are you doing?'

'Not very well. I'm getting an official reprimand on my permanent record, they're putting me on to guard duties and Blayne's booted me out of the sector house. I'm going to be assigned at Justice Central from now on,' she replied wearily. 'I just came to say goodbye. How're you doing?'

'Not too bad. I've got one of those new artificial lungs Med-Division has been developing and a complete change of blood. It's great, you should try it!' He smiled, before regret got the better of him. 'Of course they'll never let me back on the streets . . .'

'I'm sorry, Nyman, I'm so sorry. I just saw that woman's head explode and I froze – '

'Look, Castillo, stop torturing yourself. If you keep going over this again and again in your head, you'll just make matters worse. You've got to put what happened aside and start again,' urged Nyman.

'I know. I know you're right, but it isn't easy.'

Nyman nodded in agreement. 'Look, if it's any comfort, I'm as much to blame for what happened as you. I assumed the Lawgiver wouldn't fire, and assuming anything on the skeds is usually fatal.' He looked down at his wounds. 'I'm just lucky I got away with my life.'

'I've been thinking about that,' mused Castillo. 'Either the perp was actually an undercover Judge – '

'Impossible! She broke every rule in the book. You might have to act like a psycho to fit in with the "ordinary" people in this crazy city, but even the Judges in the Wally Squad aren't that crazy!'

'Guess not. Or else perps have found some way to disengage the heat signature recognition device in Lawgivers.'

'That would be pretty worrying,' agreed Nyman. 'But there's a third possibility: the Lawgiver was stolen from a Justice Department Armoury before it had a specific heat signature imprinted on it.'

14

'I thought of that too, but nobody wants to hear my theories about it. I'm not exactly flavour of the month with the Department. Anyway, thanks, Nyman.' Castillo managed a half smile. 'Look, I've got to go, otherwise I'll be late for my next assignment.'

'Bye Castillo. See you on the streets.'

ONE

Random Physical Abuse

Random Physical Abuse Test: An SJS procedure designed to prevent corruption within Justice Department ranks by virtually any means necessary. Only those without flaw or guilt can pass this rigorous and sometimes fatal interrogation.

Extract from *Justice and How it Works for You*
by Judge O'Neill, 2112AD

'If you're gonna kill me, get it over with, punks!' spat the prisoner through broken teeth, blood bubbling from his lips and dribbling down his chin, dripping onto his scar-covered chest. He was naked, strapped onto a heavy wooden chair, restraints at his neck, wrists and ankles.

'Getting impatient, are we?' smiled his captor. White teeth glistened in the darkness outside the circle of light bathing the torture chair. 'Don't worry, we're in no rush. We've got methods that can keep you in exquisite pain, just on the edge of death for days, drugs that will make this agony seem like pure pleasure.' The gloating interrogator stepped forward into the light, his wet, red tongue played over thin lips, like a moist serpent. 'Now, let's start again, shall we?'

The smallest of gestures and thousands of volts were coursing through electrodes buried deep in the captive's flesh, the smell of roasting meat and sweat and fear filling the air like some pungent, perverse perfume. The prisoner screamed, his body buckling and thrashing about beneath the restraints. The agony seemed never ending, ever-increasing in its brutal intensity.

Another gesture and the shock treatment ceased, for the moment. The interrogator leaned forward, his face just inches from that of his captive, almost able to kiss, had they been lovers. But there was no love lost here, only hatred, cold and pure, burning in their eyes.

'Now, we have evidence linking you to corruption, perjury and falsifying evidence. Confess your guilt and we might grant you a quick, painless death, the dignity of an "accident". Otherwise . . .'

SJS Judge Eliphas smirked, flecks of saliva glinting in the harsh lights burning down in the centre of the interrogation chamber. His eyes played over the tortured features of his prey.

'Otherwise, I hope you enjoy pain, Dredd. You're going to be feeling a lot of it.' Eliphas turned and nodded at the darkness. A switch was thrown and the agony returned, bursting across the prisoner's chest like shrapnel fragments from a hi-ex grenade, cutting, slicing, indiscriminate.

Judge Joe Dredd screamed, trying to block out the pain, forcing himself to concentrate beyond it, instead remembering how this ordeal had begun . . .

Dredd had been sleeping at his conapt in Rowdy Yates Block. Normally most Judges got their minimum daily rest requirement on the Justice Department's sleep machines, but Dredd was on his day's leave for the fortnight, which must be spent at a Judge's private residence in a citi-block. The majority of Judges were required to maintain such a residence and each was allocated a specific block in which to 'live'. This fostered good relations with the community and, more importantly, helped keep the crime rate down in those blocks. Rowdy Yates had the lowest crime rate of any block in the city, a mark of the deep respect perps had for Dredd's prowess as a Judge.

At exactly 0300 hours the reinforced door of his conapt was blown open with hi-ex charges and half a dozen SJS Judges burst in. Dredd drew his Lawgiver in moments but had already recognised the invaders from their jet black uniforms emblazoned with the death's head motif of the Special Judicial Squad, the Judges who judge Judges. Surrounded and out-gunned, Dredd had no choice but to surrender.

'What the drokk is going on?' he demanded but was pistol-whipped into silence by one of the SJS stormtroopers.

'We ask the questions,' announced one of the invaders before directing the others to start a rough search of the spartan lodgings. Besides the hard bed, there were just a few shelves laden with heavy tomes about the Law, a reading chair, a wardrobe packed with spare uniforms and a separate bathroom. 'Like do you always sleep with your helmet on? And where do you spend the money?'

'What money?' asked Dredd and got another faceful of Lawgiver for his trouble.

'The money from your protection rackets. Don't deny it, we know you're just as rotten as your brother Rico was: it's in your blood, clone scum!' spat the SJS Judge. One of the searchers produced a wad of ten thousand creds from the bookshelf on Dredd's wall, sandwiched between volumes 27 and 28 of *The Law*, and handed it to the squad leader who threw it in Dredd's face, along with another pistol blow.

'Blood money. You disgust me! Well, what have you got to say?'

Dredd coughed blood before speaking, his mouth full of tooth fragments. 'That's a plant, and you know it. This is just a test. I'm guilty of nothing!'

A body blow this time, to the solar plexus, knocking the wind out of the captive Dredd.

'Lie detector says different, punk – you're under arrest!'

They snapped the cuffs on Mega-City One's finest Judge and pushed him outside, taking care to ensure him

the most pain possible in the process. When Dredd
resisted another shove in the back, he was brutally
clubbed to the ground by three of the SJS.

'Resisting arrest and assaulting a Judge – now we've
really got you,' taunted the leader, trying to goad Dredd
into a major transgression.

Once outside Rowdy Yates, the captive was bundled
into the back of a pat-wagon and the beatings began
again, each blow of a daystick accompanied by a litany of
questions and threats.

'Who's your accomplice? When did you set up the
racket? Tell us names, dates, payments? Why? Why?
Why?'

Finally, mercifully, unconsciousness fell upon Joe
Dredd, black, cold and uncomfortable, like the night
outside.

He had come round to find himself alone in a bare
black cell: no bed, no chair, no toilet, just brutally harsh
lighting and the eye of a security camera watching his
every move. His demands to know the allegations against
him, who was making the charges, or how long he would
be kept prisoner were ignored. Hours passed, perhaps
even days – time had no meaning in that place.

Dredd's body craved food, rest, relief, but he ignored
all this. Instead he stood in the centre of the cell and
stared at the camera, repeating a single phrase over and
over again like a mantra: 'Somebody's gonna pay for this,
somebody's gonna pay for this . . .'

Finally the cell door was flung open and four SJS Judges
burst in armed with daysticks, quickly clubbing Dredd
to the ground, beating any resistance out of him. He
was dragged along a dark corridor into a black-walled
interrogation chamber and thrown to the floor, his dripping blood forming a pool on the white tiles beneath him.
The four Judges took up guard duty, each stationed in a
corner of the chamber. Then a tall, thin figure strode out
of the shadows and stood over the prisoner.

'Joe Dredd,' announced the figure, reading from a

hand-held data unit. 'Cloned from the genetic material of the great Judge Fargo, the very first Chief Judge of Mega-City One. Born as a force-gestated five-year-old in the year 2066, along with your clone brother Rico, and immediately enrolled in the Academy of Law as a cadet.' The leader of the interrogation unit began to walk around Dredd in a slow circle, careful to remain silhouetted by the dazzling lights set in the ceiling, keeping his identity to himself for the moment.

'After some early difficulties with your training, you and your brother were Roll of Honour graduates in the class of 2079 and went on to the streets as full Judges. Later that same year you arrested your brother Rico for corruption, and he was subsequently sent to the Judicial penal colony on Titan for the mandatory 20-year sentence.' The interrogator halted his progress and crouched down to look at Dredd's battered, bloody face. The prisoner looked up and immediately recognised his captor.

'Eliphas,' spat Dredd, his voice full of hatred. They had clashed several times before, notably over a team of SJS death squads run by a deputy of Eliphas's. The deputy had killed himself before anything could be traced back to Eliphas, who had suffered no disciplinary action for his part in the incident.

'Even then, the fatal flaw in your blood stock was evident, but somehow ignored. Interesting,' mused Eliphas as he stroked his moustache and goatee beard for a moment. Then he stood up and resumed his circular pacing.

'Interesting, too, that two of the other Roll of Honour graduates for your year have since gone bad and been struck off the honour roll. I wonder why? Sidebar: initiate proceedings against other honour roll Judge for class of 2079,' he dictated into his data unit.

'She's dead.'

Eliphas looked down again. 'What?'

'She's dead,' repeated Dredd. 'Killed in the line of fire last year.'

'Really?' The interrogator nodded to one of his guards who came over and kicked Dredd in the stomach to silence him, before continuing with the recitation from Dredd's personal file.

'Since graduation you have given meritorious service against numerous threats and have turned down the chance to become Chief Judge several times, preferring to stay on the streets. In 2099 you murdered your brother Rico upon his return from Titan – '

Dredd tried to pull himself upright. 'It was self-defence!'

Eliphas sighed and nodded to his associates again. Another severe blow to Dredd's battered body.

'You must learn to stop interrupting, really. Now, where was I. Yes! You quit the Judges after failing the Rookie Kraken, who was drawn from the same genetic clone stock as yourself. Jealous, were we?'

Dredd looked up at his accuser, but didn't bother to answer. He knew he had to save his strength for the ordeal ahead.

'Never mind. You abandoned the city and took the Long Walk into the Cursed Earth, but only after releasing dozens of dangerous Democracy activists back into the community. Later you returned and were again commended for your part in defeating the Dark Judges and stopping Mega-City One becoming a City of the Dead, a Necropolis.

'But the Dark Judges were only able to seize control of Mega-City because of the evil intervention of Kraken, with whom you share the same clone father. Since then there has been evidence of pro-Democracy sympathies, clashes with authority and even an incident where you demanded the resignation of the Chief Judge!'

Dredd ignored the accusations, the gross distortions of the truth, keeping his own counsel.

'And as for the slanderous lies directed at me by

21

yourself and that bitch Judge Hershey . . .' concluded Eliphas, tutting gently. He turned to his SJS deputies. 'I shall close my eyes for the next sixty seconds. Do as much damage as you wish during that time, but leave him alive and able to talk.'

Dredd looked up at Eliphas as the four deputies attacked, and was able to see a smile play about his captor's lips before merciful darkness came again.

Extract from the private journal of Judge Laverne Castillo:

Today was probably the second worst day of my life.

I had received an official reprimand about what happened at the New You face-change clinic and been transferred to ancillary duties for the three months since. Now I was being sent to the Chief Judge to report for duty as her personal adjutant. I had heard rumours but nobody told me the truth – the most important person in Mega-City One is a crazy woman with a beard.

I arrived at the Grand Hall of Justice early, at 1200 hours, hoping to make a good impression. Looking back now, that seems laughable, but I did it anyway. After waiting around for nearly four hours, I was sent to the Chief Judge's private quarters. They were dark and depressing, perhaps a reflection of the state of her psyche. (Grud! I can't believe I just wrote that.) I found her reading a report about my failure. She seemed fearsome and angry, but also distracted by a fly that had gotten into her quarters.

She told me the report did not make pleasant reading. Madre Grud! She didn't need to tell me, I was the one who froze on duty. I was only the one who nearly got Nyman killed.

She told me I would have to buck my ideas up if I was going to be her adjutant. I thought she was going to question me about the incident at the clinic. Instead she spent all her time chasing a fly around her quarters. Then it landed on my shoulder pad and she began reaching for her Lawgiver pistol.

I tried to persuade her not to do anything but she shot at me. Fortunately, the bullet just took a chunk out of the pad and killed the fly, but a few inches out and she could have killed me instead.

Of course two Judges from her personal bodyguard burst in, looking to see where the shot had come from. Everybody surrounding the Chief Judge seems nervous, jittery after the recent assassination attempts. She bawled them out for being too late to save her if there had been another attempt on her life and sent them away again.

Then she turned round and told me I needed to smarten myself up. What was I doing reporting for duty with a damaged shoulder pad on my uniform? I tried to protest but she was already rambling about something else. Then she sent me to go find Judge Dredd with an urgent request for him to come and see her. By this stage I was just glad to get out of the same room as her. I know I could get court-martialled for writing this, even for thinking it, but it has to be said – the Chief Judge of Mega-City One is dangerously unbalanced!

After checking in with Control I discovered that Dredd had been taken in by the SJS for a random physical abuse test. I tried to explain this to the Chief Judge but she demanded I go and summon Dredd personally. So I requisitioned a Lawmaster from the Justice Department motor pool and drove over to the Murder House, as we used to call the SJS Headquarters at the Academy.

The torture had continued for hours. Dredd was stripped naked, his clothes torn to shreds in front of him in a deliberately futile check for evidence. A full body cavity search, harsh and humiliating; forced to swallow foul-smelling liquids to purge his system, inducing involuntary vomiting so the contents of his stomach could be analysed; deloused in an ice-cold shower, being kicked and beaten. And all the while questions, accusations, lies. All part of the softening up process.

Now the electric shock treatment. Dredd had conducted thousands of interrogations himself, but none as brutal as this. Worst of all, Eliphas was plainly enjoying it all: the humiliation, the pain, the slow weakening of

Dredd's will to resist, but most of all the pain, the constant pain . . .

'Who put you up to this? McGruder?' demanded Dredd. 'I know you SJS all stick together. Is that it?'

Another blow to the face, this time fracturing Dredd's cheekbone.

'We ask the questions! Now, admit your guilt.'

'Or are you the ones behind the attempt on McGruder's life? I thought we cleaned up the SJS when we got rid of Cal years ago!'

Another surge of voltage savaged Dredd's naked body, even more powerful than before.

'If you're gonna kill me, get it over with, punks!'

'Answer the question!'

More power, more pain.

'Answer the question!'

And again.

'Answer the question!'

And again.

'Answer the question!'

As Dredd lost consciousness again, he thought he heard a voice speaking in the distance: 'Eliphas, there's a message from McGruder. Some slitch is outside and she wants Dredd . . .'

flex the muscles in your hands almost unwillingly and the talons appear: great scything blades of bone and silica and death. you reach forward to the prey, then capture and lunge fingers deep into the flesh: tearing, rending, slicing meat away from bone, the shiny red wetness glistening, inviting. but you hold back – there is better eating else-where, tastier morsels to feast upon.

and then you find the sweet treats, hidden away inside a round globe. a single slice of a talon and the skin peels away, revealing blood and bone, the skull casing. squeeze and the bone splinters, then shatters, brittle fragments flying up at you, around you, but to no effect. inside lies the prize, no longer pulsing or engorged with blood but still fresh.

24

you cannot stop yourself: grab at the soft, spongy tissue, tearing away chunks and stuffing into your mouth, chewing, sucking, absorbing. memories, feelings flood about you. the life of another, now just fodder for your insatiable hunger.

and you realise you're eating someone's brain and you're repulsed. it jolts you back, recreates the distance. you are in control, not this beast, this monster you inhabit! remember your training, remember your orders, your purpose.

you must sully the evidence, confuse those who might try to uncover you, so you pick up this corpse. it hangs under one arm like a child: limp, small, fragile. you run through the dark alleys of the twilight, unseen, unknown. then you see it, the perfect consumption, and in moments it is done, the consequences of your loss of control destroyed, but for how long? how long can this madness continue? how long can you hope to keep control of the beast inside? you gasp the words: return! return! and slump forward, exhausted, depleted, empty.

you have murdered and feasted on the flesh of your victim: how does it feel? does it make you sick, disgusted? perhaps even a little elated? you try to put the feelings away but they lurk, unbidden, at the edge of your mind. how long until the urge comes again?

TWO

First Field Test

Confidential Report for: XXXXX XXXXX
From: XXXXX XXXXX

Re: Notes on initial field testing of Prometheus Project prototypes

Aim: To collect data on actual combat scenario performance of psychological implants – nicknamed 'Skinner' – to be used in prototypes creatures, for assessment and improvement

Methodology: The Skinner imperative was 'accidentally' sent to Resyk from its 'creators', Callaghan Genetics. It was contained in a package of genetic waste, designated for complete molecular destruction. This ensured that human handling of the package was required, putting in place the conditions for the imperative to 'escape' and inhabit its first host. Then, if successful, the Skinner would proceed to move from one host to the next, absorbing knowledge and placing itself in positions of increasing importance and power. Finally the imperative would invade the body of the most powerful person in the city and begin its ultimate task, of destroying its pre-programmed target.

Throughout the field test, strict monitoring of the Skinner would be maintained at all times via the XXXXXX bio-control systems. At any time the imperative could be destroyed by remote control.

Procedure: The package of genetic material was delivered to Resyk as per methodology, where the human operative Ninestein was assigned to ensure the complete molecular destruction of the contents. Before he could finish his task, the flask containing the Skinner began to crackle and the subject opened it to inspect the contents. Then the Skinner was able to invade and inhabit Ninestein's body, creating a subservient human host for itself within moments.

[Note: Due to the 'accidental' nature of the Skinner's release, it was only through the human handler's curiosity that it was able to take control of a host and prevent its own destruction. See conclusions and recommendations below for response to this.

Also, at the time of absorption, XXXXXX picked up a massive spike in psi-telemetry readings. Although the cause of this spike was not immediately recognised by Psi Division operatives, it did betray the imperative's presence in the city. Again, see recommendations.]

The host body continued its usual duties at Resyk, leaving at 2300 hours. Unfortunately the host proved unable to sustain the life of the Skinner imperative, which seems to feed upon the physical energy, indeed the lifeforce, of the host. Surveillance noted that parts of the host body started to become transparent as the imperative began to absorb the molecular structure of the host to preserve its existence long enough to find a new subject. The Skinner was forced to 'jump' to the first available new host, which proved to be a street transient.

By now the Skinner had already absorbed all the knowledge of its first host and began to speak through its new human 'home'. At this stage it was nearly stumbled upon by a Judge on routine patrol, but exhibited strong survival instincts, hiding itself until a better escape could be made.

The Judge found the remains of the Skinner's first host, a rapidly decomposing body which soon dissolved almost completely away, leaving just a small amount of bio-organic debris. Monitoring of Skinner's 'thoughts' showed it absorbing the new host's knowledge, including information about the transient's former home, Mark Murdock Block. The imperative used this knowledge to gain entry to the citi-block and then shifted hosts again, this time to the leader of the block's Citi-Def squad, Karl Krispie.

This gave the Skinner access to the armoury of weapons held by the Murdock Citi-Defence squad and knowledge of how to use them in a conflict situation. The Skinner then triggered a block war between Murdock and the neighbouring Nial Nelson Block, forcing the Justice Department to send a squad of Judges to subdue the violence.

[Note: Each time the Skinner shifted host, it created a psi-scream from the victim. Using this to home in on the cause, a Psi Division Judge called Karyn began to investigate the incidents created by the imperative.]

While the Judges were dealing with the block war, the Skinner kept escalating the violence before 'leaping' to a new host, a Judge. We monitored its reasoning during this incident, where it chose the new host, rather than simply jumping from body to body as the old host wore out. Also, following this leap it quickly absorbed the Judge host's knowledge of Justice Department methods and realised its methods were drawing attention to itself. Before leaving the scene, the Skinner tried to destroy the remains of its last host, which were about to be analysed by Psi Judge Karyn. It shot one Judge and used an incendiary to burn away the bio-organic remains, before escaping.

[Note: Monitoring of reports within the Justice Department were able to intercept Karyn's report on the incident. She detected human DNA in the remains, but also other debris which did not match with other patterns. Most interestingly, she was unable to obtain any psychometric readings from either those remains or from a pair of handcuffs left behind by the Skinner. Not only did the Skinner not leave any psi-trace behind, it also blanked out the psi-patterns of the Judge it had invaded, wiping away any and all trace of the host's presence. The Skinner imperative was effectively invisible to psychic detection.]

The Skinner's destruction of the bio-organic remains of its previous host was meant to hide its tracks, but actually served to alert the Justice Department to what to look for. A search soon discovered previous sets of remains, leading a trail back to the first host, Ninestein. From there, Psi Judge Karyn traced the 'creators' of the organism, Callaghan Genetics.

[Note: The company had been chosen as a front for the field test, with 27 previous counts of DNA patent infringements entered into Justice Department records against it. Callaghan Genetics' role as a bio-warfare research centre made its 'creation' of the Skinner entirely logical: a simple case of scientists getting too good at their jobs, going a few steps too far. The cover story was gratefully swallowed by Karyn, thus protecting the Project and preventing the need for any 'disappearances' among those asking too many questions.]

The Skinner's trail of former hosts pointed directly towards Justice Central, such was the single-minded nature of its programming. It infiltrated the Justice Department using the host body of the Judge it had invaded at the Block War, then shifted to a Judge McKinley, absorbing his specialist knowledge about the inner workings and security patterns of the Halls of Justice. The Skinner used its authority to pull Judges away from the headquarters, thus lowering security levels and provoking a confrontation with another Judge, forcing that Judge to request an appointment with the Chief Judge.

It added to the confusion by leaking false information to the media, alleging that the Judges had been taken over by alien shape-changing invaders, and they were the cause of the 'Street Skinner' killings. This created a climate of hysteria in the city, further weakening defences within the Justice Department. Also it used its bio-chip origins to scramble computer systems within the Halls of Justice, disabling attempts to analyse or track its movements.

The Skinner now leaped to its final host, the Judge who had already made an appointment to speak with the Chief Judge. At this point, the remote-controlled destruct sequence was initiated so the field test could be aborted when the Skinner attempted to complete its mission.

Final destruct was postponed as Psi Judge Karyn burst onto the scene. She was able to detect the Skinner's host because it cast no shadow. [Note: This unexpected side effect of the Skinner imperative's body snatching remains unexplained.] Karyn 'destroyed' the Skinner imperative with an incendiary bullet – in fact, this opportunity was used to destruct the device, leaving no evidence for further examination.

The Justice Department carried out the expected purge of Callaghan Genetics, shutting down the Skinner 'programme' there, but all possible evidence leading back to this project had already long since been destroyed. No further action has been taken on the incident by the Department, which believes it to be a one-off occurrence.

Summary: This first field test was a valuable exercise, which uncovered many flaws in the bio-weapon. The Skinner imperative used up human hosts too quickly, forcing it to leap from one host to the next within hours. Also, this left behind bio-organic debris, leading to its eventual detection. While the quick change of hosts enabled it to acquire new, essential knowledge quickly, the Skinner's actions were almost too single-minded, lacking any subtlety until its mission was nearly completed.

Another obvious flaw with the host-swapping was the need for physical contact when shifting from body to body and the resultant psi-spike this created, further advertising the imperative's presence. Plus the eventual method of detection – by casting no shadow – makes this a limited weapon.

Despite these difficulties, there were many positive results. The psi-invisibility factor 'lifted' from trail with alien Raptaur creatures proved invaluable, while the rapid absorption of knowledge and exponential learning curve proved formidable assets.

Recommendations: Rather than use the Skinner imperative as a lone operator, it would be better utilised as part of a complete bio-weapon. The positives would make such a creature highly dangerous and hard to detect, while it would eliminate virtually all the drawbacks of the cuckoo-like leaping from host to host.

If the Skinner imperative can be successfully merged into the mutate creature currently in development at other sites, the resultant warriors would be virtually invincible. However, any field testing should be conducted outside the city, if only to make detection of the source more difficult, if any problems were to arise. It is recommended we work to develop a bonding mechanism to enable this merger while field testing of the mutate creature is being carried out.

Signed: XXXXX XXXXX
February 20, 2116AD

THREE

Dead in Waiting

The Apocalypse War: An unprovoked saturation attack on Mega-City One in 2104 by the Soviet State, East-Meg One. The deadly rain of nuclear warheads destroyed nearly 65 per cent of the Big Meg, killing half of its population at the time, 800 million. East-Meg One was completely obliterated in a counter-attack led by Judge Dredd.

The face of the Mega-City One was forever altered by the war. A massive rebuilding programme was begun, but such was the devastation in the north of the city and particularly in the south, that vast areas were deemed unreclaimable. More than a decade later, those areas are still classified as strictly off-limits to all citizens.

Extract from *Justice Department Case Histories*
(Volume 14; 2115 update)

The old man's body had no hands. Genya Berger looked down at the corpse and wondered which of the wild animals that roamed the zone had feasted upon it. She had seen many strange creatures over the past few months, insane mutations caused by the radioactive dust particles that still clung to the ground; the debris that had once been an area alive with people and families and businesses and hope and love.

Genya was used to death, she'd seen so much of it since the day the bombs started falling. Most of Mega-City One had still been busy fighting itself because of the Block Mania virus, but Genya was one of the few immune to the virus. She heard the first reports about the bomb attack and managed to drag her boyfriend Tony down into the Citi-Def bomb shelter in the basement of their citi-block. There they huddled together, praying to Grud to be spared. And they made love: incredible, passionate sex as if there were no tomorrow – because there probably would be no tomorrow.

She could still remember waking up the next morning to discover they were still alive. They'd both congratulated themselves on how fortunate they'd been, how lucky they were to still be alive. A bitter irony, thought Genya, they'd have been better off dead like all their friends and neighbours, than surviving to face the hell that followed.

The bomb shelter was well stocked with preserved food and clothing, but the pair didn't realise the sterilised water supply was tainted with tiny radioactive particles from above ground. They stayed underground for nearly six weeks before finally deciding to go out and investigate, to see how bad the damage really was. It took Tony nearly two days to dig a way through the rubble that had collapsed into the basement but they were finally able to find a gap and escape to the surface.

When they came out into the early spring sunshine, Genya thought for a moment Tony had dug too far and brought them up in a different sector. The ground was blasted flat, everything black with charring and the dust of millions of atomised human bodies. All that stood on the horizon were enormous metal sculptures, twisted and broken, like some crazy exhibition of post-post-post-modernist art. Then she realised the sculptures were actually all that remained of the citi-blocks, just the warped metal reinforcing frames left standing.

They walked for hours, trying to find any signs of life. Eventually, the lovers started to reach the edge of the blast zone, away from ground zero. Here some of the citi-blocks were still partially standing. On one wall was a black, life-size shadow. Tony had said it was all that remained of a citizen caught in the blast-effect, his atoms fused into the wall by the strength of the nuclear shock-wave. Genya started crying then.

She couldn't cry anymore, not even looking down at the handless body of an old man, his remains just fodder for the predators of the dead zone. Genya hadn't cried since the Judges took her baby away.

Tony had managed to navigate their way out of the desolate northern zone to an area left relatively unscathed by the war, despite feeling increasingly weak and ill. There the couple had reported to the local sector house, desperate for food and shelter. They hadn't dared eat or drink since leaving the shelter days before and were on the verge of collapse. Nearly seven weeks had passed since the bombs started falling and much had changed in Mega-City One. Millions of people were homeless, living in displaced persons camps. Food shortages were common, and crime was rife with the Judges understaffed and overwhelmed with the clean-up operations.

When Tony and Genya arrived at the sector house they were both given a thorough medical check by a robo-doc. That was when Genya discovered she was pregnant – the product of the passion shared with Tony while bombs fell. The robo-doc recommended the foetus be aborted, due to the circumstances of its conception. 'It will almost certainly be still-born anyway, because of the massive radiation exposure you've suffered.' Genya had almost agreed too, until Tony died of radiation sickness. She then decided to carry the baby to full term. It would be her reminder of the love she had lost.

The pregnancy was difficult, painful, but Genya was determined to see it through, and somehow she sensed the same determination from her baby as it grew inside her. Then, after a routine scan at seven months, two Med-Judges came to see her. Twelve years later, she could still remember every single word of the conversation.

'Miss Genya Berger?'

'Yes?'

'Under Section 42(D) of the Genetic Purity Act of

2079, we are going to take custody of your foetus. The procedure will – '

'*What?*'

'Under Section 42(D) – '

'Yes, I heard that! What do you mean "we are going to take custody of your foetus"? What the drokk does that mean? What are you going to do to my baby?!'

'Routine scans have shown genetic abnormalities inherent in the foetus. Under the Genetic Purity Act of 2079, the Justice Department has the authority to confiscate any foetus believed to have such abnormalities and deal with it as the department sees fit.'

'It's a baby, not a foetus, a baby. It's my baby!'

'Under this act you have no right of appeal, nor are we obliged to give you any information regarding the fate of the foetus.'

'It's my baby. You can't do this! It's my baby, you can't – '

They had held her down, sedated her, operated on her and taken away the 'foetus', then filled her up with anti-depressants to stop her committing suicide. Genya had spent seven years in the psycho-cubes afterwards, drugged to the eyeballs and unable to remember her own name. She could only piece together what had happened when she was ejected onto the streets, put into 'community care' where 'market forces' were to provide her with the treatment she needed. In other words, the Judges just washed their hands of her.

Genya had drifted around City Bottom for a while, before finally coming here to the dead zone: the bombed out, fallout-riddled remains of what had once been Sector 333. She didn't really know why she had come back here, back to the place she'd once called home. It was forbidden, of course, but the Judges could do nothing more to hurt her. They'd already taken away her lover with their war-mongering, taken away her baby, taken away her will to fight anymore. So she had come here, come home.

Genya turned and walked away from the old man's

handless body. He was probably only about 30, but those who lived in the dead zone always looked old beyond their years. It was the radiation again, stealing their hair, cheating them of their strength. A hundred people, perhaps two hundred had come back here to the area around major blast zone. They came to die, because they had nowhere else to go. If the effects of the fallout didn't get them, the wild animals that roamed the dead zone surely would. One day someone would come round a corner and find Genya's body lying on the ground, she knew that. What saddened her most was she didn't even have the strength to kill herself and end this purgatorial existence, bringing the nightmare to a close.

She stopped by a puddle and looked down at her reflection in the gray water. A few white wisps of hair clung to her head, her face was lined and haggard, the skin hanging from protruding bones, just a few teeth left of her once gleaming smile. Genya didn't cry, because she couldn't. She just turned away and walked back to her tiny shelter in the rubble, all the while singing an old refrain, barely remembered.

'Happy birthday to you, happy birthday to you, happy birthday dead Genya, happy birthday . . .'

It was Genya Berger's twenty-eighth birthday.

Extract from the private journal of Judge Laverne Castillo:

If my first encounter with Chief Judge McGruder was perturbing, my errand to the SJS headquarters was utterly disturbing. The building is black, foreboding, like a malignant presence on the skyline. There are no markings on its exterior, nothing to indicate its purpose, but everybody knows what it is. I noticed citizens crossing to the other side of the road, simply to avoid passing outside the entrance. In reality they have little to fear: the SJS were specifically established to police the actions of the rest of the Justice Department, not monitor the citizens themselves. Yet still the fears remain. Now, having been inside the headquarters myself, I can understand why.

The walls are all black and what lighting exists is harsh, cruel to the eyes. The death's head emblem of the SJS glares from the walls and stone-faced Judges stalk the corridors, their leathereen uniforms creaking as they walk past, heels clicking on the marble floors. To my surprise, the vast bulk of the building was underground, with twice as many levels below sked-level as above it. As I was sent from one area to another, one word kept running through my mind from an old lecture, the name of a twentieth-century department of terror from a time of war and tyranny: *gestapo*.

The forbidding environment extended to all within it. I was shunted from one part of the building to another, all of them black, foreboding and unhelpful. After nearly four hours of getting nowhere slowly, I found myself shouting at a granite-faced Judge who seemed to hardly notice my existence, let alone my questions.

I turned to find myself facing yet another SJS Judge, but this one was smiling. His black hair was slicked back and a neatly trimmed moustache and goatee gave his face an almost demonic quality. The smile reminded me of sea creatures I once saw in a history lesson at the Academy. What were they called – quarks? Sharks? They chilled me at the time and this new arrival's smile did the same.

He eventually told me his name was Eliphas, and smirked when I said I would be forced to report the conduct of his officers as direct obstruction to an order of the Chief Judge. He walked behind me and said 'we wouldn't want that to happen', speaking to me like I was some third-year cadet being humoured by a long-suffering tutor. Then he stopped behind me and pressed a hand casually on my buttocks! 'The Chief Judge has such a pretty messenger . . .' he started to say.

I turned and hit him, striking the drokker hard across the face. But then he caught my hand in his and began tightening his grip, slowly crushing my bones together. The pain was incredible.

'Don't you ever strike me, you little slitch!' he spat at me, his face red with anger, a big mark visible where I'd hit him. He just stared at me for a moment, then pushed me away and straightened his uniform. 'Tell McGruder that Dredd will be released from our custody at 0800 hours,' he announced. 'She can see him then,' he added, then stalked off as if nothing had happened.

I just stood there, not knowing what to do. I couldn't believe what had happened, couldn't believe I had hit him. Of that I'm proud: it's probably all I can ever do to redress the situation. I can hardly accuse a senior officer in the SJS of sexual harassment, nobody would take the word of a first-year Judge over that of an SJS officer, especially considering my record. If I'm lucky, Eliphas will forget about me. If not . . .

Eventually I left the SJS headquarters and reported back to McGruder's office, but she seemed to have already forgotten her request. I logged the appointment for Dredd to see her in the Chief Judge's log for tomorrow then came back here to my quarters to write this entry.

I used to believe the Justice Department was a fair, just place, full of exemplary Judges whose only desire was to enforce the Law, for the good of all. In one day I've been shot at by a Chief Judge two wheels short of a Lawmaster, spent most of the day being manipulated or ignored and nearly got court-martialled after a senior Judge sexually molested me.

I've been a naive, foolish innocent, out of my depth. It's time I talked to somebody about all this. Tomorrow I'm going to talk to an old aquaintance. I doubt that she'll remember me but I sure remember her. If I'm going to have any chance at all of surviving as a Judge in this nest of vipers and insanity, I'll need her advice. I only hope that she'll be willing to talk to me.

Mega-City One is divided into more than 300 sectors, each with its own sector house. This serves a similar purpose to the precinct houses used by police forces before the Atomic Wars. These local headquarters contain their own cells, forensic and med units and reserves of weapons and equipment. Most street Judges are assigned out of sector houses, with each building given a small team of Teks and Psis.

Sector House 66 was in one of Mega-City One's toughest areas. For a start it was sited next to the infamous Maze estate, a low amenity housing development designed by F. Lloyd Mazny. Many of the original residents had starved to death, unable to find their way out of the complex and its confusing array of pedways and skedways. Once that problem had been sorted out, the Maze became a dumping ground for low IQ residents, troublemakers and those recently released from the cubes. These factors had combined to make the sector one of Mega-City One's most lawless housing zones.

Eammon Kozwall knew this, knew it all too well. After all, he had been the Chief Judge for Sector 66 for five years. His predecessor had died during a food riot in the Maze, when citizens began hunger striking over the poor quality munce being supplied to the sector.

Kozwall could still remember his first day as Chief of 66. The sector house had been firebombed twice, and ten of his Judges were killed by extremist elements of the Killer Boy Scout Bob-a-Job assassination craze.

Since then 66 had seen one disaster after another. It seemed Kozwall had always been fighting just to keep things from going backwards in this sector, though with some successes too. The sector's bloodlust for gangland warfare had nearly been sated and smuggling of sugar, tea and coffee were down.

Eammon ran a hand over his bald pate and reflected on the cost to himself personally. A full head of red hair for a start! The deaths of dozens of good Judges. Plus all his teeth, of course: they had been knocked down his throat by a coffee-crazed killer who had run amok in the sector house one day. The Med-Judges had replaced them with synthetic teeth, but something had gone out of the satisfaction of eating when Kozwall had lost his own teeth.

Soon he would be transferring to another sector, preferably to one a little quieter, but he knew he would miss the excitement, the frenzy of old 66. There were a few things he wanted to sort out tonight, so he had stayed behind to analyse the latest crime stats. Looking at the chronometer on his desk, it was a shock to realise it was so late.

His office was spartan, unlike that of some sector chiefs he had seen – all ostentation and announcing of authority. Kozwall favoured simplicity. He knew who was boss in this sector house and so did everybody else. He felt no need to overdo it, keeping the furnishings down to a simple, sturdy desk with a holovid display set into it, some chairs and the ever-present comp-unit.

The sector chief got back to concentrating on the statistics. Rapes and murders were both down; there hadn't been a block war for weeks; missing persons – there it was again. Kozwall swivelled his chair round and addressed the comp-unit set into his desk.

'Computer on,' he said, activating the voice response units, waiting for the retina-scan and vocal analyser to confirm his identity. The laser scanner played over his freckled features before locking onto his left eye and making a positive ID on his retina pattern.

'Identity confirmed as Judge Eammon Kozwall, Sector 66 Chief Judge. Proceed.'

'What is current city-wide average ratio for missing persons reports?' he asked, already knowing the answer.

'One case per 79,000 citizens,' purred the computer.

'What is the same ratio for this sector?'

'One case per 12,000 citizens.'

'And how many outstanding cases in this sector?'

'Currently there are 108 outstanding cases.'

Kozwall was bemused and worried. He had noticed this anomaly in the missing persons stats for the past few weeks, even included it in his reports to Justice Central. But it had been dismissed as a freak numerical occurrence that would eventually correct itself. After all, 108 cases in a population of more than a million wasn't that many. But it was still a lot more than the average 16 or 17 in other sectors, and he was determined to investigate.

'Explain anomaly.'

'Insufficient data,' purred back the computer soothingly.

'Hmmph!' frowned Kozwall, then felt the hairs on the back of his neck stand up. It was as if someone was in the office with him, standing just behind him . . .

He spun round, Lawgiver drawn and ready to fire, but there was no-one there. Rising carefully, covering all the angles, he advanced into the centre of the room, calling out to the desk Judge on duty outside in the main part of the sector house.

'Symes! Get in here!'

The desk Judge burst into the room, weapon already drawn. 'What is it?'

Kozwall smiled, feeling foolish. 'Sorry, I thought there was an intruder in the sector house.'

Symes relaxed. 'I know, it gets creepy in here at night sometimes. I almost wish I was out on the graveyard shift with the others.'

'Who else is in the building?' asked Kozwall, trying to keep his voice calm and casual.

'The forensics team are still trying to make something out of those remains found in the Maze earlier today. Simpson is on guard duty down in the Holding Tanks. That's about it – everybody else is out on the streets.'

'Why so many?'

'Full moon, of course. Now, if you don't need me here . . .'

Kozwall waved the desk Judge away, feeling foolish. The graveyard shift ran from dusk till dawn and was always the busiest of the day. But there was something about a full moon that brought out all the crazies. The sector chief didn't know how he could have forgotten it but then lately the crazies seemed to be coming out in the daytime too. The human remains Symes had mentioned were evidence of that. According to forensics, the deceased had been the victim of an attack so frenzied, they doubted the killer was even human.

Kozwall went back to his desk and began running a

cross-check of the missing persons stats to see if there was any sort of geographical pattern. The results startled him: there had to be a link, it was too much of a coincidence. He was about to call for Symes when a shadow fell across his desk. The sector chief started to turn and saw something huge, shimmering and black, almost blending into the background. He opened his mouth to scream. Teeth glistened wetly and talons flew, slashing, clawing. Eammon Kozwall was dead before his cry could leave his throat.

The stab of the hypo needle into his arm dragged Dredd to consciousness again. A harsh voice barked in the background.

'Clean him up, then take him to the Meds. Tell them to use rapi-heal to fix his wounds, and make sure the dentist fixes his teeth. He's due before the Chief Judge at 0800 hours tomorrow morning.'

A hand grabbed Dredd by the jaw and shook him fully awake. He looked up to see Eliphas leering over him.

'I haven't finished with you yet, not by a long way!'

Dredd rolled some blood and phlegm around in his mouth for a moment then spat it into his captor's face. 'Drokk you,' he mumbled before passing out again.

A hand-scrawled note was taped to Dredd's chest as he was stretchered out of the interrogation room: RANDOM PHYSICAL ABUSE TEST – DREDD, J. – PASSED.

FOUR

Monkey Business Mobsters

Ape gangs: Mega-City One's talking apes are a result of genetic experimentation by scientists during the twenty-first century. Primates had long been identified as cousins of man on the evolutionary ladder and shown remarkable abilities to mimic humans and adapt to suit different environments. Scientists gave monkeys the power of speech and educated them in the ways of humans, using media fiction to give the apes an understanding of human life.

When funding ran out, the apes were released into the community. The imitative instincts enhanced in the apes enabled them to adapt perhaps too successfully, as they soon moved into criminal enterprise, adopting the guise of American mobsters from the early to mid twentieth century as their major cultural influence.

Living together in abandoned blocks, the Apes developed their own sub-culture known as Ape Town, or the Jungle. Most were wiped out by East-Meg bombs during the Apocalypse War, but some colonies have survived, mostly in run-down areas of Mega-City One, like Sector 66.

Note: All experimentation on animals was banned by the so-called Dredd Act of 2101, brought into force by the Council of Five following recommendations by Judge Joe Dredd.

Extract from *Justice Dept Case Histories*
(Volume 1, 2115 update)

'Item! Suspected gangland slaying in Sector 66, at eastern edge of the Jungle, two dead, more injured!'

It had been a long night and there was still an hour till dawn when the call came through from Control, but Judge Lynn Miller responded without hesitation.

'Miller to Control, I'll take it with Brighton.'

'Roj that.'

The two Judges swung off the overzoom and gunned their Lawmasters down to the skedways below, cutting through the near-empty avenues. At this time of the morning, Mega-City's nocturnal inhabitants were heading for bed while the rest of the population rolled over in the hope of catching a few more minutes rest before facing another day of near universal unemployment and boredom.

Miller looked over at her young partner, Judge Kevin Brighton. He was only 15 months out of the Academy but already shaping up well. She had first met him a year ago when they were both assigned to a small team sent into the Cursed Earth in search of a missing Hotdog Run squad. The task had been difficult and dangerous, every member forced to face certain death several times, but Brighton had come through it well. He'd picked up some good 'seasoning', as older Judges liked to call it.

'You been into the Jungle yet, Brighton?' she asked.

'No, I've only seen the talking apes on tri-D briefings at the Academy,' he replied excitedly.

'Yeah, well be careful. They're highly unpredictable and their slang can take some understanding,' warned Miller.

Brighton nodded. He had been assigned to the station in Sector 66 only a week before and Miller had picked him as her partner, partly to keep an eye out for him, but also because his good humour made him a pleasant change from the usual grim and gritty Judges who seemed to populate most sector houses. He had sparkling eyes and a youthful face, not yet beaten down by the harsh realities of a life Judging on the streets. Miller didn't like to admit it, but he reminded her a little of her brother

Ryan, at least the way she remembered him from when she was a child . . .

Miller pulled herself back to the present as her Lawmaster approached a makeshift sign fused to a wall, a crude warning burnt into it with a kitchen laser: WELCOME TO THE JUNGLE. She muttered a final warning to Brighton via her helmet-com. 'Leave the talking to me, and follow my lead. This place is a real banana republic.'

'Roj that,' replied Brighton, suppressing a grin at the awful pun.

In an underground chamber, a cage wall slid shut and something settled down to rest after its mission. Fresh blood dripped from red-stained claws, one talon chipped and broken at its end. Outside the cage, the head of the Prometheus Project smiled.

'So our little problem has been eliminated – excellent! A total success!' The project leader turned to look at Tek-Judge Akinsiku. 'And how is Magnus? Can I see him yet?'

The pair left the darkened chamber and emerged into a long corridor, stark and blindingly white by comparison. They strode briskly along it, heels clicking on the cold rockcrete floor.

'He finds operating the slave unit very draining, sir,' replied the technician. 'Sometimes he has to rest for several hours afterwards.'

'But I will talk to him now, won't I?'

The words hung in the air, heavy with threat.

'Yes, sir. Of course! This way, sir,' agreed the Tek-Judge hastily and led him through a side door and down some stairs to a circular mezzanine floor which looped around a huge, glowing globe-shaped tank, filled with luminous lime-green liquid.

Inside the tank floated something vaguely human.

A torso with bumps where arms and legs should have been was visible through the slimy suspension, but there were no genitalia, and a bulbous, misshapen head hung heavily forward on the creature's concave chest. From around its body dozens of wires led away like capillaries, linking it to complex banks of machinery set into the sides of the tank.

The project leader leaned forward and rapped the side of the tank with gauntlet-clad knuckles. 'Wakey, wakey, Magnus! No time to be asleep on the job!'

The lumpy head jerked upward to reveal a mournful face. The mouth was openless and toothless, sucking at the solution filling the tank as a normal person breathes air. The nose was missing and the eyes were open but glazed, no pupils, just pure white, staring.

'That's better!' gloated the leader. 'Now, how was it?'

Silence. When the creature did speak, it was telepathically, projecting his words directly into the leader's mind.

'The creature was dangerous, difficult to control . . . at times I felt myself being subsumed by its bloodlust . . .'

'Yes, yes, you've told me this before with the prototype. But this time you were properly able to direct it?'

'Yes . . . up to a point . . .'

'And the task? Completed?'

'I believe so . . . perception remains difficult whilst in control mode . . . but I believe so . . .'

'Excellent! How many more tests before we can reveal our research findings, Magnus? How long?'

'There must be more tests . . . refinements . . . all my work is not yet finished . . . it could be months before – '

'Months? We haven't got months! You told me they were almost ready, that we could go into production soon.' Now the leader of the project was angry, banging a fist against the side of the tank. Magnus crumpled himself up into a ball, trying to block out the heavy echo of the blows against his enviro-sphere. The Tek-Judge reached out a hand, tried to prevent the leader.

'Please, sir, you're hurting Magnus. I must ask you to – '

The leader whirled and smashed the technician in the face with a heavy fist. 'You must ask me what? What?'

The leader drew a Lawgiver and aimed it at the Akinsiku's head. 'Nobody knows you're here. This research centre doesn't officially exist, you know. If I killed you now, I could just feed your body to what's back there in the enclosure, and nobody would ever know what happened!'

The leader looked back at Magnus, now pointing the weapon at the side of the tank. 'Or perhaps I should just shoot a hole in the tank wall and watch as our little friend here drowns in the open air, like some beached whale? Would you like that, Magnus? Would you?'

'No . . .'

'All right then!' The leader holstered the Lawgiver again and breathed deeply. 'Let's try again then, shall we? How long until we're ready for the next series of tests?'

'Soon . . . very soon . . .' murmured Magnus.

'That's better! Make sure it stays that way!' shouted the leader before stamping out of the chamber. The Tek-Judge pulled himself to his feet, one hand held gingerly to the swelling already forming on his face.

'He'll kill you if this fails.'

'I know . . .' admitted Magnus. 'I know . . .'

Samantha Hester was a spont – a spontaneous confessor. She'd admit to any crime imaginable, if she thought it would get her any attention from the Judges. Samantha had lived in Johnny Ray Block in Sector 66 all her life, and she'd been confessing since her seventh birthday, nearly 15 years before.

At first, she'd just confessed to minor misdemeanours, like dunking in unsuspecting cits' pockets or jaywalking. Later she'd moved on to bigger confessions – body sharking, organ legging, dealing in adifax from stookies, even armed robbery with violence. Still the Judges ignored her, dismissed her as just another kook seeking attention.

She struck gold one time when she admitted to a spate of serial killings in her block, even managed to get her fingerprints on the murder weapon after she stumbled across one of the corpses in the artificial park atop the block's roof. But she had made the classic spont error of having an alibi and was quickly eliminated from suspicion. Still, it had earned her a month in the cubes for contaminating evidence in a murder inquiry, so it had been a partial success!

To be honest, Samantha didn't know why she had taken up sponting. It had been fashionable at the time to confess to crimes and when she wasn't sponting, Samantha was a great follower of fashion. She'd even joined Fashion Victims Anonymous, a group of citizens who deliberately wore expensive, high-fashion kneepads in public so they would be mugged. But the Judges had banned the club on the grounds of deliberately provoking petty crime.

Her parents despaired of Samantha's sponting. Last week, when they'd asked what she wanted for her birthday, she had requested a ten-stretch in the cubes for arson. Not that Samantha had ever knowingly committed a crime, the idea was abhorrent. She didn't even particularly enjoy being imprisoned. It was just that, well, somehow she felt responsible for all the city's ills. Maybe by confessing to all the crimes that occurred (or, at least, all the crimes that occurred to her imagination), she could help alleviate those ills . . .

Disgusted with her behaviour, Samantha's parents had signed up their deluded daughter for garbage disposal work experience. With unemployment endemic in Mega-City One, many blocks had been forced to institute Youth Training Schemes In Pointless Pastimes (or YTSIPP for short) to teach the juves how to cope with the perpetual unemployment situation. Many schools now taught Diplomas in Unemployment. Samantha had failed her diploma, but her parents managed to get her on garbage detail.

Samantha loathed the work, getting up at dawn to take the block's inorganic waste to the nearby public grinder for disposal. She didn't realise it was going to provide her with one of the most important confessions of her life, one that was almost true . . .

She had just reached the public grinder outside Johnny Ray as the first rays of sunlight began reflecting and refracting their way from window to window, shining over a new morning in the city. Samantha was carrying the remains of a disposable tri-D television set her parents had brought back from a camping holiday in the renowned Acid Lake District of northern Brit-Cit. Apparently the Brits were encouraged to destroy at least one tri-D set a day, in the interests of obsolescence, although Samantha found this hard to believe.

She was about to thrust the crumpled remnants of the mangled machine into the grinder when her eye caught a glint of something metal poking out of the grinder slot. Somebody had used the grinder overnight and not bothered to finish the job properly.

'Gruddam!' she cursed and hit the grind button violently with a tight fist. The gears bit and chewed at the metal, but instead of metal shrieking, there was a sound like curtains tearing as the grinder jammed again. Smoke billowed from the head-high machine and a smell like cooking munce emerged, as the mechanisms inside overheated.

Samantha cursed again and pulled the glinting metal from the grinder's jaws. It was torn and scarred, much of its surface ripped away but the shape was unmistakable: the badge of a Judge!

Her mind whirled about as realisation hit home: she had been grinding the body of a Judge. Even as the thought entered her brain, she was running for the nearest vid-phone, desperate to confess all . . .

Miller and Brighton rode around the eastern edge of the Jungle for several minutes looking for the crimescene, all the while aware of being watched, simian eyes looking out at them from cracks in windows and boarded-up buildings. The Jungle was dilapidated and tumble-down in many places but the Apes seemed to like it that way. Then again, no construction robots had been in this area for more than a decade to do any repairs, so maybe they didn't have a choice, thought Brighton. He was about to mention this to Miller when she pointed ahead of them.

There were a group of apes surrounding something on the ground – probably the victims – and another pair of apes standing guard over the approach road, armed with old-fashioned machine guns. When they spotted the Judges, they cocked their weapons and took aim.

Miller braked and stopped, motioning for Brighton to do the same. She pulled off her helmet and shook free her shoulder-length, shock-white hair, then put her hands over her head. Brighton followed suit, revealing his tousled fair hair. He felt decidedly nervous at making himself so defenceless.

'We's here to investigate a double-murder, we ain't got no beef witcha!' Miller shouted ahead in her best ape-slang.

'It's da Heat! Whack them out!' replied one of the apes, about to start shooting.

'Hold ya fire, ya bums. We shoot them, the whole department'll moida us!' ordered a voice from the crowd. 'Let 'em thru!'

Reluctantly, the two guards motioned Miller and Brighton to leave their bikes and walk forwards. As the two Judges got closer, Brighton was amazed to see the apes were all wearing clothes, but unlike anything he'd seen outside old vid-slugs. The male apes were clad in pinstripe suits and hats, each with a fresh paper flower in their button hole! The female apes wore dresses and some even high heels, teetering awkwardly about.

The crowd parted before them, to reveal two dead apes lying on the ground, blood in a messy pool around the bodies. The apes appeared to be older females, both wearing floral dresses. A besuited ape stood over the corpses, hat clutched to his chest, his eyes mournful. To Brighton's surprise, his partner addressed the sad ape.

'Don Uggi! What happened here?' asked Miller.

The ape shook his head from side to side slowly, trying to keep control of his feelings. Finally, he spoke. 'Moida! Those lousy dames, they whacked my mudda and her sister too! Why'd dey do this? We get no beef wit' dem!'

'What dames? Who are you talkin' about?'

Don Uggi couldn't speak, his body shaking with rage. Instead he pointed to the wall of a citi-block behind him, then slumped to the ground beside his dead mother. Scrawled on the wall in red were two words: SHE DEVILS. Tiny trails of blood dripped down from the bottom of each letter.

'Calm down, take a deep breath and relax. Now, what did you just say?' asked Judge Juneson on the Crimeline. Why did he always have to pull Crimeline duty when the nutters phoned, he wondered for the fourth time that morning. On his vid-screen, the flushed face of a young woman bobbed about excitedly.

'A Judge! I've killed a Judge! I just pushed his body down a public grinder! You've got to send someone to arrest me – right now,' she demanded joyfully.

Another Judge wandered over to see what all the fuss was about.

'Caller claims she grinded a Judge,' explained Juneson. 'I'm running her voice through the analyser now. Probably a crank call – like all the others!' The percentage of genuine calls to Crimeline was so small, he wondered why they bothered keeping the lines open. Still, when it did pay off, the results were sometimes spectacular – like that Roland Savage business last year. Juneson jerked upright in his seat as the results of the lie detector voice analyser came through: *caller speaks true*.

'Sweet Jovus, she isn't lying!' he exclaimed, before shouting to his colleague. 'Alert Control, get a trace run on her location and then get some Judges over there – *now*!'

* * *

51

Brighton was biting his lip, trying not to contribute to the conversation between his superior and the ape gangsters. Best to keep silent, until Miller indicated otherwise, he had learned after the last few days as her partner on patrol. Brighton watched for any sign of danger as she stepped forward and offered her condolences to the grieving ape.

'I'm sorry for your loss, but you must tell me – who are these She Devils? Another gang?' asked Miller.

Don Uggi nodded. 'They been musclin' in on our territory, dealin' and tryin' to run protection rackets. Just a few dames getting too big for their boots, I thought. But this . . . this means war!'

Miller stood up abruptly. 'I must warn you, any attempt to escalate this into a full gang war will not be looked upon kindly by the Justice Department. We've had a working treaty up here in 66 for more than a year. If you or any of your apes start a war – '

'We didn't start this!' exploded the ape gang leader, jamming his hat on his head. 'But I'll tell you somethin' – if those dames want a war, we'll give 'em one!' He stormed off, followed by his tommy-gun-wielding followers. Behind him, the female apes moved forward to tend to the two bodies, covering them over with coats.

'Terrif,' muttered Miller darkly, pulling her helmet back on and stalking back to her bike, Brighton trailing behind her.

'Who was that?' asked the young Judge.

'Don Uggi the third, the most important ape gang leader in the Jungle. I met him when Sector Chief Kozwall negotiated the truce between all the gangs last year,' replied Miller briskly before contacting the sector house and ordering a forensics team to the murder scene to search for any clues. 'Though what the snufflers'll find after everyone's been trampling over the site, I don't know!'

Brighton climbed back onto his motorcycle, but something still troubled him. 'I thought Justice Department procedure prohibited making deals with anyone, especially gangs?'

'Yeah, well, Justice Department procedure sometimes comes second to stopping open warfare in Sector 66. If this incident blows out of proportion, you'll soon see what I mean – first-hand,' said Miller grimly. 'Come on, we better get back to the sector house and tell Chief Kozwall what's happening – '

She was interrupted by an all-units bulletin from Control.

'Item! A Judge's body has been found stuffed into a public grinder outside Johnny Ray Block, Sector 66. Body identified as that of Sector Chief Eammon Kozwall!'

'Holy Stomm!' cried Miller, before speaking into her helmet-com. 'Miller and Brighton – we'll take it.'

Extract from the private journal of Judge Laverne Castillo:

Today I met Mega-City One's most famous Judge – and he looked like hell! I was back on adjutant duty in the Chief Judge's office, after yesterday's fiasco at SJS headquarters. She didn't seem to know about my 'encounter' with Eliphas, so it looks like I've gotten away with it. I guess if Eliphas is so busy running random physical abuse tests on the likes of Joe Dredd, he's hardly got time to be worried about me.

It was the first time I'd seen Dredd up close and somehow I expected him to be taller. He's nearly a legend in the Academy, where all the Cadets call him Old Stony Face. Having met him, I know why now. He's got a jaw like reinforced rockcrete, boulders would break on it. Some age lines are gathering around the edges of his face, but the mouth betrays no emotion. There's a rumour that he's got special dispensation to take illegal youth drugs. Whoever started that had obviously never met Dredd.

Everything about him speaks authority: his stance, his bearing, his demeanour. He must be 40 or even 50 by now, but you wouldn't know it to look at him. The body is rock hard and whipcord thin, just lean muscle, sinew and bone. Nothing flashy or excessive, not like the male

Cadets in my year who used to spend most of their time training just to get better bodies. Dredd's body is a tool, just another weapon in the fight against crime, the fight to uphold the Law.

Standing in the same room as him should make you feel proud to be a Judge, but it just made me all the more aware of my own failures, my own shortcomings. If only I could become a tenth of the Judge that Dredd is, I'd feel a lot better about myself . . .

Dredd was punctual, arriving at exactly 0800 hours, but the Chief Judge contrived to accuse him of tardiness, showing no respect for her or her authority. Dredd wasn't having a bar of it.

I respect the Law, but you're just a joke, he told McGruder. He said the Chief Judge had instituted the Mechanismo robo-judges programme which killed dozens of citizens. Then, after that, she had authorised field testing of the Mark II robo-judges. Dredd said the Chief Judge was obviously unbalanced and she should resign immediately.

McGruder was furious, jumping up out of her chair, accusing Dredd of wanting to be Chief Judge himself, plotting with others to overthrow her. Dredd just shook his head, muttering something, which McGruder demanded to have repeated, saying she was still Chief Judge and Dredd would follow her orders or face court-martial proceedings!

Dredd said she should do her own dirty work, instead of using the SJS to try and beat a confession out of him with a random physical abuse test. McGruder didn't say anything for nearly a moment, just a stony silence filled the room. I realised I was holding my breath.

Finally she sat back down in her chair and called up the latest crime briefings on her vid-screen. She told Dredd the body of the Sector Chief for 66 had just been discovered, stuffed into a public grinder. McGruder assigned Dredd to go and investigate, making him acting Chief Judge for the sector.

Dredd looked like he was going to refuse, but eventually left. The Chief Judge sneered a final comment to him: don't hurry back, Joe.

* * *

Judge Barbara Hershey was waiting when Dredd emerged from the Chief Judge's office and motioned for him to follow her.

'What's all this about, Hershey? I've got to – ' demanded Dredd, but Hershey quietened him by putting a finger to her lips. She led him into her office then outside onto a balcony overlooking the city's Southern sector, closing the door after him.

'Well?' asked Dredd impatiently. 'Why all the cloak and dagger?'

'Walls have ears round here, you know that as well as I do, Dredd,' replied Hershey, the authority in her voice belying the difference in their ages. She was barely 30, but was equal with Dredd in rank, if not yet in stature inside the Justice Department. Her jet black hair was cut in a simple fringed bob, framing her pretty but stern face and striking green eyes. 'Have you thought anymore about what we discussed last week?'

'I've already told you, I won't be part of any conspiracy against McGruder. If she goes, she goes according to the book – or not at all.'

Hershey was amazed at Dredd's loyalty to the Law, despite the flaws of their leader wielding it. 'You still say that, even after she ordered that random physical abuse test on you?' Dredd paused before replying, his features as impenetrable to Hershey as ever.

'You can prove that?'

'Niles at SJS told me the order came directly from the Chief Judge's office. And she hand-picked Eliphas to run the test, knowing how much he hates you,' confided Hershey.

'Hmmph,' agreed Dredd grudgingly, bruising still obvious around his chin from the beatings he had taken yesterday. 'As long as the Mechanismo project remains suspended, I can take a few lumps. I will not take part in a conspiracy and that's final.'

'What if the robo-judges project is still active?' asked Hershey.

Dredd scowled. 'You have evidence?'

'Nothing yet, but McGruder's been awful cocky the last few days. And she spends a lot of time in secret conference with Greel at Tek Division. Something's going on . . .'

'That could explain why she's posted me to Sector 66,' Dredd mused. 'Kozwall got stuffed into a grinder.'

'I heard,' grimaced Hershey. 'Look, I've got contacts who are looking into things. Will you at least listen if we get proof?'

'As and when,' replied Dredd and went back through Hershey's office to head out for his new posting. After a few moments Hershey stepped back inside, to find the Chief Judge's new assistant waiting for her by the door.

'Can I speak with you?' asked Judge Laverne Castillo, brushing a long, black curl of hair out of her eyes.

'Where the hell have you been? We've been worried sick!'

Gilda and Tevin had been standing outside the broken-down rockcrete building and seen Genya approaching. Gilda trotted out to meet her friend, at least she walked as fast as her weary legs could carry her. After more than a decade spent living here in the dead zone, she was bent over at the spine, her face wizened and old before its time, like her friend.

Behind Gilda, Tevin remained standing in the doorway of their home, supporting himself on a metal cane made from the buckled ruins of the bomb-blasted buildings around them. He was a little stooped, not the giant he had once been, but he still towered over his wife and her friend.

Genya took Gilda's hand and let herself be guided back into the tiny room they all shared. The walls were bare rockcrete and a corner of the roof had been seared away by the force of the shockwave from the East-Meg bombs when they fell.

The ground was hard, stony, just a few sheets of matting recovered from a pile of rubble as carpet. In two of the corners were beds Tevin had fashioned for them out of twisted metal strands, back when he had been strong, before the radiation sickness had stolen the strength from his hands and the will from his heart. Only Gilda kept him going now, and keeping him alive kept her going.

Genya couldn't remember why she kept herself going. Sometimes, she'd had a curious feeling in her bones. Almost as if there was an old friend nearby, or somebody that she knew well, and yet didn't know at all. She couldn't explain it and she hadn't told Gilda or Tevin about it. They'd think she was going crazy, and they would probably be right.

'Well? Where have you been all this time?' asked Gilda again, once they were all inside. She fussed about, stirring some weak broth in a blackened old bowl over a fire they kept lit at all times, to keep away the wild animals.

'I went out looking for shoots, from that crop we planted a few months back. I thought maybe something might have grown . . .' said Genya weakly, aware how lame it all sounded.

'Ha! We should be so lucky! What could grow in poisoned soil like this?' cried out Tevin, clutching at a handful of dust from the floor and letting it fall through his fingers to the ground again.

'I know, it was foolish,' nodded Genya weakly.

'There's something else, something you're not telling us,' probed Gilda, always the perceptive one. Genya looked away before replying.

'Tomas is dead. I saw his body by the acid pit.'

Gilda crossed herself while Tevin just looked sad. The inhabitants of the dead zone maintained a loose community, keeping in touch when they could, looking out for each other, sharing the occasional find of edible fungus or a water source that wasn't too radioactive. In an area where swallowing a single radioactive particle from the soil could be fatal, scraping a living meant a constant battle with death.

They had all known Tomas, all liked him, especially Tevin. Women always seemed to survive longest in the dead zone, while the men rarely lasted more than a year there. Tomas was the last of the men in the community to die, excluding Tevin.

'Another death,' tutted Gilda, before turning to her husband. 'Well just make sure it never happens to you!'

'I can't die! You won't give me a chance,' replied Tevin and a rare smile crept across his face. They all laughed, until the sound of a howling creature silenced them again.

'I'll stoke up the fire for the night,' said Gilda and bustled outside to collect some fuel. Genya watched her go before turning back to watch the fire. As she looked deep into its flames, her body gave an involuntary shiver. That strange feeling of familiarity was with her again . . .

Lynn Miller looked down at the remnants of Kozwall's badge and wondered how she would end up dying. A bullet in the head one day down a dark alleyway? Surviving forty years on the streets to take the Long Walk out into the Cursed Earth? Dying peacefully of old age in her sleep after a lifetime spent serving her city on the streets, then later teaching at the Academy? Or something else, something she couldn't imagine right now. However it happened, she didn't want to die like Eammon Kozwall, stuffed into a public grinder like so much garbage. No dignity, no respect, no glory, no heroics, just pain and shame and then nothing ever again.

Miller remembered her first meeting with Kozwall, the day she reported for duty at Sector House 66. She was still undergoing treatment for radiation sickness after her sojourn in the Cursed Earth but had requested a new posting to ease the bitter memories of those recent events. So she was sent to Sector 66, a hellhole that made the Slab seem like a pleasant environment by comparison.

Kozwall had called her into his office and immediately appointed her Deputy Chief Judge for the sector. Before she could protest, he explained his reasoning.

'I've read your record, Miller. You came out of the Academy with some of the best marks in your year, just missing out on the honour roll for the Class of 2012. Two years later you became the first Judge to volunteer for posting to the notorious Nelson Rockefeller Orbital Housing Estate. While there you were promoted to Deputy Station Chief, later becoming acting Station Chief during the sabotage crisis. One of only a handful of survivors when the satellite fell to Earth, you've since picked up several commendations for valour.'

Kozwall had looked up at her with probing eyes.

'Why the hell have you come here?'

'I was assigned this station,' replied Miller evenly.

'Uh-huh. Well, I've just over a year before they transfer me to another station and you're the best candidate for replacing me we've ever had through this dump. So, from now on, you'll be my deputy – end of discussion.'

'Sir.'

'Right. Come with me and I'll show you what we're up against.'

Kozwall took her on a tour of the sector. It was underfunded, under-enforced, the Judges on duty were overworked and demoralised, with little or no new equipment. The citi-blocks were dumping grounds for the scum of the city and gang warfare ran riot.

Together the pair had hammered out a treaty between the gangs and brought some law and order to the sector. It was still under-funded and under-enforced, and most of the problems wouldn't go away overnight. But they had been able to make progress.

Now Miller felt everything slipping away again. Kozwall – the true architect of peace in the sector – was dead, brutally, humiliatingly murdered and now a major gang war was brewing. Worst of all, she couldn't mourn, couldn't cry for the best friend she'd ever had, because tears would be a sign of weakness and anyway, they had long since been beaten out of her.

'Excuse me, Judge Miller?' The quiet voice pulled her

out of the reverie and back to the harsh reality of her location. The speaker was a Tek-Judge from the sector house, easily recognisable by his glasses. Only specialist Judges were permitted such eccentricities of appearance or behaviour. Miller thought she recognised him.

'Flint, isn't it?'

'Yes, ma'am. I want you to have a look at this.' He led her to the side of the grinder, which had been broken open for better examination. 'I ran the snuffler over the body and the grinder, and picked up some interesting readings. For a start, there are these long scratches in the metal around the mouth of the grinder,' he said, pointing to four long slices cut into the machine's outer casing.

'So?'

'At first I thought they were just scratches caused by everyday use. Then I found this.' Flint delicately pulled a tiny fragment of something hard and yellowed from the metal. 'I think it's part of a nail or claw, but it's not from anything human.'

'Are you saying an animal pushed Kozwall into the grinder and then turned it on?' said Miller, disbelievingly. 'That's crazy!'

'Perhaps, but there's more,' replied Flint and led her over to the hover-stretcher on which was spread what little remained of the late sector chief. 'If you look here and here, you'll see similar scratches, wounds caused by the same creature.'

Miller turned away. She wasn't repulsed by blood or the sight of death, Grud knows she'd experienced enough, killed her share of perps in her three years on the streets. But this was all that remained of Eammon Kozwall – a colleague, a fellow Judge, and her friend.

Flint knew none of this and kept burbling on relentlessly.

'Most fascinating of all, I've taken readings and there seems to be a major discrepancy with the corpse. Do we know when the grinder was last used before Kozwall was found inside it?' he asked enthusiastically.

Miller looked to Brighton for the information.

'Ah, well, we're still interviewing local cits, but no more than three or four hours before the body was found. The woman who actually phoned in the discovery is over there,' the young Judge chipped in, before pointing to a happy young woman in handcuffs attached to a holding post. She was trying unsuccessfully to push a blond ringlet out of her eyes, a task made difficult by her bondage. 'She's got a long record of sponting, name of Samantha Hester. She confessed to stuffing Kozwall in the grinder, had her story partially confirmed by vid-phone lie detector.'

Miller approached Samantha, who beamed broadly at the Judge.

'Are you sending me to the cubes now? What's my sentence? Killing a Judge is a serious offence, do you think I'll get life for it?' the captive gushed gleefully.

Miller considered the prisoner carefully before speaking. Samantha was quite thin, obviously unused to regular physical labour, and her face was wide-eyed and enthusiastic. Hardly capable of killing Kozwall, tearing his body apart then stuffing the rest down a public grinder. Grud, the woman would barely be able to lift Kozwall from the ground!

'Why did you confess to pushing the Judge's body into the grinder?' asked the Judge, carefully checking Samantha's responses on a hand-held Birdie, which was far more reliable than the vid-phone version.

'Because I did it, of course,' smiled Samantha, as if she were explaining something simple to a child.

'Lie detector says otherwise,' replied Miller, turning it round so the captive could read the screen: *false*.

'It must be faulty.'

'Maybe you did switch on the grinder, trying to clear a blockage and ended up grinding the Judge a bit more, but he was already in there, wasn't he? He was already dead.'

'No! That's not true! That's not how it happened!'

False was the Birdie's verdict again. Miller deactivated

the ultrasonic lock on the cuffs and released the captive. 'You're free to go anytime you want, Miss Hester. Thanks for your assistance.' The Judge turned and walked away.

'No, you've got it wrong! I killed the Judge! I did it!' shouted Samantha after her, but to no avail.

Back at Kozwall's body, Flint was rapt, completely in his element.

'Right. Well, that proves it, then!'

'Proves what?' demanded Miller.

'Proves my theory,' smiled Flint triumphantly. 'Sector Chief Kozwall died more than six hours ago. His body was put in the grinder long after he died, probably to try and disguise the true method of his murder, and to give the killer – or killers – an alibi.'

Miller's mind reeled, but she kept her wits enough to find a new question from Flint's final statement. 'Why do you say killer or killers?'

'Judging by the ferocity of the attack and the nature of the wounds inflicted, either there were more than one killer, or else . . .' his voice trailed away, as he realised the consequences of his findings. 'Or else we're dealing with something that's not even remotely human, with the strength of at least three men and a liking for the taste of human brains,' he concluded, smiling wanly.

Miller just stared at him, while Brighton threw-up round the corner of the block building.

Dylan Finn pulled on his new kneepads and stood back to admire himself in the full-length mirror set into the west wall of his hab-unit. Not bad, not bad at all, even if he said so himself. If this didn't get Ronetta Clobb's attention, he didn't know what would.

The kneepads were purple with bright yellow swirls set into the crushed velveteen material. Best of all, they exuded a 'control pheromone fragrance, designed to entice and excite any woman of your choice' – or so said the enticing and exciting advertisement that screened almost wall-to-wall on M-tri-D, the fave music channel on tri-D among the juves.

Dylan sniffed a little, a strange odour playing about the edges of senses. A smell like – like rotting munce! This was the fragrance designed to entice and excite? More likely to make you throw, Dylan decided and pulled the kneepads off, stuffing them back into the box and stuffing it down the mini-grinder in his hab. What a con! Well, at least he hadn't paid for them, unlike the sucker whom Dylan had relieved the kneepads from earlier.

Dylan was a dunk, a pickpocket, and a pretty audacious one at that. His proudest achievement to date was stealing six stumm gas grenades from the utility belt of a street Judge. Of course, he nearly got caught trying to sell these highly sought-after contraband items on the black weapons market, but he'd gotten away with it, like he always did.

Although it was nearly four hundred years since his ancestors had come over from Ireland as immigrants, Dylan had still grown up in a family fiercely proud of its heritage. The phrase Dylan had most frequently heard describing him as a child was 'he must have kissed the Blarney Stone at birth'. Quite what it meant, Dylan didn't know, but he was an inordinately lucky juve.

He had three things to thank for his good fortune – quick wits, a deft touch and something of the loner about him. While other juves joined gangs and got into fights with rival gangs, Dylan had concentrated on looking after one person – himself. He prided himself on his ability to talk his way into and out of any situation he was ever likely to encounter. And his fingers were subtle enough to steal the Lawmaster from under Dredd himself without the legendary Judge noticing anything was missing! Or so Dylan liked to brag.

In truth, he was a highly successful dunk, with a luxuriously furnished (if somewhat tacky) hab to prove it. The room seemed to drip gold and gilt; the walls were painted lurid shades of green and gold, while a massive hover-bed floated just off the floor, with a genuine imitation leopard-skin pattern quilt spread across its vast expanse and the latest solid-hologram virtual surreality toy lying discarded in a corner. Best of all, a wall-safe hidden behind a velvet painting of the Statue of Judgement contained nearly twenty thousand creds.

Dylan had come to the conclusion that dunking was a mug's game and he really wanted to go into a more lucrative business, like dentistry. Now there was a low-risk, high-return venture. You inflicted pain on people and they paid you ridiculously high sums of creds for the privilege! Best of all, it was completely legal. Of course, virtually all dentists were now robots, but a few human dentists remained, servicing the needs of only the richest of Big Meg's citizens. They considered it common to have their teeth serviced by a droid and appreciated the vast expense needed for a human to achieve a degree in dentistry.

Becoming a dentist was almost impossible, simply because the cost of the mental implants was so exorbitant – half a million creds. Schooling for dentistry and other such professions had long since been abandoned, because virtually all jobs were occupied by robots. It was still possible to learn to become a dentist, simply by purchasing the correct technical and skill implants and having them slotted into your brain.

Dylan was young, not yet eighteen, and he had set himself a target. If he could net just 1500 creds a day from dunking, he would have the necessary funds to buy his way into the lucrative world of dentistry within a year. He was already a quarter of the way there – just a few more months to go before the big payoff . . .

The young pickpocket slipped on a normal, nondescript pair of kneepads, a bulky jacket full of secret pockets for storing ill-gotten gains and a hefty hat to hide his eyes from suspicion. He looked in the mirror again and smiled – now he would blend into any crowd on any skedway in the city, the perfect disguise for a dunk.

'Today, I'm going to dunk me ten thousand creds!' he announced to the room and departed. Who cared about Ronetta Clobb anyway? Once Dylan was a qualified dentist, he could have any woman he wanted in the whole of Mega-City One. Such was the power of a good set of teeth!

'So what do you want to talk about, Judge – Castillo, isn't it?' Hershey sank into the high-backed chair behind her desk and regarded the woman sitting opposite her. She was young: 20 years old at the most, probably only one year out of the Academy. Her skin had a natural light-brown tint while her hair was jet black, curly, piled high atop her head. Hershey guessed she had some Hispanic ancestry in her blood, especially with a name like Castillo. Most of all, she seemed nervous.

'Yes, Laverne Castillo. I've been assigned to Chief Judge McGruder as her personal adjutant,' she replied hesitantly.

'You're a bit young for an indoors job – screw up on the streets?' asked Hershey archly. She wasn't sure whether to trust the visitor. Castillo's arrival just as Dredd was leaving their secret meeting to discuss the Chief Judge was a mite too heavy on the coincidence level for Hershey's blood, so the senior Judge decided to play it cool for now.

'Yes. I – I froze, nearly got another Judge killed.' Castillo cast her eyes to the ground, ashamed, embarrassed. Either this girl studies acting in her spare time, or she's on the level, thought Hershey.

'But that isn't why I came to you. When I graduated from the Academy, you were the senior Judge giving out the badges. You told us that if we ever had a problem, your door was open.'

Hershey smiled to herself. Now she remembered Castillo! The young woman had been just as nervous on her graduation day, even dropped the badge when handed it.

65

Still, she must have had some backbone to get through 15 years at the Academy.

'Yes, that's right,' agreed Hershey.

'Well, I think I'm in big trouble. Yesterday I was sent to SJS headquarters where a senior Judge sexually harassed me – so I struck him. And now I'm assisting the Chief Judge, who seems to be unbalanced!' Castillo nearly burst into tears.

'Who was the officer at the SJS you struck?'

'Eliphas, ma'am.'

'Hmmph! He probably deserved it. Eliphas is the worst kind of creep,' commented Hershey dryly. Castillo looked up at her, shocked.

'For Grud's sake, Castillo, pull yourself together!' Hershey got out of her seat and walked round to the front of her desk, perching on its leading edge. 'Judges are human beings too; we make mistakes sometimes, you've got to remember that. It's how you learn from those mistakes that counts. As for Eliphas, well, there are bad Judges as well as good ones and mediocre ones. Has he retaliated since you struck him?'

Castillo just shook her head.

'Well, let me know if he tries anything. Eliphas and I have had our brushes in the past, I can deal with that drokker.'

'Yes, ma'am.'

Hershey looked down at Castillo, considering.

'Now as for the Chief Judge, it's both disrespectful and dangerous to call her unbalanced – even if it is accurate! Perhaps there's something we can do about her, if you want to help . . .'

Lynn Miller sat in the chair that had been Kozwall's until a few hours ago and demanded a few straight answers.

'So can anybody tell me how Chief Kozwall's absence was not noted for nearly four hours? Well, Symes?'

The desk Judge had been the last to see the late sector chief alive, when Kozwall had called him into the office,

66

asking if there was anyone else in the building. Symes chewed on the tip of his robotic hand as he thought – the original had been shot off in action five years ago, stranding him behind the main desk in the sector house. He might not be in the thick of the action, but he still made a valuable contribution.

'I last saw him about 0300 hours. He called me into his office and I remember he seemed tense, nervous. He said he thought there was someone else in the building, but I told him just about everyone was out on the graveyard shift. Forensics were looking at those remains found in the Maze, but they were all down in the Tek section. Simpson was watching over the Holding Tanks, that was all.'

'And you didn't see him again.'

'No, that was it, ma'am.'

'Did anybody come in or out of his office?'

'Not that I noticed, but soon after Phillips and Standley brought in a bunch of old crocks from the Bingo riot in Vincent Price Block and it got pretty busy. I logged off at 0800 hours.'

'What about the sector house holovids?' suggested Brighton.

'There's nothing on the security scanner either, I already checked,' replied Symes, clutching the vid-slug in his human hand.

'Let's have another look,' decided Miller. Once the vid-slug was loaded into the holovid system, a three-dimensional hologram was projected into the air over the desk, showing in miniature the entrance to the sector chief's office. Miller stabbed a couple of controls and the image was fast-forwarded from 0200 through to 0800 hours in less than a minute. Symes was clearly seen bursting into the office at 0307, then leaving a minute later, but nothing else.

'Told you, nothing there,' said the desk Judge unhappily. Beside him, Brighton looked puzzled and began playing with the controls, winding it back to just before Symes' entrance.

'So why didn't anyone notice Kozwall's absence?' quizzed Miller, determined to get to the bottom of this mystery. She looked at the daytime desk Judge – Wallis, a bald woman who had an artificial voice-box. Like Symes, Wallis had been desk-bound since being injured on the streets. In her case, she had interrupted perps breaking into a Justice Department Armoury and her throat had been shot out.

'Kozwall wasn't missed because he wasn't expected in. He was due at a sector chief's meeting at Justice Central, but now they're saying he never turned up,' shrugged Wallis.

'Well, it ain't good enough! Judges don't just "disappear", they go missing thanks to a major lapse in sector house security. Kozwall is dead and I'm holding you two responsible until a better candidate turns up!' Miller banged her fist on the desk, her voice full of cold fury. She turned to Brighton, who was still manipulating the controls of the holovid.

'Brighton! For Grud's sake, stop playing with that drokking vid-slug!' she shouted.

'I'm not playing – look,' he replied quietly, rerunning the sequence just leading up to Symes being called into and then leaving Kozwall's office. Again, there was no other obvious movement on the hologram.

'We've seen it half a dozen times,' began Symes, reaching to switch off the holovid. 'There's nothing –'

'No!' exclaimed Brighton, knocking Symes' hand away. He altered the viewing setting. 'Now watch it in infrared.'

The same sequence began again but this time a faint red shadow appeared from the right of the hologram and entered the office. Moments later the blazing white heat signature of Symes burst into the office, then came out again. Nearly a full minute passed before the red shadow came out of the office, but this time the shadow was a different shape – bulkier, and slower moving. Once it had cleared the edge of the hologram, Brighton switched the vid-slug off, the hint of a smile on his lips.

Symes broke the silence: 'What the drokk was that?'

'Good question,' announced Miller. 'Wallis, you take that tape down to Flint and the rest of the Teks, see what they make of it. And find out what they've made of that claw fragment Flint found at the grinder – something tells me the two are interconnected.'

'Right!'

'Symes, I want to see the rest of the vid-slugs, especially those for security systems overlooking the sector house entrance.'

'That's a Roj!'

'Brighton?'

'Yes, ma'am?'

'Good work – but don't let it go to your head. You ain't sector chief yet, you know!'

'No, ma'am!'

'That's good advice,' offered another voice from outside the office. 'But neither are you, yet!'

Miller got up out of her seat and started towards the door, but the owner of the new voice was already stepping into the room. He was tall, he was grim and he wasn't very happy to be there.

'Judge Dredd!' spluttered Miller.

'Glad you still recognise me, 'cause I'm the new sector chief for 66. Now what the hell's been going on here?'

FIVE

Second Field Test

Confidential Report for: XXXXX XXXXX
From: XXXXX XXXXX

Re: Notes on secondary field testing for Prometheus Project prototypes

Aim: To collect data on actual combat scenario performance of mutate creature, from which the prototype creature will be developed.

Methodology: The hybrid creature was being transported from the orbiting satellite laboratory where it was developed to a new location. However, the lock on the creature's cage was to 'malfunction' during the flight, allowing it to escape at a pre-designated point. This gave it the opportunity to use its physical abilities in a harsh environment, in this case, the Alaskan tundra.

Throughout the field test, strict monitoring of the hybrid was maintained at all times by XXXXXX. A remote-controlled destruct device was implanted in the creature before the flight, to enable its complete destruction should the field test be detected by the wrong authorities.

Procedure: The shuttle craft Erasmus left the Aarcom-Zeitz satellite orbital research laboratory on schedule, the cargo's installation overseen by the project leader, Darius Flaw. The two-person crew were kept unaware of the true nature of the cargo, merely being told they were shipping crystal minerals Earth-side. Once the shuttle had entered the Earth's atmosphere, the pilot Newey was contacted by ATC, Atmospheric Traffic Control. This is standard procedure, but this time the XXXXXX team initiated the contact, whilst jamming the presence of the Erasmus from standard Earth-side scanning systems.

The Erasmus was granted air corridor clearance and given a course heading to take it over the Alaskan wastes. At this point the 'malfunction' in the cage locking system was initiated. The creature moved to the front of the shuttle craft and quickly disposed of the two crew. [Note: see onboard security scans for graphic demonstration of its raw power in close quarters conflict.] The creature was unable to pilot the shuttle and it soon crash-landed in the pre-arranged drop-zone, several hundred klicks north of Uranium City.

[Note: it was later discovered the crash was observed by a local prospector, Jethro Muvalve, who returned to his home in the small mining service community of Misery, a hundred klicks to the south. He informed several other individuals of his sighting, which led to the events detailed later in this report. Muvalve subsequently died while undergoing 'debriefing' in a special cell in Uranium City. Nearly all the other inhabitants of Misery who knew about the shuttle crash have also since been silenced.]

Within three hours of the crash, the head of the Geno-Tech division of Aarcom-Zeitz (the 'creators' of the prototype creature) was notified of the 'incident'. Flaw briefed a pre-selected team of highly experienced security troopers, all former members of deep space search-and-destroy teams. He told them they were going on a 'bug-hunt', searching for a new hybrid creature called the Mark 12 design. The team were told the hybrid had chameleon abilities and were given movement sensors to track it. Flaw ordered the hybrid be retrieved and delivered to its destination unharmed. The squad immediately left in a camouflaged drop-ship, with precise co-ordinates for the crash-site.

[Note: By this time the prospector Muvalve was back in Misery, and had told two individuals about the shuttle crash – a small-time mutant grifter called Zeke, and a local gun-for-hire, Harmony Krieg. The pair were forced to leave Misery after a fire-fight on the main street and headed north on sleds drawn by cyber-huskies. Muvalve had told the mutant he believed the crashed shuttle might contain valuable cargo they could salvage, if he got a share of the profits.

Soon afterwards a freelance operative for the Uranium City Justice Department named Havoc arrived in Misery, looking for Krieg. Muvalve approached Havoc and sold him information about Krieg's whereabouts. Havoc immediately began pursuit of his quarry, travelling in an All Terrain Vehicle (ATV).]

The bug-hunt team of Moore, Hamsund and Pethon arrived at the crash-site to discover stark evidence of their target's abilities. A scrambled report back to Flaw reported the cockpit of the Erasmus had been shattered from inside. The body of co-pilot Purvis was still in its seat, ribcage ripped open by huge claws, the top of his skull pulled back, the brain completely missing. Further inside the downed shuttle was a mess of blood and flesh fragments, metal shards and shreddings – all that remained of the pilot Newey and her craft's interior, both butchered. The report also stated that the motion sensors were only partially effective in tracking the hybrid.

[Note: See summary for more details. The following information was gleaned from standard surveillance cameras set into the hunting team's helmets, as well as secret scanner and sensor implants grafted onto the hybrid itself.]

The hunters quickly became frustrated, facing a foe they could not physically see and which frequently eluded their motion sensors. They also quickly realised they were under-equipped, armed with a titanium net projector and

72

one small-calibre machine pistol. One of the team, Pethon, began to panic and tried to return to their dropship, ignoring a warning from his comrades that the hybrid might be inside the craft. Before Pethon could react, his head was cleanly sliced from his body by one swipe of the hybrid's talons. The creature was sprayed with its victims blood, the splashback making it partially visible against the snow-white background [Note: See vid-slug play-back for illustration of this phenomenon].

The team member with the machine pistol, Hamsund, began firing indiscriminately at the hybrid, despite warnings from Moore that he could hit the drop-ship, their only means of escape. Hamsund kept firing but the bullets were having no effect against the hybrid's silicon-bonded outer 'armour-plated' skin. It attacked the hunter, slashing his chest open with its claws, but he kept firing, his shots now flying wildly around, several hitting the engines and fuel storage areas of the dropship. The damage initiated a chain reaction, which caused the drop-ship to explode 24 seconds later. Both Hamsund and the hybrid were consumed by the explosive fireball and flying shrapnel it generated.

The final team member, Moore, survived the explosion. Unfortunately for him, so did the hybrid, which swiftly pressed its attack and began to feed upon his still living body. Within an hour, night fell over the snowy tundra. The hybrid spent the evening cleaning, licking the last of its victim's blood from its body, gradually restoring its invisibility.

Next morning the pairing of Harmony Krieg and the mutant Zeke reached the downed shuttle. Krieg accessed the ship's onboard computers and discovered the true cargo was a battle hybrid, not diamonds as stated on the manifest. Realising the danger they faced, the pair were about to flee when Havoc arrived at the crash-site in his ATV, using a sonic shockwave projector to incapacitate them. He emerged from his vehicle and began to arrest Krieg when she told him about the danger. Havoc remained dismissive until he turned to see the creature unveil itself momentarily, standing between them and the ATV, their only escape.

The three individuals quickly decided to work together against the hybrid, realising team-work would give them their only chance of survival. The woman Krieg noted that her cyber-huskies were able to sense the creature's presence. The mutant Zeke tried to make a run for the ATV but was struck down by the hybrid; not a killing blow. Havoc tried to shoot the creature but was stopped by Krieg, who believed the prototype was merely toying with them. The trio used the enhanced animal senses of the dogs to follow the hybrid's movements.

One of the dogs attacked the hybrid and was struck down, brutally mauled. Surveillance cameras set into the drop-ship recorded the creature as it feasted on this new morsel. Krieg noticed the inside of the creature's mouth was visible when it was opened. She released the rest of the cyber-huskies and told Havoc to fire at the hybrid's mouth, but the shots went wide. Meanwhile the mutant Zeke took this chance to sneak into the safety of the ATV, Havoc following him.

Now the hybrid turned on Krieg, striking her to the ground, ready to tear her body apart. But this had given Havoc enough time to get an anti-tank bazooka from his ATV, loaded with armour-piercing shells. He fired once at the hybrid to get its attention, then – just as it reared up, mouth drawn open in a snarl of triumph and bloodlust – he fired again, directly into its open mouth.

The shell exploded in the hybrid's head, blowing most of it backwards across the snow behind it. The prototype was dead. Krieg double-crossed her two new partners and departed in the ATV, leaving them in the snowy wastes to start the long trek back to Misery.

A second drop-ship landed at the crash-site soon after Havoc and Zeke had departed. A clean-up crew removed all trace of the crashed shuttle, the dead humans and cyber-huskies, while a scientific team took the remains of the hybrid away for further examination. The entire site was wiped clean within three hours, no trace remaining of what had taken place there should there be any investigation. All records of the flight of the Erasmus have been wiped from travel logs. According to all known records, the 'incident' never happened.

The three survivors have also been silenced. Harmony Krieg was captured one month after the events described above and given a complete memory wipe by authorities in Uranium City, while Havoc has been 'persuaded' to forget the incident. The mutant Zeke has been threatened into silence, assisted by a small payoff in creds. All traces of this field test have been wiped away.

Summary: This exercise provided much valuable data on the abilities and flaws of the Mark 12 design prototype mutate creature. The chameleon talent combined with an ability to mask its movements made it almost impossible to track, although animals were still able to sense its presence. Also, the mouth was uncovered as a potential Achilles' heel, giving away the hybrid's presence when open, as did any external matter splashed on it, such as blood.

The hybrid displayed considerable aggression, although this contributed to its eventual destruction. It also recognised the blood-splash as a potential recognition marker for either its prey or predators, and cleaned this away on its own initiative.

The creature's major drawback was a lack of total reasoning intelligence or strategic goals. Aggressive and quite deadly, it was content to hunt and kill within a limited area, but lacked any ambition to move beyond this area. Equally, it failed to adapt, using the same tactics repeatedly. At best, it displayed a malicious streak to toy with its victims, but little other useful intelligence.

Recommendations: Just like the Skinner imperative tested in the first field experiment, the hybrid is better utilised as part of a complete bio-weapon. Combining the reasoning intelligence of the Skinner (with its exponential learning curve, knowledge absorption and Psi-invisibility) and the physical prowess, aggression and chameleonic abilities of the mutate creature would create a near-invincible weapon.

This should be the next stage of development, with the end result again tested in a hostile environment outside Mega-City One to prevent detection of this project. The major obstacle to overcome will then be controlling the product of this research, so it can be used for our own purposes, rather than anyone else's – or even its own.

Signed: XXXXX XXXXX
April 02, 2116 AD

SIX

Less than Zero

Iso-Block Zero: probably the most feared place of incarceration in Mega-City One, this forbidding black building stands in the exact geographical centre of the city. At any time it houses never more than a hundred perps, but has the capacity for up to two thousand. The reason for its seemingly wasteful emptiness? Iso-Block Zero is the modern equivalent of Death Row. This is where convicted criminals come to await execution. It is rarely full because the most dangerous perps are rarely captured alive, or else the death sentence is passed and executed on the streets.

No perp transferred to Iso-Block Zero has ever escaped, been reprieved or released. The building is the final stop on the way to the execution chamber, from where the body is taken to Resyk so the perp may give the city some benefit in death that they rarely did during life. Due to its location and special purpose, Iso-Block Zero has a rather morbid but appropriate nickname: the Dead Centre.

> Extract from *Justice and How it Works for You*
> Judge O'Neill, 2112 AD

Bruno 'The Bomber' Chuckowski was bitter, and not without reason. He had been brought to the Dead Centre five days ago after his final appeal for clemency to the Chief Judge had been gruffly rejected. Now he was waiting to die, sentenced to execution by lethal injection.

Sometimes the irony of his situation brought a laugh to his throat but it never got past his lips. Sure, he'd been a bad citizen, some might even call him evil. Sure, he'd killed a few people – 217 to be precise, but who was counting, Bruno told himself. But now he faced execution for a crime he didn't commit and nobody would believe him!

Drokk! He wasn't even in Sector 99 when the sector house was blown up, killing more than a hundred Judges. He hadn't been in the sector for more than two months before the explosion, but his record counted against him. When the Judges had interrogated him about the crime, every lie detector backed him up, so the Judges decided Bruno must have developed some special system to beat the 'Birdie'.

Eventually they found him guilty on circumstantial evidence. Sure, the bomb that blew up the sector house was one of his, but it had been stolen from his conapt three days before the explosion. Was it his fault the thief decided to use the device to wipe out a sector house? Bruno realised the answer to that question was a big yes when he was transferred to the Dead Centre. He knew he should have had better security at home.

'There's just no justice,' he muttered to himself for the twenty-seventh time that morning. He was about to repeat the statement just for effect when the miracle happened. The iso-cube door slid open and a Judge-warder walked inside.

'Bit early for lunch, isn't it?' asked Bruno, before a chill thought ran through his mind. 'It's not – now – is it?' He wasn't ready yet; he hadn't prepared himself; he didn't really believe it was going to happen; oh Grud, he didn't want to die, please don't let it –

'No,' smiled the warder. 'It's good news. We're letting you go.'

Bruno couldn't believe what was he was hearing. 'What?'

'We're letting you go. Apparently some perp's just confessed to the bombing in 99, put you in the clear. Seems you were telling the truth after all – for once in your life!'

Bruno just sat on his bunk, dumbstruck, his mind reeling. It was impossible, it couldn't be happening, nobody was ever released from the Dead Centre. Could it actually be true? He stood up and almost fell back down again, his knees were so weak. His mouth opened and closed but no sound came out.

'Come on, get your things together, Chuckowski! We haven't got all day, y'know,' hurried the warder. 'Unless you want to stay here . . .'

That settled it! Bruno grabbed the handful of personal possessions he'd been allowed to retain, jammed them in his pockets, and bolted for the door before someone changed their mind. As he was led down a corridor to be released, Bruno didn't notice the Judge-warder shielding his face from the security cameras and scanners. Bruno was too busy trying to stifle any premature celebration; he just couldn't believe his good fortune. It was some cruel trick and any moment they would take him back to his cube, or worse . . . But that moment never came and soon he found himself outside the entrance to the building, saying goodbye to the warder.

'Well, er, thanks!' he laughed at last. Before he turned to go, there was one final question nagging at him that he had to ask. 'You're new here, I haven't seen you before today . . .'

'Y-Yes,' replied the warder, as if he hadn't been expecting the question. 'That's right. Just started. Well, keep your record clean from now on and you'll never see me again.'

'I hope not!' smiled the reprieved man and walked away from the dreaded building, a spring in his step and plans for a new crime already forming in his mind.

'I guarantee it,' muttered the warder to himself before stepping back into the iso-block. He strode through the building's back corridors before using a turbo-lift to drop down into the basement. There he stepped into the Judge-warders' locker-room, peeled off his uniform and slipped it into an automated laundry chute. Making sure he was not observed, he opened an unmarked locker, removed a standard Street Judge's uniform and pulled it on with quick, practised movements.

One final act: just before he rode out of the basement parking zone on his Lawmaster, the 'new' Judge slammed a fist through a glasseen window and punched a red alarm button. Klaxons wailed and blast-proof metal doors slammed down to the floor throughout the iso-block, cutting off any possible means of escape. But the mysterious saviour of Bruno 'The Bomber' Chuckowski was already gone . . .

'Anything out of the ordinary? The Psis have scanned the room already and picked up nothing unusual. Could you be a bit more specific, sir – this is Sector 66, after all.' Miller had updated Dredd on the events of the past 24 hours but was becoming exasperated by his oblique, almost monosyllabic replies and questions.

'Had there been any threats made against Kozwall or the sector house? Any unusual deaths or sudden changes in the stats for the sector?' he persisted, arms folded as he sat back in the dead man's chair.

'Threats – no, none more than those from the usual crazies. We've got one woman who sleepwalks to the sector house every Wednesday in the nude, but I don't think she's much of a threat, except to traffic perhaps,' mused Miller. 'Certainly no threats against Chief Kozwall himself that I know of, and we worked quite closely together.'

'Yes,' said Dredd, his voice heavy with disapproval.

Miller could feel her face flush with anger. 'If you're suggesting there was anything – '

Dredd held up a hand to silence her. 'No, I just believe Judges shouldn't form emotional links of any sort; it interferes with their ability to uphold and enforce the Law.'

Miller scowled, then thought back to Dredd's inquiry.

'Unusual deaths . . . Well, besides Kozwall being

stuffed into the grinder, there were a set of badly savaged human remains found in the Maze yesterday. The Tek boys are still examining those.'

'Savaged?'

Miller nodded. 'There was barely enough left to half-fill a body bag. The victim had been torn apart by some kind of crazed animal . . .' She ground to a halt, realizing the significance of her words. 'Tek-Judge Flint examined Kozwall's body where it was found. He speculated that the killer could be an animal of some sort, with a taste for human brains.'

'Brains?' Now it was Dredd's turn to think. 'There was a case three years ago, an alien killer that fed on the brains of its victims – Raptaur, the Teks called it.'

'What happened?'

'It was destroyed using a sonic disruptor in the sewers. At least, it seemed to have been destroyed . . .'

'You think it could have escaped?' asked Miller anxiously.

'Unlikely. But its true origins were never discovered.'

'I'll have Wallis pull the files from MAC at Justice Central.'

'Good.' Dredd got up and walked over to the side wall of the sector chief's office, examining a tri-D projection of the sector housed there. 'That could explain the body found in the Maze, but not Kozwall.'

'Why not?' wondered Miller aloud.

'His death was deliberate, he was singled out when half a dozen other potential victims were in the building. His death had to be premeditated.' Dredd turned round, pointed at the desk of his predecessor. 'Has anything been touched on this since Kozwall's disappearance?'

'Just the tri-D screen, we used that to view the vid-slug from the security scanner.'

'If Kozwall's death was premeditated, someone had a reason to kill him, a motive. The Raptaur killed randomly, so it seems likely . . .'

'Unless someone had found a way to control it,' suggested Miller. 'I wonder what Kozwall was doing here so late? What was he working on?'

'Too many questions, not enough answers,' decided Dredd. Before he could elaborate, Brighton appeared at the office door.

'Tek-Judge Flint wants to see you – both of you. He thinks he's found something!'

Hershey was not happy. While most divisions of the Justice Department had their own divisional heads – Niles for the SJS, Greel for Teks, Shenker for Psi Division – some areas didn't warrant a full-time chief. As a senior Judge, it was Hershey had held responsibility for many of these sub-groups, including the Academy of Law, the undercover Judges of the Wally Squad, and the Judge-warders. So when the alarm was raised at Iso-Block Zero, it was ultimately her responsibility to find the cause.

'Let me see if I've got this straight,' she grimaced. On her vid-phone she could see the nervous face of the head Judge-warder for the Dead Centre, a normally jovial, round-faced woman called Zandell. 'A prisoner responsible for the bombing of a sector house and the deaths of more than a hundred Judges just walked out of your maximum security iso-block?'

'Yes, ma'am,' stuttered the head warder.

'From which nobody is ever released and from which nobody has ever escaped?'

'Yes, ma'am.'

'And how do you explain this?'

'Umm, I can't, ma'am.'

Hershey tried a different approach. 'Who raised the alarm?'

'We, er, don't know that either, ma'am.'

The senior Judge just rolled her eyes. 'Didn't the security scanners pick up anything at all?'

'There seems to have been a, er, systems-wide failure during the escape, ma'am.' By now heavy drops of sweat were dripping into the head warder's eyes from her eyebrows, falling from Zandell's nose.

'Really? How convenient,' fumed Hershey. 'This smacks of gross incompetence and perhaps even conspiracy. I am hereby relieving you of duty until a full inquiry can be concluded. Put your deputy on please.'

'But, ma'am – ' protested the former head warder.

'*Do it!*' snarled Hershey. A new face appeared on the vid-phone, this time male. 'Well, what's your name?'

'Er, Lannock, ma'am.'

'Lannock, I hereby appoint you acting head warder for Iso-Block Zero, effective immediately. I hope you're one helluva lot more competent than your predecessor.'

'Yes, ma'am. Thank you, ma'am,' stammered the new head warder.

'Hershey out.' She fumed for a full minute before stomping her way to Control, to oversee the search personally. Bruno 'The Bomber' Chuckowski might have escaped through the incompetence of a few fools, but he wouldn't get the better of her!

Carl Chimpanzini – or Crazy, as he preferred to be called – loved Bananarak. That was hardly uncommon among the denizens of the Jungle. Of course consuming the heady mix of synthetic banana extract and alcohol was highly illegal. But Crazy did not have to worry about minor irritations like the Law, not as long as he stayed inside the Jungle, where Judges rarely patrolled. And the Jungle was Crazy's home, so why should he go outside?

Crazy loved his job, first lieutenant to Don Uggi the Third, strong-arm ape and enforcer of the Don's will. Crazy liked violence, some even said he had some wild orangutan blood in him. Of course, they didn't say it to his face, not if they wanted to keep their own in one piece. Crazy loved the sound of bones breaking and heads smashing and screams in the night, the jolt of his tommy gun as it spat death, the sight of blood and brain as it splashed against a wall.

But most of all, Crazy loved dames. Not female apes (although he didn't say no if one threw herself at him), but human women – real dames, he liked to call 'em. There was something about the sight of their hairless bodies, those gorgeous curves squeezed into clothing just half a size too small that wiped at Crazy's imagination, drove him mad with lust. Some said it wasn't natural for an ape to go with a skinface, but Crazy didn't care. He knew what he loved and where to get it – in abundance.

Crazy's favourite haunt – when he wasn't working for the Don – was a little speakeasy on the border of the Jungle, name of Kadie's. Kadie's catered for the most bizarre and baroque tastes of Sector 66's underworld. There was a full harem of prostitutes – aliens, apes and humans – illegal substances in abundance and an open all hours policy that extended to the all-female serving staff too.

Kadie's had the decor to match its decadent services (with the emphasis on the vice aspect). The ground floor was dimly lit, with a long imitation wooden bar running down one side on the left of the establishment, saloon style. Behind that was a room-length mirror with dozens of dubious draughts held in strange-shaped bottles and containers. Around the room were a series of tables and chairs, each alloted to a regular patron. There were no physical markings to tell whose table was whose, but anybody who came to Kadie's more than once knew exactly who sat where. Those unsuspecting visitors who had made the mistake of taking somebody else's table never made it back for a return visit. Kadie's was that kind of place.

Along the bar sprawled a selection of serving staff, each clad in as little as legally permissible. All the woman had faces that could fit into a church choir and bodies that would surely see them burn in hell for a very long time, if such a place existed. Most of the serving staff believed they had already arrived in hell, but Kadie's was not a business that accepted resignations easily.

At the back of the speakeasy a winding staircase led up to the first floor, where a balcony wound round the top of the central room, a series of black, unmarked doorways leading off it. The sound of screams or sobbing could sometimes be heard from those rooms, frequently with the two sounds merging together, growing ever louder and faster and more insistent until a final, juddering silence hung in the air.

No Judges darkened the doorstep of this establishment. It was considered a safe haven for perps, punks and escaped prisoners. Before any gang truce had ever been negotiated in Sector 66, this speakeasy was a sanctuary – no gang would ever attempt a hit here, it was tradition. Kadie's was the roughest joint in town and Crazy Chimpanzini loved it.

He was having a little get-together at Kadie's with some of his boys, to discuss the emergence of the new threat to Don Uggi's authority in the sector. All the apes were dressed in sharp, pin-stripe black suits, their jackets hung over the back of their chairs. Each kept a battered violin case close to their side, but the only musical accompaniment for the tommy guns inside was the sound of death and screaming. Crazy's brother Kookie was doing the talking.

'I say we hit 'em back now, hard and fast, show these dames who's top banana round here! If they can whack the Don's mother in da heart of da Jungle and get away with it, who knows where they'll stop?'

The other apes banged the gingham tablecloth in appreciation of his sentiments, until Kookie had a hand to silence them.

'I say we go out and teach the She Devils a little respect, show these dames their place!'

'Yeah – in da bedroom!' yelled Crazy. He slapped the well-rounded and scantily-clad thighs of a passing waitress, grunting lustily at her. Looking round, his eyes lit on a particularly alluring redhead waitress by the bar. He called over the owner of the joint. 'Hey, Kadie! Com'ere!'

A buxom woman of 50 with a face like a bear-trap approached. 'Yeah?'

Crazy jerked a thumb towards the redhead. 'Who's da new girl?'

'We call her Red, coz she's got a temper to match her hair colour.'

'Is that right? Well maybe she needs some taming – send her over!' Kadie departed to summon the new waitress, while Crazy turned back to his fellow gangsters. 'Now I'll show ya how to treat a dame!' The others howled and laughed, jumping up and down on their seats.

Red appeared beside Crazy, carrying a silver tray with a small cloth draped over the top of it, and wearing not much more. Tiny pieces of red silk and lace held her costume together, but barely kept her well-rounded curves contained. Tall red leathereen boots reached up her legs, and her lips shone crimson in the candlelit speakeasy.

'Can I get your something?'

'Yeah – you!' replied Crazy and burst out laughing, as did his five associates. He began to slide a simian hand up the waitress's thigh, brown and hairy against her smooth pink flesh. 'Well, howza bout it?'

Red smiled sarcastically and reached under the cloth on her tray. 'I don't think so, chimp! Or should that be chump?'

Crazy was shocked. No skinface had ever dared insult him like this. He started to get to his feet – he was gonna hafta teach this smart-mouth slitch a lesson. He pulled back a hand to slap the waitress to the ground and was even more surprised when a bullet blasted through his skull, scattering bone and brain over the rest of the apes.

Before the others could even start scrabbling for their weapons, the 'waitress' pumped a round into each of them, coolly, dispassionately, the silencer on her weapon keeping the gunshot noise to a minimum. She waited for a moment, put another bullet into Kookie who was still thrashing around, then pulled off her red wig and threw it on the table.

Black hair cascaded down to her shoulders as she pulled on a knee-length coat from a hook on the wall. Her long fingers dug a crumpled note out of one of the pockets and she slid it into the top pocket of Crazy's blood-speckled suit jacket. Casually she swivelled on the stiletto heels of her boots and marched from the silent speakeasy, pausing only to throw a roll of creds onto the bar in front of the shocked Kadie.

'For the damage,' announced the assassin and departed.

Kadie stumbled forward to the six corpses, disbelieving. One of her real waitresses had the presence of mind to pull the note from inside Crazy's pocket. On it were two words: SHE DEVILS.

Bruno heard the alarm being sounded when it was less than two blocks from the Dead Centre and he'd been fleeing ever since. He knew it had all been a trick! They'd let him out just so they could hunt him down, have some sport with him on the streets. Shot while escaping, it would read on his file. Well, not if he could help it!

Bruno wasn't without influence among the seedier elements of Mega-City One's gangland. Killing more than 200 people earns you a certain respect, especially since the slayings had been done individually. Any idiot could wipe out a hundred, even a thousand people with a well-placed bomb. Bruno knew that, hell, he'd made enough bombs for just that purpose, hence his nickname.

But in his spare time Bruno liked to keep his hand in when it came to murder, so he had applied for membership in the Huntin', Shootin' and Fishin' Club – or Bloodsports, as it was better known. His speciality was shooting, and he liked to keep a full range of high calibre weapons at his home. But as he walked – don't run, you draw attention to yourself if you run, he thought over and over again – away from the Dead Centre, he realised he couldn't go home, that would be the first place the Judges would look for him. Better to head for somewhere he could lay low for a day or two, until it was safe to visit a few of his 'friends' and sort out a new identity for himself.

So instead Bruno Chuckowski headed for the Wasteland, a bombed out part of Sector 66 where the twin towers of Tom and Viv Eliot had once stood. Both had been blown apart by one of the clients from Bruno's bomb-making days, over some long-standing argument among Mega-City's literary circles. The area was still awaiting reconstruction and the Bloodsports Club liked to use it for hunting practise. Bruno knew he'd be safe there, where Judges never bothered to patrol and no block security systems could accidentally pick him up. Besides, he had a secret cache of supplies hidden in the Wasteland, in case of emergencies. Bruno figured this qualified as such a case.

Soon he was clambering over the rubble at the edge of the Wasteland, assessing the landscape for a suitable hiding place before night fell. He didn't notice the hover-wagon high in the air above him, or the eye-in-the-sky cameras monitoring his movements from a discrete distance. Standard Justice Department surveillance techniques were never that subtle . . .

'Both murders were committed by the same killer, or creature,' announced Tek-Judge Phillip Flint smugly, adjusting the high-powered glasses perched on his nose.

'Prove it,' growled Dredd, arms folded in front of him. He was standing in Sector House 66's forensic lab on the third floor, flanked by Judge Miller. Flint wiped the smile off his face, swallowed hard and began to explain.

'Well, for a start, the wounding pattern is nearly identical in both slayings. If you look here,' he said, drawing back a body bag fastening to reveal a pile of human remains loosely reassembled to resemble a corpse, 'there are these large slash marks. Now, if we look at the body of Chief Kozwall – '

'We'll take your word for it,' broke in Miller. She had no great affection for corpses, especially those of people she considered friends, unlike the forensics members of 66's Teks.

'Er, yes, of course,' nodded Flint.

'What about the nail fragment? Have you analysed it yet?' asked Dredd, his voice deep, full of authority and impatience.

'Yes! This was most fascinating,' enthused Flint, leading them over to a tri-D screen set into one wall. With a voice command he activated it and called up the results of the analysis. A three-dimensional image of the claw fragment appeared, along with a flurry of statistics flowing down one side of the glowing screen. 'The fragment we found was definitely non-human in origin, although I was unable to firmly identify against any previously logged alien species.'

'What about Raptaurs?' pressed Dredd. 'Alien predator, killed more than two dozen cits two or three years ago.'

'Wallis was supposed to be pulling that data from MAC,' chipped in Miller helpfully.

'I don't recall that on the system,' replied Flint, activating a terminal and calling up the name. A red light flashed, accompanied by the words *classified information: level AAA security clearance required*. 'That would explain why I didn't make any connection: I don't have access to those files.'

Dredd slipped off a gauntlet and pressed a thumb against the terminal's ID pad. 'Authorisation: name, Dredd, Joe. Clearance: AAA.' A pause, then acknowledgment. 'Now run your checks,' Dredd told the Tek-Judge.

'Yes, there seems to be a connection,' announced Flint soon. 'Although not an exact match, our fragment correlates with samples taken from the disintegrated Raptaur creature up to 83 per cent.'

'Hmmph,' grunted Dredd unhappily. Now Miller spoke up.

'Could the creature have survived, recreated itself in an evolved form? If it's managed to lay low for three years, that would indicate a greater reasoning intelligence than the original Raptaur had, according to MAC's files,' she suggested.

'Yes, but why start killing now?' asked Dredd reflectively.

'Maybe it has been killing all the time, but was able to cover its tracks. We could check back on the missing persons stats – ' Miller fell suddenly silent, then slapped a hand to her head. 'Of course!'

Dredd and Flint just looked at each other quizzically, then both looked back at Miller who was smiling broadly.

'When I first went into Kozwall's office, he had a bunch of Sector 66 statistics called up on his terminal – the missing persons stats! Maybe he had already discovered what we have, and that's why the creature killed him!' she exclaimed.

'But how would an alien predator know that? Unless it had access to our computer system,' mused Flint.

Dredd rubbed his chin thoughtfully before speaking. 'We've got the pieces of a puzzle, but only a few pieces. There's more to this than meets the eye. One thing is certain – we've got some sort of alien menace on the streets, killing cits. If news of this leaks out, we'll have mayhem. This conversation does not leave this room – understood?'

Miller and Flint nodded gravely, but before either could speak Control broke through on their helmet-coms.

'Control to all units, Sector 66. Six ape gang members slaughtered by a lone female at Kadie's Speakeasy in the Jungle. Judges on the scene require back-up now!'

Dredd and Miller were already running for the turbo-lift before the message ended. 'Sounds like another She Devils hit,' Miller shouted into her helmet-com as they rode their Lawmasters out of the sector house parking zone, up onto an overzoom. It was twilight outside and street-lighting was flickering on across the sector.

'She Devils?'

'Sorry, I forgot to mention it in my briefing before. At the gangland slaying in the Jungle this a.m., two words were written on a nearby wall, using the victims' blood: She Devils. We think it's the name of a new gang that's trying to provoke a war with the ape gangs,' she explained.

Dredd was silent for the rest of the journey. Miller decided she preferred it when he was talking, at least then you had some idea what was going on behind the visor of his helmet. After being so close to Eammon, working with Dredd was a bit like holding a conversation with a rockcrete wall – very one-sided.

you pound the walls which vibrate around you, but will not open or tear or rend, no matter how you slash at them. noise assails you, screaming wind and metal shrieking. then you are falling, air flying past you, darkness rushing up from below.

you fall to earth, the breath knocked from you, but no matter, you have little need of it now. already you smell the blood on the air, the scent of fear and terror, the ultimate aphrodisiac. you're running, padded feet slapping on the uneven ground, barely audible against the thrill of the chase, the thrill of the kill to come.

you sense the prey ahead of you and alter direction, gradually circling around, assessing the quarry, deciding tactics, choosing the best method of attack. you concentrate and tingling sensations run out along your arms and legs and torso, muscles flexing, epidermis shifting and altering its pigmentations to match the tiniest variations in background. you are invisible, your thoughts cloaked, your presence hidden from the eye, the ear, all the senses.

then the ground shifts beneath you – disaster! you scramble for sure footing and are betrayed. now the prey knows it is being hunted. but it doesn't know it's already as good as dead. masks stripped away now, you howl at the single moon above and move in for the kill; the taste of

*blood and flesh already sending you crazy with desire, with
bloodlust . . .*

Bruno was scared, more scared than he'd ever been
before. Five days in the Dead Centre was nothing compared to this naked terror clutching at his chest, pulling
the breathe from his lips in heavy, hungry gasps. Sweet
Jovus, what was out there?

The fugitive had been resting against a tumble-down
wall when he felt the hair on the back of his neck begin to
rise up. Bruno knew better than to ignore that feeling, a
sixth sense he liked to call it. Grud knows, it had served
him well in the past. But this time it was tingling like
crazy. He'd looked around but could see nothing as the
last dim illumination of twilight faded away.

Then he heard the sound away to his left and nearly
jumped out of his skin. There was something out there,
something big too, from the sound of it. He patted the
barrel of his Widowmaker 3000 – once 'liberated' from a
Justice Department Armoury by an associate in part
payment for an explosives consignment – which he had
recovered from his secret storehouse. Inside his pocket
now was a bundle of thousand-cred notes and a false ID
chip he'd been storing in the cache for a rainy day. At
least with the Widowmaker by his side, he stood a chance
of seeing another rainy day. Then he heard the howl of
his hunter and the blood drained from his face faster than
his bowels emptied into his u-fronts.

'What the stomm is that thing?' he hissed to himself
and scrabbled around in his hiding hole for the other item
stored there. Got it! He removed the slim metal tube of a
nightscope and slotted it into the top of his weapon, then
peered through it. His eyes widened in horror and he
looked again through the nightscope. 'Drokkin' hell . . .'

It was huge, standing nearly three metres tall judging
by its silhouette, which seemed to be constantly shimmering and changing shape. The body was massive, more
than a metre wide, standing atop two enormous legs.

From the upper body two arms were raised, nearly as thick as the creature's legs. The arms turned into hands which turned into long talons, flexing and clacking together. It was hard to tell in the dark, but Bruno thought he could make out extra arms or perhaps even tentacles and what seemed to be a third leg, or tail.

Then it started running towards him, crushing rubble underfoot as it raced at him with incredible speed. Bruno's hands were shaking so hard he could barely hold on to his gun, but he forced himself to stand up, take aim and firmly squeeze the trigger. A solid burst of pulse-beam plasma shot out of the gun, its red energy lighting up the ground between them. It hit the creature in the chest and the attacker screamed . . .

you bound towards your prey, foul black tongue licking at razor-sharp fangs, howling with delight, the thrill of the chase, blood on the wind. then light blazes towards you and burns at your chest, you fall to the ground screaming . . .

'Yes! Yes, yes, yes!' shouted Bruno, punching the air with a fist. 'Take that you demonic stomm-sucker!' He watched the creature carefully through his nightscope but it did not move, just lay perfectly still, the red glow on its chest slowly fading away over several minutes. Finally, when he was absolutely sure it was dead, he advanced slowly towards it, gun still held ready for another burst if it was just playing dead.

Bruno slapped his gun with satisfaction, almost pride. 'Yep, the salesman was right – the Widowmaker 3000, don't leave home without it!' He approached the creature with caution but it was plainly dead. A nudge with a boot brought no response, a full-blooded kick to the head nothing. Bruno smiled and rested one foot on the chest of his catch. 'The boys at the Bloodsports Club are never going to believe this one!' he laughed. 'I wonder if I can get it stuffed and mounted?'

Then the tip of the creature's tail impaled him through the chest.

you scream and fall to the ground, the light burning at your chest until you concentrate and close together the blastproof scales of your skin. you lie still, not breathing, no movement and sure enough your prey comes to you, begging for the slaughter.

so you oblige it, first the killing blow to its chest, injecting your paralysing poison directly into its blood-stream. then you stand up and while the whimpering creature still hangs in the air, you flick out a talon, slowly extend it before the terrifying, streaming eyes of the living feast.

you slowly, almost delicately use the talon to slice open the skin around the meat's head, then peel back the hair and scalp. one punching stab and then the skull rips open, revealing the prize inside. you gorge yourself and howl at the moon again, despite yourself, blood dribbling down from your black lips onto the ground below . . .

Bruno 'The Bomber' Chuckowski screamed and screamed and screamed and screamed and screamed and screamed and screamed . . .

'She only started work here today; I'd never seen her before. It isn't easy getting staff for a place like this who are willing to put up with the clients, let alone a looker like her! So when she turned up this morning asking for a job, well, I could hardly refuse now, could I?' smiled Kadie weakly.

Dredd said nothing, gave the speakeasy's proprietor the silent treatment, enough time to get nervous and say something, anything to break the awful silence.

'I thought it was a bit strange when she asked me about Crazy and his mob, what time they come in normally, but everybody knows about Crazy and his liking for girls. Human girls, if you know what I mean.'

Still nothing.

'Look, I didn't know this was going to happen, did I? I'm just trying to run a respectable place, ain't I?' Now Kadie was getting angry, her Brit-Cit accent starting to get more pronounced by the pronoun.

Dredd just sneered and walked over to Miller, who had been interviewing some of the waitresses. She looked up and gave a quick report of her findings.

'All the other customers had fled by the time the first street patrol had gotten here, no chance of tracking any of them down. Not that they'd talk anyway, even if we could find them.'

'What about the staff?'

'Pretty much the same story as we've already gotten from the owner. But get this! One of them swears she got a good look at the murder weapon – she says it was a Judge gun! A Lawgiver!'

'Hmm.' Dredd went back to the unfortunate Kadie. 'You're under arrest for running a disorderly house, storing and serving alcoholic beverages, allowing the consumption of tobacco and aiding and abetting murder – six counts.'

'Aiding and abetting! But I didn't know she was gonna kill those apes!' protested Kadie.

'Perhaps, but you didn't try to stop her, nor did you notify us of the incident. If we hadn't had an anonymous tip-off, you probably would have covered the whole thing up,' replied Dredd stonily. 'Better add obstructing the course of justice to that charge list. Sentencing: three years for the whores, two years for the alcohol, one year for the tobacco. Ten years for each count of aiding and abetting, plus four years for the obstruction. All terms to be served consecutively.'

'But that's . . . that's . . .'

'Seventy years,' chipped in Miller, snapping a pair of handcuffs on Kadie. 'And we're closing down the speak-easy too. Move it!'

'But I'll be an old woman by the time I get out, I'll be over a hundred years old!' protested Kadie forlornly.

'Then you'll have plenty of time to ponder the error of your ways, won't you?' Miller cuffed Kadie to a holding post outside until a pat-wagon could pick her up. Then the Judge directed two others to start shutting down the speakeasy, while she went back inside to talk to Dredd. 'Well, what do you make of it all?'

Dredd stood over the bodies of the six dead apes, surveying the scene. 'A professional hit, almost too professional . . .'

'What do you mean?' asked Miller, taking the opportunity to sit down for a moment. She'd been on duty for nearly 48 hours, with only five minutes rest snatched in a sleep machine. Right now, she felt she could sleep for a week.

'The killer was cool, quick, efficient. No wasted energy, no fuss, just seven rounds used to kill six targets. From the statements you took, she didn't flinch once, not even when the apes were going for their guns after the first shot was fired, just concentrated on her task.'

'So, she's a good assassin,' said Miller wearily.

'Too good. And what about the weapon? Lawgivers are hardly standard issue for gangland slayings. Then there's the name on the note – She Devils. I've heard that name before.'

'Yes, I told you it, that was the name that – '

'No,' interrupted Dredd. 'I mean before, years ago. The Wally Squad once ran a team of undercover Judges, all women. They worked as a gang, buying and dealing in longevity drugs. I worked with them on a case about seven years ago. The gang had a code-name: She Devils.'

Miller sat up at this news. 'You think this is part of a Wally Squad operation?'

Dredd shook his head. 'The She Devils were broken up after their leader, Amos, shot another Judge. Seemed at the time she was taking the pretence a bit too far.'

'What happened to her?'

96

'Captured, tried and sent to Titan, standard 20 year term.' Dredd held the note from Crazy's jacket pocket in his hands. 'But now somebody calling themselves the She Devils are back in circulation. They've got Justice Department weapons, Justice Department methods and they're about to start a bloody gang war.'

He crumpled the piece of paper into a tight ball.

'Well not in my sector, they won't,' he vowed.

Cosmo Murdoch was fat. Not just overweight, or plump, or big-boned, or any other euphemism, but fat. Really fat; in fact so fat that he could could no longer walk without the assistance of a belliwheel – a unicycle-style device to keep his blubber off the ground as he waddled along. He weighed in at about half a tonne, but it didn't worry him at all.

In fact, Cosmo was happy to be fat. He'd worked damn hard force-feeding himself to achieve his flabby balloon appearance, studiously avoiding any exercise or lapsing into bad, non-eating habits. He stuck to his diet of a dozen munce-burgers every meal, supplementing them with popular anti-slimming products like Otto Sump's Flabbon™ when he was failing to meet his target weight.

Every month he attended his Flab Watchers meeting, where an atmosphere of support and positive reinforcement helped reassure him of his goal, trying to achieve his target weight of a full tonne. Sometimes the pressure got too much for Cosmo and he'd go on a starvation binge, but then one of his friends would come round and talk him back onto the blubber wagon. It was so easy to fall off and slip into old, slim habits but Cosmo was resolute; Cosmo was strong; Cosmo was determined.

Cosmo was a fattie.

The fattie craze had started more than a decade before, but unlike most Mega-City crazes which lasted a week then faded from memory, this fad had become a new way of life. Just as the slimming industry had grown into a major source of economic growth in the late twentieth century with vast sections of the population virtually brainwashed into believing only the slim and petite could be beautiful, so the bloating industry took a similar grip on the population's psyche in the early twenty-second century.

No-one was sure how the fattie craze had started, but like most crazes in the Big Meg, it was fuelled by the business genius of Otto Sump. He recognised a (quite literally) burgeoning market for a range of fat-increasing products after the emergence of the League of Fatties in the shadows of the Apocalypse War. This terrorist organisation fought for the right to be fat during food shortages and rationing, but was quickly defeated by the Judges.

But a demand for add-flab-fast foods remained and Sump serviced that need, adding to his own enormous wealth through the gluttony to others. Since then fatties had become celebrities, like Two-Ton Tony Tubbs, the first man to tip the scales at two tonnes. He now had his own chat show, fashion line of tastefully tailored marquees and a special fragrance – Eau de Blubber. Eating contests were common with some entrants consuming an entire hover-bus to prove their prowess.

It was the success of Two-Ton Tony Tubbs that had particularly inspired Cosmo Murdoch. From an early age he'd kept pin-ups of Tony (actually, just one pin-up but it covered three whole walls in his hab-unit in order to display Tony's titanic girth). And he'd had to make sacrifices. His first marriage had broken up on the grounds of infidelity, when his wife proved in court that Cosmo loved food more than her. Then, there was his tragic second marriage, when he accidentally rolled over in his sleep and crushed his new bride to death.

And Cosmo had been forced to shift to a ground floor conapt in his home block of Robert Maxwell, simply because the turbo-lifts broke whenever he tried to use them. Getting the entrance to his home replaced with double-doors to allow him to go out had also been expensive, but Cosmo believed it was his destiny to become famous as the biggest fattie in Mega-City One. Sadly, fate had another role lined up for Cosmo Murdoch.

Cosmo rolled out of bed into a standing position, taking care to ensure his belliwheel was in place for his blubber to fall on to – it was the only way he could get upright any more without the assistance of a dozen house-droids. He slipped on a highly fashionable kaftan, the fabric's design featuring broad, horizontal stripes to make him look even bigger than he really was.

Last, but not least, he slipped a well-stocked eating tray over his head and rested it on his gently sloping chest. It was essential to keep food ready for immediate consumption, should he feel at all faint or need his energy restored after a particularly energetic pace or two.

Now, he was ready! It was time to leave for his meeting of Flab Watchers. The meeting itself was not due to start for another three days, but it was going to take Cosmo that long just to transport his vast bulk to the WG headquarters three skeds away. He always liked to get an early start for the monthly gathering, but just then he caught sight of his wristwatch wrapped around a pudgy wrist.

Just time for a quick snack.

SEVEN

Random Crime Swoop

Random Crime Swoop: A Judge may enter a citizen's home at any time, under the provisions of Section 59(C) of the Mega-City One Criminal Code. The citizen has no rights in this matter.

Crime swoops are useful both in uncovering criminal activity and discouraging potential lawbreakers. The random nature of the search gives perps no chance to disguise their offences and frequently reveals the makings of minor breaches of the Law which could lead to major trouble unless nipped in the bud. Crime swoops are generally conducted late at night, to catch perps quite literally napping.

One drawback of this preventative measure is the resultant cluttering of iso-blocks with citizens on relatively minor charges. More frequently those serving less than 60 days in a cube are kept in the holding tanks at the local sector house.

Extract from *Justice and How it Works for You*
Judge O'Neill, 2112 AD

Kevin Brighton looked to the Judges standing either side of the conapt doorway. They nodded their readiness. He drew a large breath, pulled back a leg and then slammed his boot hard against the door to conapt 279, smashing the lock and forcing it inwards. Within seconds half a dozen Judges had burst into the small apartment, Lawgivers drawn and ready.

'Crime swoop!' yelled Brighton and began to look around the room. It was typical of most Mega-City One dwellings: small, cramped and sparsely furnished. With unemployment about to top 90 per cent again, the vast majority of citizens depended upon means-tested welfare benefits to get by. But the rates paid were rarely better than subsistence level, so home decorating was never a top priority for most citizens.

Aside from the ubiquitous tri-D viewer in a corner, just a handful of pieces of run-down furniture were scattered about the conapt. In a corner, next to the bathroom, lay a heap of clothes and rubbish – at least, that was what Brighton thought until he realised it was moving. It was a bed, and someone was sleeping in it! The young Judge stomped across the room and delivered a hefty kick to the side of the rubbereen mattress.

'Wake up, sleeping beauty – crime swoop!' he yelled, trying to keep his voice deep, resonant and full of authority, like he'd been taught at the Academy. The lump stirred briefly then fell back asleep, a steady snoring rising from the pile of debris.

Behind Brighton the other Judges were sorting through the sordid mess, checking for infringements of the Law, evidence of wrong-doing. As they found items of interest, they yelled the details to Brighton.

'Possession of goldfish without a licence – six months!'

'Prohibited ultra-violent vid-slug – *Noddy Goes Shopping* – twelve months!'

'Illegal foodstuffs – evidence of sugar cube possession – two years!'

'Bingo cards, five of them – illegal gambling – twelve months per card, that's five years in all!'

Brighton contemplated the snoozing lump before him. 'Quite a little den of vice and iniquity you've got here!' Still no response. Another kick, harder this time, neatly directed into the back of the sleeping citizen. 'I said *up*!' barked Brighton.

A frantic clawing of arms and hands from underneath shifted the pile of clothing and rubbish away to reveal the occupant of the bed – a sour-faced woman with all her blue hair shaved from the right side of her head.

'Another crime swoop? Don't you creeps have anything better to do than keep hassling us Walter Mittys?' she demanded. 'This is the third time you've busted our block this year!'

'My heart bleeds,' replied Brighton sarcastically, jerking a thumb towards the broken door. 'Out – now!'

The protesting citizen got up and wrapped a thin robe around herself, indignant at how she was being treated. 'I've got rights, y'know!'

'Actually, no, you haven't,' smiled Brighton and propelled her towards the doorway with a well-placed shove. Outside in the corridor she joined two dozen other citizens, all waiting to be taken in for processing. Brighton called for a pat-wagon to make a pick-up outside Walter Mitty Block. 'We've got 25 cits, all to be taken to Sector House 66.'

'Roj that,' replied Control.

The female tenant from 279 was still protesting loudly, trying to rouse the other citizens into action. 'We don't have to take this! We could stage a citizens' protest, right here!' The others did their best to ignore her.

Brighton couldn't stand the woman's belly-aching any longer. 'You, bigmouth! What's your name?' he demanded.

'Scarotti, Judy Scarotti,' she replied diffidently.

'Well, keep your mouth shut or else by the time you get out of the cubes, you'll be the late Judy Scarotti. Got it?'

She opened her mouth to protest, then thought better and shut it again, glaring at the young Judge violently. If looks could kill, she would have been pulling 30 years for killing a Judge.

Genya dreamed she was in the war again, but this time she was trapped outside with the bombs falling around her. Tony was running ahead of her and then a bomb fell in front of him and she watched in horror as he burned away into a skeleton and then nothing –

She woke with a start to find Gilda shaking her. 'What? What is it?'

Tears were streaming down her friend's face. 'It's Tevin. He's dead.'

Genya pulled herself out of bed and went over to the other bed, where Tevin's body lay perfectly still. His eyes were open, seeming to stare at the ceiling but no breath from his nostrils was moving through the white hair of his moustache. Genya put a hand out to touch his face – it was cold, hard, almost like marble. 'What happened?'

'I went out to see if I could find some food, left him sleeping. When I came back, I found him like this,' Gilda said, trying not to sob. 'He looks so noble – as handsome as the day I first met him.' She could hold back the sobs no longer. Genya hugged her friend as she cried, but could find no tears of her own.

Gilda recovered enough to speak again. 'How will we bury him? The ground is too hard and I have no strength for digging.'

'I don't know, Gilda, I don't know. But I promise you this, I won't let the animals feed on him like some common carrion. He deserves better than that,' vowed Genya.

Gilda thought for a while. 'A fire, perhaps? We could burn him, like a funeral pyre. I remember Tevin telling me about it, he had read it in a history book once!' Then the grieving woman remembered her husband was dead. 'Oh Genya, how will I live without him?'

'We'll stick together, you and I, we'll survive. We have to,' replied Genya as convincingly as she could.

'Why?' asked Gilda, hollowly. 'Tell me why?'

But Genya couldn't think of a reason, so she changed the subject. 'I'm going out to get some fuel, so we can give Tevin a proper send-off. Will you be okay here?'

'Yes, I'll look after him. We'll be together again soon,' smiled Gilda.

Genya frowned at the remark, but ventured outside their makeshift home anyway. When she returned an hour later, Gilda was lying in the bed beside Tevin, hugging her husband. She was smiling.

She was dead.

Desmon Stich was scared, nervous and very tense. They came for him at night, always at night. He hadn't had a decent night's sleep since, since . . . Since he couldn't remember when. They seemed to have been working on him for months. During the day they left him alone, but always that damned light blazed in his special room, filling every corner with light, with blinding brightness.

Desmon's skin was pale and wan, from having spent some many months in cells just like this, his face haggard, heavy black shadows round his eyes from exhaustion and stress and worrying. He had been balding before his incarceration, now what little of his black hair that remained was heavily flecked with silver. He was clad in the grubby white garb of a psycho-cube inmate. Desmon Stich was a broken man.

He couldn't sleep during the day and they wouldn't let him sleep at night. Every night he hoped, prayed to Grud above – if there was a Grud, Desmon couldn't be sure of anything anymore – they would leave him alone. Just one night's rest, a few hours blissful release from this torture, the questions, the shouting, the demanding voices. Always the same thing, over and over again.

Desmon cursed the day he'd ever had the idea of creating the Mechanismo Project. Remembering back now, it had seemed so obvious, so simple it was a wonder nobody else had ever thought of it. Then again, looking at the state he was in now – drokk it, the padded cell he was in now – perhaps others had thought of it too and never taken it any further. But he had felt compelled to; his ambitions had got the better of him.

He'd been a Judge then, a rising star in Tek Division and part of the team responsible for creating the special unbreakable globes the Judges had used to capture and imprison the Dark Judges after the horrors of Necropolis. As the city began to pull itself back together and the massive rebuilding programme was begun by the towering construction droids, Desmon had had an idea: if robots could rebuild the city, why couldn't robots become Judges?

Robo-Judges could be programmed with all the information, tactical knowledge and know-how of a Cadet, but that could be down-loaded into its memory chips in 15 minutes, instead of taking 15 years to instil in a human. Being robots, they would have quicker reaction times than humans, be one hundred per cent accurate when firing, have access to every single file on the Justice Department computer MAC in microseconds. They could do things a human Judge could never achieve: walk into a blazing building to save trapped citizens, or fight long battles without ever getting tired or sick or frightened, or ever questioning their orders, their motivation, their authority to enforce the Law.

Once he'd had the idea, it just seemed to grow and grow within Desmon's head. Finally, after several weeks of careful development work in his spare moments, he'd presented the plan to Coker, then head of the Tek Division. It was given a cautious go-ahead, which had been a frustration for Desmon – why couldn't the whole project just be approved and production started straight away? Still, it was a start and with the funding he attained, he gathered a team of eager young Teks around him to develop the future of Law enforcement, as they liked to called it.

Then came the zombie war with Sabbat and in just the first day, hundreds of Judges were dead. By the time the conflict was over, the Judge force had been cut by a third with no way to replace the losses quickly. Desmon's ambition got the better of him and he went over Coker's head, presenting his plan directly to Chief Judge McGruder.

She had welcomed it with open arms and the first field tests were taken during a hostage situation. It was a complete success and Stich was the star of the Justice Department overnight! Desmon had never been so happy. Of course, there had been doubters – that old fool Dredd had been among the most vocal against Desmon's project – but success silenced them at the time.

Desmon remembered all this and smiled, his worries, his incarceration in this padded cube forgotten for a moment as he felt the warm glow of popularity and success. But then his mood soured again as the memory of what happened next crushed his fragile happiness.

The robo-judges began to malfunction. Just little things at first, but Dredd was always there, demanding the Mechanismo units be withdrawn. Desmon had refused, and tragedy struck. There were fatalities and eventually the ten Mark I robo-judges had to be withdrawn. The fault was soon found, just a small circuit overheating, leading to an overdose of aggression and machismo in the robots' behaviour; behaviour patterns ironically based on those of Judge Dredd!

So Stich and his assistant Quiggly began work redesigning the robo-judges, to correct the flaw and improve on the original version. They were urged on by Greel, the new head of Tek Division who had replaced Coker, a victim of a deadly clone virus that had further depleted Judge forces. But one of the decommissioned Mark I Mechanismo units was not completely disengaged and it revived itself, escaping from its holding area. Due to damage sustained in a previous confrontation with Dredd, the unit turned rogue and killed dozens of citizens and Judges.

After that, events went hazy for Desmon. He knew now that he'd had a nervous breakdown, the doctors had told him that. He'd been committed to a psycho-block for treatment, but the obsession to find and recapture the rogue robo-judge drove him on. He was determined to exonerate himself, prove all the doubters wrong, most of all to prove Dredd wrong!

So he started escaping, going down into the old sewer system beneath Mega-City One where the rogue robo-judge had last been sighted. It was down there that the incident had happened, the one they kept asking him about, the incident with Dredd . . .

Desmon started at the sound of heavy footsteps coming down the corridor outside, coming towards his cell. Please, Grud, let them pass me by, please Grud, please Grud, please Grud, he prayed, eyes clenched tightly shut, hands clasped together fervently, his whole body shaking, ears straining to hear the footfalls outside.

He thought the steps had gone past his cell for a second and elation began to surge through him, only to be replaced with fear and hatred and loathing as the steps stopped. There was the murmuring of a voice and then the electro-magnetic locks pulled back, the door to his cell swinging open. A figure stood in the doorway, silhouetted by the light shining in from the corridor. The tell-tale eagle-shaped shoulder pad on one arm betrayed the identity of the visitor: it was a Judge. He stepped forward into the cell, a hungry smile on his face.

'Hello, Desmon. It's time for another of our little chats,' announced Todd Greel, head of Tek Division.

Desmon Stich screamed.

Dredd watched with interest as the perps collected from the crime swoop on Walter Mitty Block were brought into Sector House 66. He had ordered the swoop to catch a very special perp, and now he was waiting for that perp to make herself known.

At the back of the queue of prisoners, a bedraggled looking woman with blue hair on the left side of her head began shouting and screaming, thrashing her handcuffed arms around and generally making life very difficult for her escort, Judge Kevin Brighton.

'Let go of me, you thug, I've done nothing wrong! I'm

a true believer, I don't deserve to be treated like this!' she howled in protest.

The last sentence seemed to catch Dredd's attention and he strode over to get a closer look at the situation. 'Brighton, what's wrong here?'

'We brought her in on a random crime swoop, name of Scarotti, a real rotten egg. Found enough at her conapt to put her away for nearly ten years,' explained Brighton. He'd be happy to see Scarotti take up permanent residence in the cubes, anything to get her whining voice out of his ears.

But still the wild-eyed citizen persisted with her complaining, her nasal voice cutting through the air like a buzzsaw. 'I said I'm a true believer, you can't treat me – '

A heavy cuff to the side of her face from Dredd's fist shut her up. He leaned in close, getting a good look at Scarotti. 'I don't care what you believe in, punk! Scum like you make me sick.' Dredd looked up at Brighton. 'I'm going to deal with this piece of filth myself!'

Brighton was suddenly unsure, Dredd was pushing the limits of the Law already. What sort of beating was he going to give the irritating woman in private? 'Er, sir, according to procedure – '

'I don't care about procedure!' barked Dredd. 'This little slitch needs a lesson and I'm gonna give her one!' He turned to glare at the other prisoners. 'And I'll do the same to anyone else who wants to take me on – tell your friends, punks – if you've got any. Judge Dredd is in charge of Sector 66 and I don't take stomm from anybody.'

'Y-Yes, sir,' muttered Brighton under his breath and uncuffed Scarotti, releasing her into Dredd's custody before leading the other perps away. Dredd shoved the perp into his office and slammed the door shut behind himself. There was a female cry, then ominous silence . . .

* * *

Whiti Vitaliev had emerged from the iso-cubes triumphant. His six month's incarceration for interfering with a Judge while working as a roving reporter for tri-D 23 had turned him into a *cause célèbre* among civil rights activists in Mega-City One. The fact that the Judge who arrested him was Joe Dredd – long a target for complaint from such activists, or bleeding-heart liberals as Chief Judge McGruder preferred to describe them – only made Whitti's case more famous.

When he had been released after serving his full term, the half-Russian, half-Maori journalist with the blond hair and handsome brown skin, had found himself the subject of a bidding war among the city's leading 24-hour tri-D news networks. Celebrity reporters were all the rage, so having a celebrity reporter with some training and talent had been considered a major bonus. Finally, after three weeks of luxuriating in the joy of being wanted and sought after, Whiti had plumped for tri-D 27. Sure, they were his old station's bitterest rivals, and yes, they were owned by Ned Kerner, media mogul supreme with some interesting interpretations of the Law. But most of all, they were rich and they had wanted Whiti to share in those riches.

Now, nearly a year on from his arrest, Whiti found himself back on the streets, searching for scoops. Initially his reports were the top stories in every bulletin, regardless of content. But the novelty of his name and notoriety waned for the millions of viewers constantly searching for relief from the interminable boredom of life in a city of 400 million people.

Soon Whiti was just another news hound fighting for the latest angle of a story somebody else had already broken. Sure he was hungry but the breaks just didn't seem to be coming his way anymore. It was when he was summoned before Ned Kerner himself and told to get busy or get lost that Whiti realised drastic action was necessary.

'If I can't break the news, I'll make the news,' he told himself. After all, wasn't it his brush with the Law that had gained him his fame in the first place? Armed only with his hover-camera globe, he had set out to create news where there was none, or else find some minor incident and blow it out of all proportion. In another century, it was called tabloid television – right now, Whiti called it survival of the fittest.

It was a headline on D-fax that caught his attention: *Second slaughtered corpse found in Sector 66!* Immediately his mind was racing for the angle. Could it be a serial killer? Someone with a nice catchy name like the South-Am Slayer, or the Eldster Eliminators. Of course, that was it: the Sector 66 Slasher! Rolled off the tongue well, very alliterative, contained the right element of terror in a localised area. Now he just needed to make the story his own . . .

For the past day since seeing the headline he'd been stalking the streets of Sector 66, hover-camera following close behind, waiting for his chance. He'd crossed a few palms with creds and got all his sources primed up, ready for the first whisper of another killing. If it came to the worst, he was willing to hire someone to do the killing himself if necessary – after all, why let the facts get in the way of a good story? In the end, the bribe money paid off. He got a call from a source within the Department with a dubious liking for sweet substances, earning the reporter some reported stomping grounds of the beast. Whiti didn't know how reliable the info was, but at last it lead indirectly to his scoop. Ironically, it was Whiti himself who found the third victim of the newly-christened Sector 66 Slasher.

Just after dawn, Whiti Vitaliev was crossing the Wasteland area of the sector as early morning light spread over the city. It was still quite dark and making his way across the shifting rubble was tough going. He was nearly clear of the ruins when a foot slipped out from under him and the roving reporter stumbled forward, falling to the ground heavily. His camera floated down to the ground beside him, as always staying within its electronic 'tether' distance of two metres.

Whiti waved it away and felt his hand touch something wet and soft, almost like the pulp of a wet fruit he'd once touched while in Ned Kerner's palatial office. He rolled over to see what it was and found himself face to face with the crushed-in head of Bruno 'the Bomber' Chuckowski. The top of the head was missing, almost like an egg with its shell cracked open allowing access to the contents. The dead face was covered in claret-red moistness, the one remaining eye staring intently at the reporter. He looked down and realised his hand was plunged inside the crumpled chest of the dead man.

Whiti Vitaliev tried not to vomit on his scoop.

'You can cut the act, now,' grunted Dredd, slumping into his seat behind the sector chief's desk and gesturing for Scarotti to take the chair opposite. 'Screaming won't help you here.'

'I should hope not,' replied the now smiling captive, her annoying accent wiped away without a trace. 'I thought nobody was ever going to recognise the codewords – I must have shouted true believer at least half-a-dozen times.'

'Well, Brighton didn't seem to realise he'd arrested the head of the Wally Squad for this sector. Better we keep your true identity as secret as possible, otherwise you'll be no use to us at all,' grumbled Dredd.

'I know you don't really approve of undercover Judges – '

'It doesn't matter what I think,' cut in Dredd. 'I had you brought in because I need some information and according to Kozwall's files you're not due to report in for another 15 days.' He jerked a thumb at the vid-screen on the desk, where Scarotti's file was visible.

'You have been busy since Eammon's death,' commented Scarotti wryly. 'He's only been gone, what – a few hours? – and you're into his personal files already.'

'Cut the chat, Scarotti. My predecessor might have appreciated your lax ways but I don't. In case you haven't noticed, we've got a major gang war brewing in this sector and the provocateurs seem to be undercover Judges. Got anything you want to tell me, or should I just send you straight to the Titan shuttle?' growled Dredd.

That drained the colour from Scarotti's face. 'No, sir!' she replied briskly. 'I mean, yes, sir – I have some information.'

'Good – make your report.'

Scarotti swallowed hard then began speaking. 'I've been investigating the She Devils for more than a month, since my last meeting with Sector Chief Kozwall. He had identified them as the source of a tide of new drugs hitting the skeds and also as a rising threat to the fragile peace between the gangs in this sector. Kozwall wanted me to find out more about them.'

Just silence from Dredd. The Wally Squad leader continued.

'The gang seems to consist of about a dozen women, all highly trained and motivated. Each has adopted a code-name to protect her real identity. The leader calls herself Fury, but little else is known about her. I believe the woman who made the hit at Kadie's was a new recruit called Scarlett, the attack was her initiation to the gang. The gang seem to have access to Justice Department weaponry but I've yet to discover from where.' Scarotti looked at Dredd, waiting for questions.

'Are they Judges?' he asked finally.

'Impossible to tell at this stage, but it seems highly likely. The precision of their attacks, their methods and weapons all point to them being Judges. Or rather, rogue Judges.'

'Are they Wally Squad Judges?'

'Not from this Sector, that much is certain – all my Judges have been accounted for at the time of She Devil attacks,' affirmed Scarotti.

'I know, I've already checked,' growled Dredd. 'You'd

already be on your way to Titan if that wasn't the case.'
He sat silently before punching a control on his vid-phone. 'Dismissed. I'll have Brighton take you down to the Holding Tanks – we don't want anyone suspecting your arrest wasn't real, do we?'

'This is Whiti Vitaliev, broadcasting to you live from Sector 66 with a news exclusive to tri-D 27 viewers! This reporter has stumbled upon a gruesome discovery – the badly dismembered body of a dead man, the third victim of the Sector 66 Slasher!'

The news hound stepped aside to melodramatically reveal the corpse of Bruno 'the Bomber' Chuckowski in all its gory glory. Whiti continued his voiceover from one side as the camera-globe slowly moved around the remains in a specially pre-programmed three hundred and sixty-degree revolve shot.

'That's right! A serial killer stalks the streets of Mega-City One and the Justice Department has been covering up this murderous monster's nefarious deeds. You didn't realise your lives and the lives of your families were in danger until this shock revelation, made exclusively – *live!* – here on tri-D 27, where the news is always the newest!

'I stumbled upon the body of this poor soul not ten minutes ago and had the regular programming on the station interrupted to bring you this special bulletin. Beware, the Sector 66 Slasher might strike at you next! Now, just time for a word from our sponsor . . .'

Dredd activated the scrambler before contacting Hershey on the vid-phone. She looked red-faced and flustered.

'Yeah, what the hell is it? Oh! It's you Dredd!'

'Something wrong?'

'I've spent the past few hours sorting out a mess at Iso-Block Zero. Why are you calling on a scrambled frequency? Is it about McGruder?'

'No, but it probably involves Judges. Do you remember

113

a Wally Squad operation from a few years back, nick-named the She Devils?'

'Sure, we had to disband it after the leader shot another team member, Amos, I think her name was. She got the standard twenty on Titan, as I recall. Why do you ask?'

'Well, the She Devils are back in business, and they seem intent on starting a gang war here in Sector 66. You got any secretive Wally Squad operations going here you'd like to tell me about?' demanded Dredd.

'None that I know of, but I'll have it checked out. You got any more details you can give me?'

'There's about a dozen women in the gang, they've got department weapons and methods. If they ain't Judges, they're a pretty good imitation – and I don't want them in my sector!'

'All right, all right, keep your helmet on!' replied Hershey hurriedly. 'I'll look into it, personally, but you know what the Wally Squad is like. They go deep cover for years at a time – hell, even we don't know exactly where most of them are all the time! Hershey out . . .'

Miller burst into Dredd's office and switched on his tri-D viewer before he could protest. Roving reporter Whiti Vitaliev was just beginning his first report from beside the corpse of Bruno 'the Bomber' Chuckowski on the screen. When it finished, Dredd switched off the viewer and turned back to look at Miller, lip curling with disgust. 'Terrif.'

'I've already sent three teams of street Judges and a forensics team over to the site. We should have a cordon up within the next sixty seconds. Unfortunately, we can't bust the reporter – he phoned us with his find before he went on the air,' said Miller sternly.

'Well, if he's disturbed a hair on that corpse we'll have him anyway. I'll take the interrogation myself,' grunted Dredd with relish.

'What did Scarotti have to say?'

'Nothing more than we already knew. The leader of the

She Devils is called Fury, not much more.' He looked up at Miller thoughtfully. 'Ever been undercover yourself?'

'No, I prefer wearing a badge,' she replied.

'Maybe it's time that you tried it. You might enjoy it!'

Within minutes of the cordon being established around the Wasteland, dozens of tri-D news crews were buzzing around the perimeter, desperately trying to get a piece of Whiti's scoop. Each had picked up on his name for the killer, the Sector 66 Slasher, and were re-broadcasting it over and over again. The only reporter inside the cordon was Whiti himself who was getting a rough time from Judges on the scene.

'Look, I told you twice already, I fell over, I rolled down here and found the body, okay? I didn't have nothing to do with it!' he insisted. Beside him a Judge tested the truth of his words with a hand-held lie detector device.

'Birdie checks out, but we're taking you in for questioning,' announced the stern-faced Judge.

'Suits me,' smiled Whiti, happy to be the centre of attention again. Just like the good old days.

Behind him, the Tek-Judge forensics team were busy transferring the remains of the unfortunate Bruno into a series of black body bags. Flint was overseeing the operation, having examined the corpse carefully before it was shifted. He activated his helmet-com.

'Flint to Sector 66 Control: tell Dredd I've had a prelim exam of the body. Looks like our alien predator's handywork again!'

Whiti's ears pricked up at overhearing this snippet, but he was shoved away to a pat-wagon before he could hear anymore. Flint picked up the crushed remains of Bruno's Widowmaker 3000 from the ground.

'And tell Dredd our dead man was packing a Justice Department Widowmaker 3000 – looks like he got a couple of shots off from it too! No sign of our killer though . . .'

* * *

Extract from the private journal of Judge Laverne Castillo:

This is the first time I've been able to grab a few moments to write down what's been happening over the past couple of days; it's just been crazy round here! I'm beginning to understand that that's normal . . .

I went to see Judge Hershey, to talk with her about my problems, my worries about Eliphas and the Chief Judge. She told me not to worry about Eliphas, if he tried anything against me then I should just tell her and she would sort it out. I believe her.

But she was also very interested in my feelings about the Chief Judge. I could be mistaken, but I got the impression she wants me to spy on the Chief Judge for her. I know McGruder is a bit crazy, but that things should come to this, with senior Judges spying on each other!

Still, the way Hershey explained it, it seemed to make sense. After Necropolis, McGruder pretty much abolished the Council of Five, only calling them together for big emergencies like something she called the 'Savage Incident'. That means there's no legal way the Chief Judge can be voted out of office. She can only go by resigning or dying.

Hershey says the Chief Judge has been making irrational decisions, decisions that are costing lives. Unless something is done to persuade her to step down, things could get a lot worse.

I agree with Judge Hershey, but I can't help feeling I'm just a pawn in all of this. Nobody really cares what happens to me or the city, they just care about themselves. And that's frightening.

I almost told Chief Judge McGruder about all this today when the head of Tek Division came in, Greel. I don't know why but he gives me the creeps – I don't like him. He's balding, with jet black hair and a sinister air of menace and naked ambition exuding from his every pore. His mouth is saying one thing but you can tell from his eyes that he's thinking another. He was nice and friendly to the Chief Judge, supporting her, backing her up no matter what crazy things she was saying – and they were pretty crazy, too! But I could tell he was just lying, just trying to get his own way.

He doesn't really care about her, he just wants to be Chief Judge himself. He scares me, much more than McGruder does. She's a crazy old woman, but she means well. Greel just wants power.

He came in to tell her about some secret tests they're doing in the Tek Division. He said the latest test had gone extremely well and the new prototypes should be ready for use on the streets very soon. There was something else about some old field tests, but I didn't catch that. I almost thought Greel suspected me of listening for a minute; I'll have to be more careful, or else I'll get caught in the middle of all this.

The other thing he talked about was somebody called Stich. Apparently they've being interrogating him for weeks without any success. Just the same old story, Greel said, something about Judge Dredd and something going wrong.

McGruder was furious, banging her fists on the table and demanding results. We'll have your badge for breakfast otherwise, she told Greel – that shut him up! Then he asked for authorisation and McGruder agreed – use the drugs, she said, whatever it takes.

I don't know who this Stich is, but I sure feel sorry for him. I think he's in even more trouble than me!

Gotta go now, McGruder wants me . . .

Unable to get much of a story at the Wasteland, the media pack had shifted its attention to Sector House 66, setting up camp outside and demanding information. Dredd looked out of the interrogation cell window at the crowd of hover-cameras and reporters gathering in front of the building, before turning round to regard the captive.

'This is all your fault, Vitaliev,' growled the Judge.

'I was just doing my job – you're the ones with the problem,' smiled the reporter. Dredd slammed a fist down onto the desk in front of him.

117

'I'll give you a problem, punk! How does five to ten in the cubes sound to you? Perhaps you'd prefer 15?'

'On what charge? I've done nothing wrong. I discovered a dead body, I immediately reported it to the proper authorities, then I went about my business, which happens to be breaking and making the news,' replied Whiti tartly.

'It's the part about making the news that worries me! How do we know you aren't behind these killers, that you're not responsible for creating all this simply to compensate for a slow news day?'

'I'll take any lie detector test you want,' smiled the reporter.

'Hmmph,' grunted Dredd unhappily, before looking up and nodding at Brighton, who stood behind Vitaliev.

'Am I under arrest? What charges are being brought against me?' asked Whiti.

'We ask the questions!' shouted Brighton, slamming a fist into the journalist's back. Whiti collapsed forward onto the desk, gasping for air.

'Judge Brighton! Consider yourself under severe reprimand!' yelled Dredd. He went to the reporter's side. 'You're not under arrest yet, but if we should gather further evidence against you . . .'

Whiti pulled himself to his feet. 'In that case, I'll be leaving. And next time, keep your dogs in a muzzle!' He stormed out of the cell and down the corridor. When his steps had gone out of earshot, Dredd looked at Brighton for a moment.

'Well?'

'Tracer stuck on like a charm,' smiled the young Judge.

'Good. Get the Teks to keep a constant fix on Vitaliev's whereabouts – I want to know where that little creep is every minute of the day.'

Brighton went to the window and pointed outside. 'Well right now, he's addressing the assembled rabble of media vultures.'

Whiti smiled and signalled for silence from the throng of fellow reporters. 'I have just been consulting exclu-

118

sively about the Sector 66 Slasher slayings with Judge Joe Dredd, who is acting Sector Chief. Although most aspects of our conversation are classified, I will be able to reveal part of what is going on – '

'When? When?' screamed the other reporters, desperate for more information, some facts to flesh out the latest update.

'I will reveal all that I can exclusively on my next bulletin on tri-D 27. Until then, my lips are sealed,' smirked Whiti. There were howls of protest from the media rabble, but to no avail.

Whiti had the greatest exclusive of his life, and by Grud, he was going to milk it for all it was worth.

Miss Muriel Baynes worried a lot; she was good at it. At night she'd spend long hours worrying about what was going to happen tomorrow, in the day she would fret about why she hadn't slept a wink the night before. If worrying had been a legitimate event in the Mega-Olympics (it had only been an exhibition event for the past three Mega-Olympiads), Muriel could easily have taken the gold medal.

Standing barely five foot tall, she wore an appalling bad-taste ensemble in brain-curdling clashes of colour and style. Her grey hair exploded in a shapeless frizz from her skull, like crazed antennae fighting each other to pick up some important signal from outer space. She worked with a constant stoop that was purely psychosomatic, brought on by trying to carry the cares on the entire world on her shoulders.

Miss Baynes worried about her hearing, which was poor at the best of times, despite the giant leaps in technology medical science had made during the last few wars. She worried about subsidence, which had badly affected the small housing block she had inherited from her late father, Barnum Baynes, king of the flea circus impressarios. Barnum Baynes Block had been gradually sliding away to one side for decades.

When Miss Baynes employed some construction droids to correct the subsidence, they had left the job half-finished to return to their places of manufacture following scares about a new robot revolt among some construction mechanoids. It had proved to be a false alarm, but the droids had their memories wiped anyway and never returned to finish the work. That just gave Miss Baynes something else to worry about.

She would have been better off worrying about the decor of the block, which mixed styles from different centuries, different cultures, even different planets! Thousands of yellowing old periodicals stood in teetering piles up the sides of walls, growing ever ceilingwards, while dust settled on every surface. Quaint dried flowers shed their petals from ill-matching brown glasseen vases atop green synthi-leather pedestal tables next to lurid claret flock wallpaper. Her block was an interior decorator's ultimate nightmare, but that didn't worry Miss Baynes – she thought it all matched perfectly!

Instead, she worried about the tenants in her block, who seemed a surly and ungrateful lot in her eyes. Just because they were paying unusually high rents, they seemed to expect extra services and quicker maintenance as a result! The youth of today, you just don't know who to trust, Miss Baynes was always telling herself. Wasn't the fact that the block was in a prime location in the heart of Sector 66 enough for them? The neighbours were very quiet, hardly a peep out of them. This was probably because the Barnum Baynes Block was surrounded by municipal graveyard buildings, but some people found that a bit creepy too.

There had been a bad run of tenants who absconded in the night, some leaving outstanding bills running into thousands of creds, so Miss Baynes worried about that too. She worried about pollution; declining standards of education; the weather; the price of munce liver oil; the dramatic drop in hairdressing standards among house-droids; the way a slice of bread always seemed to land synthi-spread down and never up; the way those talking apes seemed to be taking over the area; the end of the world; the beginning of the world; you name it, she worried about it.

In short, Miss Muriel Baynes worried about everything.

Besides being deaf as a munceburger, she was also short-sighted. But the idea of surgery worried her too much to get those new-fangled bionic eyes fitted, so she made do with a complex pair of optical enhancers hanging in front of her face, supported by a head band. She worried this made her look stupid and she was right to worry.

She worried the Justice Department would decide she could no longer cope by herself and place her in a home for eldsters. She'd heard about what happened to old women in Crock Houses, as the ladies in the Sector 66 Gossip-Mongers Association liked to call the eldster homes. Rape, murder, or something worse, they said over cups of synthi-tea and copies of the *Megapolitan for the Post-Menopausal*. Muriel didn't know what the something worse could be, and she didn't want to find out.

So she rarely ventured outside her own door, only making a skittish trip away from her home to catch up on events at the Gossip-Mongers, or to stock up on oil for her pet, a robo-parrot named Major Barnum in honour of her dear, departed father. It was the parrot's behaviour that was causing her most worry right now.

He hadn't been right since she took him to the robo-pet veterinarian mechanoid repair service six months ago. His voice loop had somehow become wiped of its charming range of expressions. ('Oh dear, how worrying' had been one of Muriel's favourites), with just a cacophony of obscenities being bellowed at awkward moments. And he'd started escaping from his cage and flying round the room, bombarding her with sump oil from his system.

Miss Baynes sat in her favourite chair and eyed the rogue robo-parrot, which stared back at her beadily from atop a towering pile of back numbers of the *Mega-City*

Times. There was nothing else to do, she would have to venture out and get help, before something worse happened. But what if something worse did happen, while she was out?

'Oh dear, how worrying,' she shouted to herself.

'Shut the drokk up, you stupid old bat!' bellowed Major Barnum.

Miss Baynes shook her head sadly. Such vulgarity! Father would never have approved, never. She looked over at her father, standing resolutely in the corner, one finger held up in front of his face, a little flea jumping up and down in the air, before landing on the finger and jumping up again. It was unfortunate how the finger extended and its positioning had combined to turn this loving illustration of her father's love for fleas into an obscene finger gesture at the world in general.

Muriel had wanted to have him stuffed properly when he died, even toyed with the idea of taking the job to the great Jacob Sardini, but the expense had worried her. Instead one of her friends had recommended a small, private firm of taxidermists, whose work on stuffing humans was almost the equal of Sardini, or so her friend had said. But Muriel had been left with another half-finished job and the stuffed and mounted body of her beloved father giving her the finger from a corner of the room.

Muriel sighed and took another sip of synthi-caff. You just couldn't get the workmanship anymore . . .

EIGHT

Third Field Test

Confidential Report for: XXXXX XXXXX
From: XXXXX XXXXX

Re: Notes on further field testing of combined prototype

Aim: To collect data on the actual combat scenario performance of the new bio-weapon, combining aspects of the Skinner Imperative and the mutate creature trialed in previous field tests

Methodology: The bio-weapon was released into the Badlands outside Texas City in a location specially chosen so it would be quickly 'discovered' by a routine patrol from the city and then taken back there for further study. It would be up to the creature how it would respond to this situation – would the Skinner Imperative drive the bio-weapon to escape and move rapidly from one source of knowledge to another, gathering information until it was ready to seize control of the city? Or would the more base hunter/killer instincts of the mutate creature and its genetic-sample 'parents' turn it into a rampaging murder machine?

Throughout the field test, strict monitoring of the bio-weapon would be maintained at all times via the bio-control systems. At any time the bio-weapon could be destroyed by remote control.

Procedure: The bio-weapon was released in the Badlands surrounding Texas City, where it was soon 'found' by a routine patrol from the city. The creature killed four of the six team members before they were able to pump it full of enough stun charges to subdue it.

[Note: According to information accessed from the Texas City Justice Department files, the creature required nearly six times the amount of voltage necessary for a normal human being to render it unconscious. Even then, the two survivors swore the creature still allowed itself to be captured. They said it seemed almost 'curious' about them, and only became subdued after it had bored of slaughter.]

The bio-weapon was subjected to dozens of complex tests by Texas geneticists within the Justice Department. The best answer they could find was to call it a freak 'super-mutant', the rogue result of a one-in-a-billion DNA variation. Psychologists had a field day, finally agreeing a diagnosis of 'deepcore homicidal psychosis with multiple split personalities, each more malevolent than the last'.

[Note: It seems that while the bio-weapon was being studied, it was actually studying its captors, absorbing their combined knowledge and then using this to project whatever signals they wanted back at them. From the patrol Judges it learnt of department tactical and weapons capabilities; from the psychologists it gained important insights into both human madness and the analysis of that madness; from its captors the bio-weapon plundered backgrounds about their plans for itself and possible future threats; and so on . . .]

Next, the bio-weapon was subjected to an intensive psychic probing by Texas City's top Psi Judges. The first two died just trying to scan its mind, cut down by a complex web of psychic defences. Eventually the creature allowed the Psi Judges access, but only to what it wanted them to know. Then it was the turn of the Exorcist Judges, one of whom was babbling about 'demonic possession' before dying of massive heart failure. At this point the creature uttered its first spoken words: 'Burn in Hell!'

[Note: Again, the creature kept control throughout of what little information it let its captors glean, while draining them dry of all increasing data. Interestingly, the exposure to the religious knowledge and beliefs of the exorcists seemed to have a profound effect on the bio-weapon, as will be demonstrated later in this report.]

Eventually, the department admitted defeat and locked the bio-weapon away without food or liquid in a maximum security padded cell, more for the protection of the captors than for the captive. According to security-scan logs, the creature spent time giggling to itself or howling at the Moon when it was out – despite the cell being completely sealed, without windows or any way the creature could know of the lunar cycle. Some nights the bio-weapon would consume parts of its own body, but these would have grown back by morning.

[Note: Was the bio-weapon feeding upon itself for nourishment, for pleasure or merely to pass the time? It could be speculated it was testing its regenerative abilities.]

Finally, the Chief Judge of Texas City sanctioned the execution of the creature. It was decided to electrocute the bio-weapon. The Judges electrocuted the creature five times, increasing the voltage on each occasion. But the more intense the jolt, the more the creature laughed at them. It also chose this moment to make an announcement: 'My name is Legion, for we are many.'

By now, the authorities were rapidly coming to some unpleasant conclusions. They couldn't cure Legion, they couldn't seem to kill it and they doubted the creature would allow them to keep it in captivity much longer. They had to get rid of it. Papers were hurriedly signed and Legion was to be shipped off-world, to a maximum security penal colony near Luna-City on the Moon.

[Note: This was a 'cover story' planted into the flight recorder of the shuttle *Morning Star*, which was to transport Legion to the Moon. In fact, this unlisted, unmanned flight was deliberately under-fuelled so its engines would cut out just before it achieved orbit. As a result, the shuttle would fall back into the Earth's atmosphere and burn up on re-entry. Even if Legion somehow survived all of that, the Texas City authorites reasoned the creature would fall to Earth somewhere else and become somebody else's problem.]

But the *Morning Star* began to malfunction soon after take-off, never reaching the edge of the atmosphere. Instead it fell to Earth on the edge of the Badlands, deep in gila-munja territory. Legion emerged from the burning wreck seemingly unscathed and was immediately surrounded by gila-munja. The chameleon-like creatures are normally invisible to the human eye, but Legion's gila-munja ancestry enabled him to see his 'cousins'. He killed several of the creatures, and sustained two bites from their normally fatal poison tipped fangs without suffering any ill effects. Instead, he let them drink of his blood, forming a telepathic bond with them.

[Note: From here on, most of Legion's early actions in the radioactive wastes of the Cursed Earth were observeved by satellite. But an h-wagon with long-range scanning and sensors was despatched to the area immediately, arriving within a few hours.]

The fall of the *Morning Star* was observed by a former Texas City Outlands Marshal turned Bible-basher, Preacher Cain, and his tracker deputy, Resurrection Joe. But they were several hours from the crash site and by the time they arrived Legion had long since departed for the Gerasenes Badlands with his new brethren of gila-munja.

[Note: At this time a massive dust storm blew up in this area, making scanning by satellite difficult. Although the storm was monitored by weather control in Texas City, no natural explanation for its occurrence could be deduced or discovered.]

On their way to the Gerasenes Badlands, Legion and

his hordes stopped at a small community church on the edge of a mixed norms and mutants settlement. All inside were brutally slaughtered. The bells of the church were rung, calling out to those willing to listen. The ringing appears to have had an hypnotic effect on certain sections of the population of the Cursed Earth, bringing forth killers, criminals and even raising the dead from their graves in response. Legion was gathering a flock, a following for his crusade of murder and conquest.

[Note: The following information is drawn from reports submitted by Preacher Cain and his deputy about their search for and fateful encounter with Legion, the bio-weapon.]

The two lawmen discovered the horrors perpetrated in Legion's name at the church, then followed the trail of destruction from one dead place to another. Legion's army left a long trail of burned-out farmsteads, ambushed wagon-trains and entire settlements razed to the ground. Blighted crops, poisoned water-holes and dead cattle marked the horde's passing, like a dark stain spreading across the land. But the pair never found a single body, until they reached the Cactus Badlands, a mile-long stretch of poisonous cactus surrounding the worst country in the radioactive wasteland.

There Legion and his followers had hung the bodies up on the cactuses. Despite being dead, some were able to speak, taunting the two lawmen – apparently a residual mental projection left by Legion to dissuade any who might follow him. Finally they tracked Legion and his followers to the Golgotha Heights, the toughest mountain range in all of the Texas City Territories. There they confronted the bio-weapon near a molten lava pool fed by the volcanic mountain range.

In a brutal battle Preacher Cain was able to fight his way through Legion's hordes to face the leader of the pack. Despite blowing a fist-sized hole through the bio-weapon, Cain was unable to defeat it and buried both himself and the creature under a massive rockfall as a last resort. But Legion merely pushed the boulders aside and walked away.

Cain too emerged from beneath the rockfall and the pair fought again, this time the lawman used silver bullets melted from a holy cross and a crucifix to try and exorcise the 'demon'. Legion was disabled by Cain's deputy who paralysed him by shoving the broken crucifix into the creature's back. Then Cain threw the bio-weapon into the molten lava pool, watching Legion burn away.

With the bio-weapon dead, his followers disappeared into the early dawn's light. Cain and his deputy submitted reports about the incident but these were duly filed away and ignored, with Texas City denying any knowledge of the creature and the *Morning Star* disappearing from any records. Within weeks the incident was gone, forgotten, just another sorry chapter in the history of the Badlands around Texas City.

Summary: This field test was the first of its kind, combining the psychological advantages of the Skinner Imperative with the physical strength and near invincibility of the mutate creature. The marriage of these two elements was not entirely successful. By comparison with the actions of the Skinner Imperative as a solo entity, 'Legion' was quite happy to take his time absorbing knowledge before acting upon it. Like the mutate creature, it displayed a highly malicious streak, revelling in toying with its victims.

Certain elements of the Skinner Imperative were lost in the transfer to a single host – Psi invisibility was replaced by Psi impenetrability (not the same thing by any means) – while other aspects such as the lack of subtlety were reversed to an almost overwhelming degree.

Equally, some advantages of the mutate creature were lost with the addition of the Skinner Imperative. Legion was not able to maintain chameleonic blending into any background, but he could perceive other creatures with that ability. In exchange, his physical invulnerability was greatly enhanced, but there were still weak points. More of the natural silicon 'armoured' skin of the Raptaur creatures needs to be genetically introduced into the make-up of the bio-weapon.

Most significantly of all, Legion's rapid absorption of the knowledge of others around him proved to be a disadvantage, creating a mentally warped creature bent on inflicting pain and great suffering, rather than setting any goals and attaining them. The bio-weapon proved to be incredibly single-minded and completely unpredictable and probably uncontrollable. Legion was almost invincible, but could never have been usefully employed against an enemy, except as a dangerous diversion dropped behind enemy lines that could easily backfire.

Recommendations: While the combination of the two elements highlighted many difficulties within the design and make-up of both, it also proved the positive points of each. Certain flaws need to be resolved – the loss of both psychic invisibility and physical 'invisibility' via the gilamunja chameleonic talents; the need to eliminate weak spots in the physicality of the bio-weapon, such as susceptibility to a single, well-placed shot or projectile; the malicious tendency towards toying with victims, rather than simply utilising them as necessary then discarding them.

The most important question to resolve is that of controlling this weapon. A Lawgiver would be no good if it only fired when it felt like it, then kept firing at the same target again and again, just for the hell of it. The same applies to the bio-weapon. A method must be found to control and direct the actions of the weapon, or else it shall be useless to us.

The good news is that such a method of control already partially exists – the bio-control system. This was installed to provide opportunity to destroy the bio-weapons if necessary during these field tests. If this system can be extended to give some psychic control of the bio-weapon, then we are very close to achieving the aim of creating a viable tool against our enemies, be they zombie army, human warriors or even alien superfiends such as Judge Death and the Dark Judges.

The Prometheus Project stands at an exciting cross-roads. Given the go-ahead, it is believed our first, new-look prototypes could be ready for testing in live situations within a month, the final version ready for unveiling and full-scale production within three months. This may seem ambitious but this bio-weapon is the future of all conflicts.

Signed: XXXXX XXXXX
May 19, 2116 AD

NINE

Talking Pinstripe Freak

Narks: Also known as grasses, supergrasses, and a variety
of other, less pleasant names. Paid informants have been
a fact of life in law enforcement for hundreds of years and
still play a useful role in the work of the Justice Department, even now in the twenty-second century.

The best informants are able to pass on a valuable
stream of information about planned crimes as well as the
names and locations of those responsible for law breaches
already committed, while still working within the criminal
organisations they are 'betraying'. Such informants are
financially well rewarded, as compensation for the sure
knowledge that one day their 'treachery' will be discovered, and a swift, painful death become inevitable.

Such informants work best when in contact with only a
single Judge representative of the Justice Department,
thus enabling them to develop a rapport of mutual trust.
Such relationships can take years, even decades to evolve.
Among the most infamous narks of recent years are 'Eggs'
Benedict, Bill 'The Confessor' Windsor-Smythe and
Steven 'Bigmouth' Morris. All are now missing, presumed
dead.

Extract from *Justice and How it Works for You*
Judge O'Neill, 2112AD

'Hey, Joe! Where you going with that Lawgiver in your
hand, man?' The voice was pure cool, smooth, silky,
deeply resonant. The face was synthicaff brown, a few
smile lines around the eyes but still that broad smile, the
gleaming white teeth, the impeccably trimmed mous-

tache, the eyes twinkling with excitement and hidden knowledge. As always, the black bowler hat was perched at a jaunty angle atop the head, a head that held more secrets than most of the files in the Justice Department computer systems put together.

'Long time, Max,' replied Dredd to the fresh face on the vid-phone monitor set into his desk. 'You're a hard man to track down.'

'Gotta keep movin' on, baby, know what I mean?' smiled Max, brushing a speck of lint from his immaculate pin-stripe three-piece suit. 'I've been in semi-retirement since that incident with that little lady friend of yours, need I say more.'

Max Normal was one of the Big Meg's most eccentric characters. Nicknamed the Pinstripe Freak for his love of twentieth-century clothing and mannerisms, his sked-wise savvy had turned him into a prime informer for the Justice Department, with Dredd as his main contact. If there was anything going down, Max was the man with the plan.

Eventually, word spread of his links with the Justice Department, but his connection with Judge Dredd generally kept him safe from any major acts of retribution by the gangland underworld. He even acted as an unofficial two-way conduit for information, when the Judges wanted a particular perp and were willing to make the occasional trade-off.

But Max's fame nearly proved fatal. A martial arts assassin used him to lure Dredd into an ambush, brutally beating the Pinstripe Freak and nearly killing the Judge too. That was nearly three years ago and Max had been keeping a very low profile since. It had taken Dredd nearly two hours to track Max down for this conversation.

'What can I do you for, anyway?'

'I need some information.'

'Well, you came to the right place dude – exactly what do you want to know?'

'There's a new gang in Sector 66, the She Devils. Heard of them?'

'Hell, yes! Those are some dangerous ladies, but I've got a few inside scoops on their sweet selves. You got the readies?'

Dredd was slightly perplexed. Max's use of a highly individual patois merging street slang and anachronisms frequently made him a hard nark to understand. 'Readies?'

'The dough, the bread, the bucks, the moolah. Y'know, man, the *creds* for this valuable information that the Max is gonna lay on you!' Max rolled his eyes. 'Boy, will you ever get hip to the groove, Joe?'

Dredd just grunted.

'I guess not. Anyway, just transfer the creds into my regular account. My bank will advise me of the deposit immediately, then we can talk, okay?'

Dredd pressed a button on his vid-phone console, activating the automatic cred transfer. Seconds later, the smiling informant's face was back on screen. 'Okay, let's talk!'

'Who are the She Devils? Where did they come from? Where do they get their weaponry from? How – '

'Hold it, hold it, hold it, baby! One question at a time, my man,' spluttered Max, one hand held up in front of his face on the vid-phone.

Dredd paused, then asked again. 'Who are the She Devils?'

'Good question,' replied Max, ''coz that's what everybody on the skeds wants to know. They ain't yours?'

Dredd shook his head. 'Not that we know of.'

'Well, they sure act like Judges. They kill like Judges too. Word on the skeds is they're some new Justice Department offensive against the mobs, trying to provoke a gang war so they can wipe out a few problem individuals – starting with the ape gangs in Sector 66. But if they ain't Judges . . .' Max mused, '. . . then I don't know what they are. And as you know, it ain't often old Max here will admit that.'

'You better have something else for me, or else that deposit could easily become a withdrawal,' threatened Dredd.

'Be cool, Joe! I got more,' the king of cool assured him. 'The She Devils started appearing about two months ago. There were just a handful of them at first, but they seem to have been on a recruiting drive – last I heard, the gang was up to 15 tough ladies.'

'I heard a dozen.'

'Old news, Joe! If you want the cream, you got to come to the top cat. Who told you a dozen?'

'Let's just say someone who ought to know.'

Max smiled. 'No need to be coy, boy! We both know who you're talking about – Judy Scarotti, head of Wally Squad operations for Sector 66. I'd keep a close eye on her if I was you.'

'Why?'

'Don't trust her, man. You may have noticed the She Devils are packing some of the Department's finest weapons – well, word is she's the source. Hell, there's even been some Widowmaker three-thous on the market for those with a few extra creds to spend,' stated Max sagely.

'We found one on a corpse in the Wasteland this ayem.'

'The girl's trouble, Joe – been out in the field too long, acquiring a few too many bad habits, if you know what I mean. Got a bit of a sweet tooth, or so I hear . . .'

Sweet tooth was sked-slang for sugar addiction. Sugar had been outlawed for more than thirty years, due to the extreme rush it created in citizens. It was number one on the Judges' list of prohibited drugs, just ahead of old favourites like coffee, tea and most forms of tobacco.

'So she's doing a little arms dealing on the side to support her habit,' concluded Dredd aloud.

'Got it in one, Joe.'

'Scarotti says the leader of the She Devils is codenamed Fury. You know anything else about her or where she could be found?'

'Fury's a bit of a mystery, like the rest of the She Devils, but I hear she's got an eye for the ladies. As for the gang, my friends in the murder business tell me that the top floor of Bet Lynch Twin Towers Hotel is where all the prospects go first. But you better be careful if you're planning to send someone applying for membership, shall we say . . .'

'Why?'

The informer smiled thinly. 'Nobody ever comes out alive – either they join the gang, or they seem to suffer unfortunate accidents. And I wouldn't advise an aerial assault either. The penthouse is apparently laden with enough defence systems to take out an h-wagon at five klicks.'

'Thanks for the info, Max.'

'Just doing my job, Joe, just doing my job. Be seeing ya,' replied the nark and disappeared in a flash of static. Dredd swivelled his chair round to look at Miller.

'You get all that?' he asked.

She nodded. 'So when do I pay a visit to Bet Lynch?'

'Tomorrow,' replied Dredd. 'You'll need to get a new identity, some memory implants, a trip to the face changing machines. Better choose a neutral sector house for the transformation, Scarotti will obviously have a few contacts here. I'll spread a cover story, you've been shot by a revenge-seeker while on routine patrol and are being treated at a secret location, in case the shooter tries again.'

'I better disappear then,' agreed Miller, preparing to leave. 'How will I contact you?'

'Use your initiative,' barked Dredd.

Don Uggi's mother and her sister had been lying in state at the palatial family conapt in the Jungle since being brought home from the mortuary. Now it was time for their final journey, to be laid to rest in the Uggi family plot in the Sector 66 Municipal Graveyard Block.

Full funerals including a proper burial were relatively rare in Mega-City One. For a start all deceased people – ape or hume – automatically became the property of the city. Standard practice is for a formal service to be held at Resyk, after which the corpse is put on a giant conveyor belt leading into a total recycling centre. Resyk's motto: We Use Everything Except the Soul.

To avoid what some consider a grisly fate, it was possible to pay a standard release fee, recently increased to 1000 creds. Then there were the burial charges. The cheapest service was offered by Amber Fields out in the Cursed Earth, an economy shared burial plot for just under 6000 creds. For considerably more a citizen could be buried within the city walls, either at a municipal multi-story graveyard block (prices starting at 15,000 creds) or in a private cemetery (from 50,000 creds). Throw in the cost of hover-hearses, the reception afterwards and the hiring of a religious speaker, and the total cost of a funeral had been known to top 100,000 creds for even a modest burial.

But Don Uggi III believed that money was no object when it came to deciding upon his mother's final resting place. Daughter of the original Don Uggi, she had survived the bombs that fell during the Apocalypse War, destroying most of the original Jungle. The first Don Uggi and his son, Don Uggi Junior, were among those driven mad by radiation from the fall-out. They were culled by Judge Dredd in the aftermath of the Apocalypse War, a crime that still brought an angry rush of blood to the heart of every member of the Uggi crime family. One day they would avenge that butchery . . .

Now Don Uggi III's mother was dead: brutally, callously murdered by the She Devils, while the Judges stood by and did nothing – another wound, another crime waiting to be revenged. She had brought up the young ape, taught him the difference between right and wrong

136

and how to exploit it, turned him into a leader among apes. At the very least, he owed her a send-off to rival all send-offs.

The Don considered all this as he stood by the side of his mother's casket, a hairy hand gently stroking the side of her face, the hairy skin cold to the touch, almost like marble. One day he would be with her again, in the great Jungle of the Beyond. One day he would –

'Father! Father!' Don Uggi IV burst into the room, his young face contorted with rage. In ape terms the son was in his mid-teens, not yet an adult but now faced with taking on some of the responsibilities of one. 'On da tri-D, dey just announced who da new sector chief for 66 is – Judge Dredd!'

The Don gasped in shock and anger, the hand that had rested against his mother's face now tightening into a clenched fist. 'Have dey no sense of honour, dese Judges! Are dey determined to force us into war again?' he thundered.

His son began to jump up and down excitedly on the spot. 'Are you going to whack dem out, father? Will you ice dis Dredd, da one who has caused our family so much pain?'

The Don looked down at the lifeless body of his mother. 'First, we must lay da mother of us all to rest. Den Judge Dredd sleeps with da fishes!' He looked up at his son again. 'It is time I showed you something, da secret behind da power of da Uggi crime family.'

The Don led the young ape to a wall covered by a massive painting of a real jungle: green, lush, beautiful. 'What is dis?'

'A jungle, a real jungle, like dey have in Pan-Africa. Mother Uggi told me about it often. She said one day we would return dere and da apes would reclaim deir natural home, deir birthright as simians.'

'Very good,' nodded the Don. 'But dis painting also hides something, as well as showing us something.' He leaned forward and pressed against a small section of the painting, showing the face of an ape. The section slid away to reveal a touch-sensitive pad. The Don held his son's hand up to the panel which glowed red for a moment, then the light behind it faded away. There was a grinding of machinery from behind the huge painting as it slid away, up into the ceiling!

The young ape looked on amazed at the small secret room that had stood behind the painting all these years without him knowing. The walls were lined with complex machinery, a chair sat before the central control unit, which was formed by a bank of tri-D projection units. The Don walked forward into the small chamber and pulled a necklace from around his throat, on which two small metal keys dangled. He inserted one of the keys into a slot in the central console unit and the projectors came alive, throwing a series of solid light images up into the air.

'Dis is what has made the Uggi family top bananas among da ape gangs since my grandfather first became Don: a bomb, exactly like da one dat killed so many of our kind during da Apocalypse War, like da kind dat drove so many of our kind crazy, so dat Judge Dredd moidered dem. A bomb – hidden in da top of dis building – it could wipe out half a sector if we launched it,' explained the Don. He pointed at his son. 'Around your neck, you wear two keys on a chain, exactly like mine. Dey operate dis machinery. With dose keys and da correct codeword, you have da power of life and death over tens of thousands, skinfaces and apes alike.'

Don Uggi IV held the keys in his hand, looking down at them with reverence. 'What's da codeword, father?'

'A name from da past, da place where some of our first ancestors came from: Congo.' The Don pulled his key from the wall and the circuitry went dead again. He looked at his impetuous son. 'Just pray dat we never have to use it.'

They stood silently, thinking, before the Don brought

them out of their respective reveries. 'Come on, it's time for da funeral procession to begin. We better get going.'

Samantha couldn't believe it. Not bad enough that she had failed to be cubed for her obvious crime of grinding a senior Judge into a pulp, now she had been sacked from the unemployment opportunities programme. Worst of all, her parents were sending her to the other side of the sector on some ridiculous errand.

'I want you to go and visit that nice Miss Baynes from the Gossip-Mongers Association, take her this leaflet about upcoming activities. She never seems to come out to meetings much anymore and I do worry about her,' Samantha's mother had cooed. She was one of the organisers of the association, and liked to maintain a matronly concern for its members.

Samantha had thrown her usual tantrum. 'For Grud's sake, mother, I'm 21, I shouldn't be running errands at my age!' But to no avail. Now she found herself on a cross-sector hover-bus, heading towards Graveyard Alley, as the suburb was commonly known. Why the old crock had to live between two municipal multi-storey graveyards was beyond Samantha's understanding. And why was this hover-bus taking so long, when they were only two skeds away from her destination?

Samantha walked to the front of the vehicle to quiz the driver droid. 'Why are we taking so long?'

'There is a large funeral cortège on the skedway ahead, it is causing some impediment to our progress. Please return to your seat. Blue Moon Hover-Bus Inc would like to take this opportunity to apologise for the delay and any possible inconvenience it might cause you. If you would like to take a leaflet all about our Citizens' Charter, it will explain how you can – '

'Save it, motorhead, I'm walking!' Samantha stabbed at a public door control, but got no response. The head of the driver droid swivelled to look at her.

'I'm sorry, young lady, but no member of the public is

allowed to alight from this vehicle unless it is properly stopped at an authorised hover-bus alighting point. If you – '

Samantha glanced around wildly before her eyes lit upon a more promising button marked EMERGENCY EXIT ONLY. She stabbed it and the doors swung open with a satisfying hiss. She ran down the steps and out into the stalled traffic.

'Please return to your seat, we hope to be continuing with our journey shortly,' cried out the plaintive voice of the driver droid behind her. 'Blue Moon Hover-Bus Inc would like to take this opportunity to apologise for the delay and any possible inconvenience it might – '

'I take it you're not enjoying life in the big chair then?' Judge Hershey smiled at the scowling face of Dredd on her vid-phone monitor.

'I'd be more use to this sector and the city if I was out on the streets,' he grunted. 'Is there a reason for this call?'

'Actually, there are three reasons. I checked out your request for further information on current Wally Squad deep-cover operations. There's definitely nothing being run in your sector.'

Dredd nodded. 'That confirms my sources, too. Whoever these She Devils are, they definitely aren't official undercover Judges. What about the Amos connection?'

'Yes, I've pulled her file from the Titan records. Things are still a mess there from the Grice incident, but I managed to get something,' offered Hershey. Typically, Dredd remained silent. Don't thank me out loud, thought the female Judge resignedly before continuing.

'Judge Toni Amos was the leader of the Wally Squad operation known as the She Devils, who masqueraded as potential drugs buyers. Seems Amos got a little too involved with one of her acquaintances and ended up shooting a Judge. She claimed the killing was necessary to maintain her cover, but the Council of Five wasn't

140

convinced. It sentenced her to the standard 20 year sentence to be served on the Judicial penal colony on the Saturn moon of Titan.

'Amos had spent just over five years of her sentence there when Grice led his break-out last year. The authorities on Titan believe Amos died during the prison revolt but they can't prove it. They estimate a three per cent chance she hitched a lift back to Mega-City with Grice and his cronies. Either way, she hasn't been seen since.'

'Hmmph,' grunted Dredd. 'What was the other reason for your call?'

'I thought you might be interested. We had a break-out from the Dead Centre, but it seems the perp had help – from a Judge. We're close to tracking them down now. The trail of the perp leads right to your sector,' Hershey explained.

'What's the creep's name?'

'Bruno "The Bomber" Chuckowski. He was pulled in for the Sector House 99 bombing – '

'I think we're a step ahead of you,' Dredd interrupted. 'What's left of Bruno is currently being examined by our forensics team. They barely found enough to half fill his body bag,' he muttered grimly.

'Ah! The mysterious third victim of the Sector 66 Slasher?' asked Hershey. 'It's all over every tri-D newscast.'

'Terrif.'

'Better switch to scrambler now, I've got an update on our earlier conversation about You-Know-Whom,' suggested Hershey.

Dredd nodded and activated the special device to prevent any possible interception of their conversation by outside sources.

Elsewhere, static filled a special screen that had been secretly monitoring the dialogue between Dredd and Hershey. The watcher swore beneath his breath, tried fruitlessly for a minute to break the scrambler code before abandoning the task.

From the sound of it, the two senior Judges had moved on to another subject, and the leader of the Prometheus Project could guess what that was. Chief Judge McGruder was becoming a very unpopular woman in the Justice Department.

Good! That suited his purposes. Once the old crone was out of the way, making the project a reality would be even easier, with nobody to stand in his way. But another aspect of the conversation between Dredd and Hershey left him worried and angry.

'We had a break-out from the Dead Centre, but it seems the perp had help – from a Judge. We're close to tracking them down now,' Hershey had said. That meant the fool he'd assigned to finding a suitable subject for the latest field test had given himself away somehow.

'Sweet Jovus, do I have to do everything myself?' asked the project leader rhetorically. Obviously the answer was yes, from now on he would have to take even more control of proceedings if the Prometheus Project was to succeed. But first of all, there was the little matter of removing all trace of that bumbling fool.

A quiet, almost serene smile spread across the leader's face. Of course, if the technician was unable to find a suitable subject for the prototype to hunt down and slaughter, perhaps he would be better able to fill that very role himself . . .

On the scrambled channel, Dredd and Hershey were continuing their conversation. The younger Judge had an update about the Mechanismo programme, which had been officially suspended nearly a year ago after an incident involving Dredd, Desmon Stich and two robo-judges in the city's old sewer system.

'I've got Niles checking out the whereabouts of a few of the Tek-Judges who were involved with the programme. None of them seem to be involved with the normal duties of the Tek Division,' she said.

'Doesn't prove anything,' grumbled Dredd.

'Yeah, well how about this. Seems the unfortunate Desmon Stich is being interrogated day and night about whatever happened down in that sewer with you and the two robots. Guess who's asking the questions?'

'Todd Greel.'

'Got it in one,' affirmed Hershey. 'Look, I'm still gathering facts, but the evidence just keeps getting stronger. I'm sure McGruder has secretly revived the robo-judge programme and I'm picking Greel to have pushed her into it. He's just waiting for her to fall, so he can take her place.'

Dredd gave no response, no hint of his feelings. Impenetrable as ever, thought Hershey. She tried another approach.

'Some of the senior Judges are planning an informal gathering soon to discuss what we've found out – Niles, Plaski, possibly Shenker, maybe even Herriman. Will you at least come to that?' Hershey knew those she had named had some influence within the Department, but the bulk of the force were street Judges, and they looked to Dredd for guidance. Without his support, moves to usurp McGruder would never succeed.

'If she goes, it's got to be according to the rules. She must resign – I won't be part of a coup,' grimaced Dredd. 'I've done enough to violate the Code already.'

Now it was Hershey's turn to be perplexed. What did he mean, violate the Code? The Judges' Code of Conduct? The Mega-City One Criminal Code? What could Dredd of all people possibly have done to break his oath?

'Look, Dredd, I'm not talking about any sort of coup. But I am really worried about McGruder. You've said it yourself, she's becoming increasingly irrational. For Grud's sake, she can't even say "I" anymore! How long before she turns into another Cal?'

That got Dredd's attention. Judge Cal had been head

of the SJS more than 15 years ago, but his lust for power had driven him mad. He used a robot double to frame Dredd for murder, forced the Chief Judge out and assumed control of the city himself. Cal hijacked the daily hypno-briefings given to every street Judge to update on the latest crime events, instead using it to brainwash nearly the entire force into following his orders. Dredd had escaped in a shuttle to the Judicial penal colony on Titan and gathered a small group of unaffected Judges, forming a rebel resistance. At the height of his madness, Cal made a goldfish his deputy, reduced some Judges to going on duty in their underwear and hired alien mercenaries to help enforce his will. He was eventually toppled from power and the rules of office were altered to prevent a reoccurrence.

But the parallels between Cal and McGruder were becoming more and more uncomfortable each day. She too rose from being head of the SJS to Chief Judge, and now she seemed to be succumbing to the same madness and paranoia that afflicted Cal. Her disbanding of the Council of Five after Necropolis made it legally impossible for her to be removed from office, unless she died, resigned or reinstated the Council and was then voted out of power by its members.

'All right,' decided Dredd finally. 'I'll try to make it to this meeting, but events are boiling over down here. Let me know the details as and when, Hershey. Dredd out.'

His transmission cut off abruptly, leaving her with a screen full of static. Well, she had managed to nudge him a bit further along. Now she needed to gather some hard evidence against either Greel or McGruder. She reactivated the scrambler channel and started making a few calls.

Genya had spent hours trying to find enough fuel to make the funeral pyre before finally coming to a sad conclusion. She would never be able to shift both Tevin and Gilda outside and up onto the pile of paper and rags. Better to burn them where they lay, in their beds, burn the little shelter they had all called home with them. She couldn't face living there anymore: it was too full of memories.

So Genya took one last look at her two dead friends, their smiling contented faces. Would she ever know such happiness again? Doubtful. She'd probably be dead herself in a day or two, caught out in the open by one of the wild animals. There was nothing left to live for, no reason to go on, despite what she'd tried to tell Gilda.

Genya struck the firelighter and worked its flame into the rags by the bed, before walking out of the shelter, being careful not to look back. Never look back, Tony always said. You'll just end up living in the past.

Genya felt the strange tingling up the back of her neck again, as if someone was trying to reassure her. Maybe there was hope, after all . . .

Funeral Row is probably one of the most expensive pieces of real estate in Mega-City One. Considering the cost of an individual plot in the massive multi-storey graveyard, buildings could easily fetch 20,000 creds, and each of the ten buildings that lined the artifical tree-lined avenue had a hundred such plots on each of their fifty floors, the total worth of the skedway came in at a cool billion creds.

Despite that, Funeral Row was also one of the ugliest skeds in the city. Each of the ten towers might be worth a fortune, but the builders had invested none of that potential profit in subtle architecture, catering for the grieving families who came here to lay their loved ones to rest or softening the environmental blow to the landscape caused by these rockcrete edifices.

In short, the buildings were ugly – drokking ugly. Grey slab of rockcrete stood upon grey slab of rockcrete; each of the graveyard towers best resembled the ugliest of multi-storey car-park buildings from the twentieth century. But none of this architectural and aesthetic anarchy made any impression on the bulging blubbery bulk of Cosmo Murdoch, because Cosmo was late.

He had been making slow, unspectacular progress along the skedways towards his Weight Gainers meeting, but there was nothing new about that. Today, he had an excuse for taking so long to get anywhere, as the pedways were clogged with citizens all out watching a parade of long, black vehicles moving along the sked.

Finally, Cosmo could resist the temptation to rubberneck like everybody else no longer, so he simply barged his way forwards to the front of the kerb-side crowd. One of the reasons he liked being so big was that few people every tried to stop you getting to the front of a queue, not unless they wanted to be squashed beneath half a tonne of pure blubber.

Soon the kaftan-clad fattie was at the edge of the sked, getting a great view of a funeral cortège of sleek hoverhearses gliding slowly by. The first of the hearses strained beneath the weight of a massive floral tribute, the word MUM spelled out in a mountain of the finest paper roses creds could buy. Slightly less ostentatiously but nearly as nice was the tribute on the second hearse: AUNTIE ETHEL.

'What's going on?'

Cosmo managed to turn his head and its five double chins enough to see a small, nondescript juve beside him, watching the cortège pass by. 'It's a funeral procession, but I don't know whose.'

Dylan Finn nodded his head understandingly. 'Boy, I bet this all set somebody back a few creds!'

'Yes, I'm sure it did,' agreed Cosmo. He was finding the procession very moving, tears beginning to well up in his eyes. He reached a pudgy hand into the pocket of the kaftan – only to find another hand already inside it! The fattie pulled out the invading hand and found it attached to Dylan's arm.

'Oops,' smiled the dunk apologetically. 'Sorry, thought it was my pocket, sorry, it won't happen again – '

'You're a thief! A dunk!' Cosmo was outraged that someone could be using a funeral procession as a cover for crime, especially on a day so beautiful as this. He kept

146

hold of the struggling juve's arm. 'Help! Help! Somebody send for the Judges – I've caught a pickpocket red-handed!' shouted Cosmo at the top of his voice.

Dylan realised the jig was up and began pummelling the fattie with blows, anything to try and dislodge this huge, clammy grip on his hand. Alas, Cosmo's sheer magnitude defied simple body blows, which merely bounced off his rotundity. 'Oh, stomm. Jovus, Mavis and Jonah, get me out of this one and I swear I'll never dunk again,' he prayed quietly, still throwing blows vainly at his captor.

Samantha managed to fight her way through the crowd on the side skeds, only to be confronted with masses of people lining the street leading to Miss Baynes's block. For Grud's sake, anyone would think the world was coming to an end, the way everyone was acting.

She was particularly annoyed by two tall women directly in front of her, blocking any possible view of the funeral cortège. Finally exasperation got the better of the spont and she jabbed one of the women in the back.

'Could you please move along? I'm trying to have a look too . . .' Her voice faded away as the duo turned to reveal chunky machine guns hidden inside their trench-coats. 'Er, I'll go look somewhere else.'

The bullet spat quietly from one of the weapons and neatly divided the space between Samantha Hester's eyeballs, which crossed themselves trying to look at the wound. Then she realised she was dead and promptly dropped to the ground, her body gently lowering near the two women.

The assassins turned and walked away, leaving the first victim of the Funeral Row Massacre lying face-down on the pedway behind them. The other citizens simply assumed Samantha had passed out in the crush and nimbly stepped over her body, grumbling about the lack of space and couldn't she go collapse somewhere else please.

* * *

In the hover-limo behind the two hearses, Don Uggi III sat grimly in a jet black double-breasted mourning suit and matching trilby hat. The procession was slow but it gave him a chance to contemplate what revenge he would exact upon the She Devils for what they had done to him and his family. But first he would deal with the accursed Judge Dredd.

There was shouting from the side of the skedway, distracting him. He turned to look, to see what the noise was and couldn't help laughing out loud. A skinface fattie was shouting and waving his arms in the air, the scene made more comic by the presence of a small juve clasped in one of the fattie's hands, the youth being waved about like a piece of cloth.

The Don was still laughing when the first bullet thudded into the limo's upholstery just a hair's breadth away from the side of his head. 'It's a hit! Everybody down!' He threw his son to the floor of the limo, then threw himself on top of the young ape, shielding him from the gunfire.

Another bullet took the top off the limo driver's head, covering the inside of the front windscreen with blood and brains. The dead driver's foot pushed down hard on the accelerator and the limo surged forward, smashing into the back of the hearse in front, before cartwheeling through the air towards the teeming crowd of bystanders on one of the pedways. More than a dozen citizens were crushed to death immediately, as a hail of bullets filled the air: the Funeral Row Massacre had begun.

TEN

Funeral Pyre Maniacs

A Judge should never show fear, he should inspire fear in others. Controlling your fear will make you stronger, while in turn making perps fear you. Fear is the greatest enemy for a Judge, and also his greatest weapon. Fear is the key to every situation.

Never back down, always be your own person. Make a reputation among the citizens as a Judge to avoid, and that reputation will serve you well on the streets.

Extract from *Dredd's Comportment*
Volume III (revised 2116 edition)

'The Sector 66 Slasher is, in fact, a deadly predator from outer space, preying on the citizens of this sector like common carrion! That exclusive inside story from our ace reporter on the skeds and peds of Mega-City One, Whiti Vitaliev, coming up in a moment!'

The man in question smiled to himself. The words 'ace reporter' were music to his ears. He was back on top of his profession, with the hottest scoop of the month, possibly of the year. Now it was time to deliver the goods, safe in the knowledge that every other newscast in the city would be poaching his story for the lead story in their next three major bulletins, possibly even overnight – depending on how slow a newsday it turned out to be.

Around him hovering a battery of mini-cameras and a blaze of lighting to give his face that larger than life quality required for a good tri-D image on-screen. Beyond the halo of lights stood a production droid in direct communication with the ratings bureau. That supplied a moment by moment assessment of the viewers reaction to the news, so any item that caused ratings to dip could be cut off within seconds if necessary. But the ace reporter doubted anyone would be switching off during this item.

'Hello, I'm Whiti Vitaliev and I have just returned to our studios after an exclusive consultancy session with the acting sector chief for the beleaguered Sector 66, Judge Dredd. He told me that the Sector 66 Slasher is, in fact, a deadly alien predator that is feeding upon the citizens of this mighty metropolis!

'During our two-hour discussion, I was privy to much information which must, at this time, remain classified, due to the sensitive nature of the material. However, I can reveal that the Slasher has struck at least three times and possibly more. Indeed, I understand that Dredd has stood in for one of the unfortunate victims, the late sector chief for 66, Eammon Kozwall.

'This story burst onto your vidscreens this ayem when I exclusively revealed the discovery of the –'

Suddenly the auto-cameras on Whiti went dead, the lights in the studio dimmed and he was left talking into thin air.

'What the drok happened? Why did you cut away from me? I was barely getting started!' he demanded furiously. The voice of his producer buzzed into his brain from a tiny implant in his ear.

'Sorry, Whiti, we had to cut away to another story. There's a bloodbath going on at Funeral Row, apparently gang-related, but at least a dozen cits have already been caught in the crossfire. We've cut across live to the scene. Sorry, but you've just become old news . . .'

It was at this point that the 'ace reporter on the skeds and peds of Mega-City One' threw a major trantrum. Sweet Jovus, all his glory was stolen away by some sordid shoot-out, just because somebody was lucky enough to have a camera on the scene when it started – typical! Well, he wasn't going to stand for it, he was the star of this station and if he had to go out and find the alien predator himself, he drokkin' well would!

Judge Kevin Brighton had been assigned to help cover the funeral security by Miller just before she suffered her mysterious 'attack'. Normally, a funeral cortège was ignored by Judges, unless it was likely to cause major traffic congestion. But in view of the spate of attacks on the ape gangs by the She Devils and the sensitive nature of the situation in the sector, Brighton and a team of five other Judges had pulled corpse escort duty.

Unusually for a Judge, Brighton had passed through the Academy and graduated while suffering from a physical disability – he had no sense of smell. Normally, a disability discounted a Cadet from becoming a full street Judge. Instead they would be directed into one of the specialised divisional roles, like Tek- or Med-Division. But when Brighton's lack of olfactory sense was discovered – and that wasn't until his ninth year in the Academy – he was given a special dispensation to continue with standard street Judge training.

Since then it had rarely been commented upon. He was always conscious of the need for extra vigilance, he had no urge to burn to death in a building on fire just because he couldn't smell the smoke. But the lack of smelling was compensated by his four other senses being unusually enhanced, compared to normal standards. So when the first shot was fired, it was Brighton who knew immediately from where the bullet had come.

'Sniper! Top floor window, east side of the sked!' he shouted into his helmet-com. While the other Judges were still scanning the graveyard blocks for confirmation, the young Judge was already calling in the incident to Control.

'Brighton to Control! We've got a sniper attack on the Uggi family cortège, Funeral Row, Sector 66!' Before he could speak again, the single shot turned into a thunderous volley of gunfire and then the hover-limo was flying through the air, into the crowd of bystanders, and exploding, all in a matter of moments.

'We need major back-up and we need it *now*! Sniper attack has turned into a full-scale war down here! Send us meds, fire crews, and meat wagons, lots of 'em! You copy that, Control?!' He was screaming into his helmet-com now, unable to hear his own words over the sound of bullets and explosions and people screaming, crying, dying.

Directly in front of him the last hover-car in the cortège blew up, killing the line of people in front of him and blowing Brighton off his Lawmaster. By the time he pulled himself up off the ground, shaking his head to clear the fuzziness of the blast's concussion wave, his own bike was burning. Fortunately the safety system prevented the fuel rods from exploding.

Brighton gave up waiting to hear a reply from Control and ran into the heart of chaos, shouting to the other Judges to follow him. There had to be a way to stop this madness, or at least cut down the number of casualties and outright deaths.

The Don and his son were both thrown clear as their hover-limo crashed into the crowded pedway. Within moments the vehicle exploded into a ball of flame as its fuel rods were ignited by a peppering of incendiary and hi-ex rounds fired by the She Devils. Thirty-seven citizens were roasted alive where they stood, another fifty-two suffered fatal burns and hundreds more were severely injured. But worse was still to come.

The Don kept his son hugged close to the ground and swivelled his head around to see where the attack was coming from. Bullets seemed to be flying from everywhere. He guessed there were at least three or four shooters in the crowds, two on each side of the skedway. Another couple seemed to be stationed up in the municipal graveyard buildings lining either side of the sked. Still more hovered above the chaos on hover-bikes.

'Where da hell are my shooters?' he demanded. As if in response, answering fire began spurting back from the dozens of apes in the rest of the cortège. But they were pinned down by the covering fire from above, which started picking them off one by one. Then the following cars began to explode, one after another, showering the panicking crowd with white-hot shrapnel and burning debris.

The Don watched in horror as the attackers trained their weapons upon the hover-hearse carrying his mother's coffin, which was stalled in the centre of the sked.

'No, not her too!' He got up and started loping towards the vehicle, but was thrown backwards as it too exploded, sending a massive fireball up into the sky. The Don fell to the ground, unconscious and completely undefended. Two women dressed in long black trenchcoats and carrying Widowmaker 3000 weapons stepped out of the crowd and approached the comatose ape.

'Time to die, monkey,' smiled one, her eyes glinting excitedly behind black, shoulder-length hair.

Dredd almost smiled when the alarm came through about the massacre. Within moments his Lawmaster was tearing out of the sector house, along with that of almost every Judge in the building. As he sped to the scene, Dredd barked orders into his helmet-com.

'Dredd to Control! Scramble every Judge in Sectors 64, 65 and 69 and get them down to Funeral Row in 66 now! We're going to need every badge we can get to clean this mess up!'

'Roj that Dredd!'

Another stamp of his boot on the accelerator pedal and the bike surged forward, pulling ahead of the others. His trigger finger had been itching for days . . .

When the first shot was fired, Dylan Finn knew exactly where to put himself – behind the considerable bulk of his corpulent captor, Cosmo. The dunk wisely decided that the fattie would make a much bigger and better target than himself, and could provide some useful protective coverage as well. Then the juve watched as a hover-limo – seemingly in slow-motion – drove into the back of the hearse ahead of it before cartwheeling through the air into the crowd away to his left. When the limo exploded, Dylan decided that would be a good time to move on.

In front of him Cosmo was still looking around himself at the action, quite fascinated, as if he were experiencing a Surround-Yourself-Experience™ movie, with all five dimensions working at once. His attention was distracted when the first bullet hit him in the stomach, but it merely got lodged in the lard-like excesses of his abdomen. Then the tiny charge within it ignited and a large portion of Cosmo Murdoch's half-tonne body was spread across the skedway in front of him.

Dylan decided just a moment too late to leave the area, maybe even the entire sector if this kept up. He turned to go and found himself lying flat on his face, covered by what seemed to be a huge, heavy blanket. He couldn't move his legs and he could barely breathe. Then he made the horrific realisation that he was actually trapped under the fallen body of the fattie-and-proud-of-it Cosmo. Dylan screamed, but nobody could hear him, nobody at all. They were all too busy screaming themselves.

The Don opened his eyes in time to see his assassin's hand burst into flames, the mini-cartridge of napalm-19 inside the incendiary bullet that had hit her arm expanding in moments to engulf her whole body in flames. The other woman turned and began firing blindly towards the source of the bullet before she, too, was transformed into a blazing human torch. The pair writhed around before collapsing to the ground, dead hands still trying to beat out the unquenchable fire.

The ape gang leader turned to see which of his lieutenants had saved him, and gasped in astonishment as a

Judge got up from a crouching position behind the wreckage of the burnt-out hover-hearse. Keeping all angles covered, the Judge crept towards him cautiously, one hand extended towards the Don.

'Are you okay? Have you been shot?' asked Brighton.

'Not yet,' replied the Don gruffly as he climbed to his feet, ignoring the helpful hand offered him. He squinted at his saviour ungratefully. 'I knows you – you were dere wit' dat dame, Miller, when my mutha died da other day, weren't you?'

'Yes,' replied Brighton, pausing to return a volley of fire from one of the snipers in the multi-storey graveyard blocks around them. 'Please, we've got to get you to cover, otherwise they'll try again.'

'Who'll try again? Da Don don't run from nobody!' He stood resolute in the centre of the sked, bullets whizzing around them.

'I guess it's the She Devils, they seem determined to provoke a gang war with you and your family,' said Brighton.

'Oh yeah? Well, dey's gonna get one after dis! Look what dey did to my mother, she never hurt nobody!' protested the Don. 'De She Devils are gonna pay for dis, or my name ain't Don Uggi da Third!'

He was still protesting when Brighton threw him to the ground while firing round after round at an oncoming hover-car as it zoomed low over the ground towards them on a suicidal final flight. A stray bullet caught the pilot in the forehead, throwing her head back, jerking the controls out of her hands. The hover-car swerved wildly through the air, then began falling to earth again, this time heading directly for a small citi-block dwarfed by the graveyard buildings around it . . .

Miss Muriel Baynes thought she could hear a faint popping noise from outside the windows, but she ignored it. In the back of her mind it triggered a memory, a tiny fragment of thought from years ago, before the Judges, before the war even, from when she was a child. There was a day, once a year, when the people would celebrate. They used to mark the occasion with lights in the sky, now what were they called? She could still recall having to hold her hands over her ears to drown out the noise. That was it – fireworks. They were called fireworks.

The eldster turned around and started walking towards the windows that faced out onto Funeral Row. Funny, but she almost thought she could hear fireworks now, from outside. She pulled aside the curtain and looked with horror at the carnage outside. There was a particularly loud explosion and a hover-car began to fall from the sky, burning and blazing its way directly towards Barnum Baynes Block.

As it tumbled towards her, turning end over end gracefully through the air, the noise seemed to fall away and time itself slowed to nearly a stand-still. Muriel knew she was about to die, but she couldn't turn away, couldn't run, couldn't move from the spot. A single thought ran through her mind like the refrain from some long-lost melody, eluding identification, just nagging at the subconscious.

'I wonder who'll look after my cyber-parrot now I'm dead,' she whispered to herself. Then the world exploded through the window and she was incinerated in seconds, the blackened clothes and frying flesh flying away sizzling from her bones, the white skeleton turned to dust and ash, then floating apart, just atoms in a world of death and destruction.

The cyber-parrot died with her. And outside on Funeral Row, the death toll reached six hundred . . .

This was not the way Dylan had expected to die, slowly suffocating beneath the remains of a half-tonne tub of lard with a taste in loud kaftans.

Like most juves, he actually believed that somehow he was immortal, or that some miracle cure for ageing would be found in his lifetime. Of course, at the back of his mind, he knew that that would never happen and one day his heart would stop beating and the blood would stop pumping oxygen to his brain and all the thoughts and feelings and hopes and dreams and memories he possessed, that were unique to him and nobody else, would be lost forever.

So when he thought about dying on those long, dark nights when sleep would not come and his brain wouldn't shut up, he considered all the ways he might die and gave them a favoured order. Generally he confined himself to a Top Five Favourite Ways to Cark It. One night he'd gotten the list up to 39 but was utterly frustrated at trying to come up with a number 40 to round out the tally.

Of his top five, number five was usually dying quietly, in his sleep, at some incredibly ripe age, having lived a life so full and famous he would never be forgotten. Even if he couldn't achieve actual immortality, by Grud, he wanted some kind of eternal presence in the scheme of things.

Numbers four and three sometimes swapped places in the pecking order, but were always the same. In no particular order – dying whilst making mad, passionate love with the most desirable woman in the galaxy (hey, this was his fantasy list, right, so it didn't actually have to be overly realistic) or dying just after making mad, passionate love with the most desirable woman in the galaxy. He knew this was a bit one-track-minded, but he was only a juve, Dylan rationalised, and hormone season was at fever pitch inside his body.

Number two was actually a former number one that had slipped from the top slot only a few weeks before after a record-breaking stay at the top of the chart – dying at the moment of his greatest triumph. Dylan had loved that one for a long time but eventually realised that he wouldn't know it was the greatest triumph of his life because he'd be dead, and even if somehow fate got it right and claimed him at the appointed moment, he'd never get the satisfaction of savouring his greatest triumph. Either way, it seemed to suffer from major drawbacks and would be lucky to stay in the top five for much longer as its appeal grew thinner.

But straight in at number one was Dylan Finn's absolute favourite way to die – temporarily. He figured that even if the afterlife or the concept of reincarnation were utter stomm, as most people believed, it didn't hurt to keep up a vague belief in them, if only as an insurance policy if they should ever pan out.

Yet in all the times the self-proclaimed finest dunk in Sector 66 had contemplated dying, slowly suffocating beneath the remains of a half-tonne tub of lard with a taste in loud kaftans had never figured in his thinking. Oh well, mused Dylan, at least I've got something to fill out the top forty now. He gasped thin breath as another thought crossed his mind. So now he was going to peg out at number forty, only just creeping on to the foot of the chart. Perhaps all his family's talk about divine retribution and the like had actually meant something. Guess crime doesn't pay off, at least in the long run, decided Dylan.

He was just contemplating ways of increasing the chart to a top fifty to make the manner of his death a little less uninspiring when the Judges discovered him, barely alive, gasping for breath and babbling about new entries at number sixteen.

Three hours later, Dredd looked along the death-strewn skedway aptly named Funeral Row and shook his head. 'All this, just to provoke a gang war. I'll give 'em war if they want it,' he muttered darkly.

'Sorry, sir, you were saying?' asked Brighton.

'What's the damage?' replied Dredd, countering a question with another question. Brighton looked at the latest tallies on the compu-monitor built into his replacement Lawmaster bike.

'Still counting, but currently 1093 dead. Another 3000-plus injured, about 600 of them not expected to last the night. Property damage is estimated at nearly half a billion creds, mostly due to the three multi-storey graveyards downed in the fighting. We lost five Judges, we estimate eight of the She Devils are dead and more than half the members of the Uggi crime family are deceased.'

'Terrif,' growled Dredd unhappily. 'We manage to take any of the She Devils alive?'

'One was captured but she committed suicide before we could question her – believed to have a cyanide pill embedded in her teeth. Our ID record shows her to be a Belinda Sisko, a.k.a. "Bliss", aged 92, a former mercenary and convicted murderer. She got a thirty years sentence for various offences, chose to take it on the time stretcher,' replied the young Judge, before looking up from the print-out. 'The weird thing was, she looked more like 22 than 92 – maybe the records are wrong.'

'Time stretcher,' mused Dredd. Perps given a sentence of twelve years or more were given the option of serving their time in an iso-cube, or going on the time stretcher. This accelerated the rate of ageing in their bodies, so one minute in the time stretcher was equal to one decade in confinement. Besides being psychologically crushing, the process was also incredibly painful, so few perps took this option. 'Of course!' shouted Dredd.

'Sir?'

'She must have been using stookie – the adifax drug! The whole gang probably does,' realised Dredd, thinking out loud. Just as a time stretcher accelerated the ageing process, so was there technology to reverse the process. Called stookie or adifax, an expensive and highly addictive serum had been discovered nearly twenty years before which stopped and sometimes even reversed the ageing process.

It was prepared from the adifax gland found only in a small, cuddly alien creature called the Stookie. The discovery of this life-enhancing property made the Stookies hunted creatures, with Stookie Glanders willing to battery-farm them on secret ranches in the Cursed Earth. The process was highly illegal, but this didn't stop desperate addicts and only drove the price of the drug higher. A recent haul of stookie seized by the Judges had an estimated street value of nearly twenty billion creds.

'What about the Don?' asked Dredd.

'I managed to keep him alive until back-up arrived. He's over there, in that pat-wagon,' gestured Brighton at a black Justice Department vehicle, hovering by the side of the sked. Dredd marched over and pulled open the door.

Within moments Don Uggi III was flinging himself towards Dredd, trying to stretch his bonds far enough to get his hands around the throat of his family's greatest enemy.

'You! I'll kill you! I'll kill you wit' my bare hands!' screamed the Don, rage driving him quite crazy.

'Hmm. You seem a little disturbed,' commented Dredd. 'In view of the attempts upon the lives of you and your family, I'm taking you into protective custody. Consider yourself under arrest.'

'What!?! Dose bitches take a shot at me, dey ice half my family, and youse arrestin' me!? Why you – '

Dredd swung the door shut on a howling torrent of obscenities. 'Quite a temper he's got. Brighton, I want you to escort the Don to the Holding Tanks back at the sector house. Better give him one on his own, we don't want any mysterious 'accidents' happening to him while he's in custody, or else things could get ugly.'

'Get ugly! Pardon me, sir, but what do you call all this?' asked the young Judge, gesturing at the carnage around them.

'Boy, we're just warmin' up,' replied Dredd.

Brighton could almost have sworn there was something resembling a vague smile on the Dredd's face. But he must have imagined it – Dredd never, ever smiled, hence his nickname among the Cadets at the Academy: Old Stony Face.

ELEVEN

Call Me Cherry

Wally Squad Judges: The Undercover Division of Mega-City One's Justice Department. These are Judges who live under false identities, playing out the part of ordinary citizens. Of course, ordinary can mean incredibly outlandish in appearance and outrageous in behaviour when it comes to the citizens of the Big Meg. Thus Wally Squad Judges are better able to detect and infiltrate criminal operations. However, at no time are such undercover Judges allowed to compromise the Judge system or break the Law by their own actions.

Taking on a new identity can require a range of procedures. For extreme cases, the Judge would require not only a completely different wardrobe and a temporary facial restructuring using face change technology, but sometimes also needs a complete memory wipe and psychological implant therapy to set the new persona in place, unshakeable in its permanence. Such extreme measures are usually only necessary on deep cover 'sleepers', who are then made aware of their true purpose through a trigger mechanism, which restores their original persona.

Extract from *Divisions of the Justice Department:*
A Tutorial
Judge tutor Marcus, 2115AD

Lynn Miller hated to admit it, but she had quite enjoyed her startling transformation from being a tough street Judge to become the sex-bomb assassin, Cheryl 'Cherry' Lane.

The hardest task had been choosing the identity of her

161

new guise. It had to be a real person, with a real background to make the persona believable, give it the necessary depth and background. And the identity had to already have a reputation as a smooth, deadly operator if she was to have any chance of gaining admittance to the select membership of the She Devils. But most important of all, there had to be no chance of the real person turning up and blowing her cover story, otherwise Miller could quickly find herself on the wrong end of an assassin's bullet.

A trawl through MAC's files had located the perfect fit – Cherry Lane, a former Brit-Cit Judge turned bounty hunter. She had slipped into Mega-City One a week before and already been responsible for the deaths of more than a dozen Brit fugitives, retaining only their bottom jaw-bone for proof of identity from the dental records. Unfortunately for Cherry, she was discovered by a street Judge removing one such trophy from a target and panicked, killing the Lawkeeper.

Judge murder can carry a death penalty, but perps caught rarely made it to the Dead Centre for the sentence to be executed. So it was for Cherry, who caught several rounds in the back and was now lying in the vault beneath Sector House 44. Each sector house keeps aside an area where severely injured criminals are kept in suspended animation until they can be cured, and made to serve their rightful sentence. It was a mark of the pettiness of some Judges that they were willing to keep Cherry 'on ice' until surgical techniques were developed to save her life, just so she could be executed straight afterwards.

The unfortunate Cherry's presence in sus-an not only prevented her from inconveniently blowing Miller's cover, it also gave direct access to what remained of her memory. This was downloaded into the compu-system and placed on an implant, which was then transferred into Miller's mind, giving her the feelings, thoughts and memories of the very deadly Cheryl 'Cherry' Lane.

Like almost all Judges, Miller had been well trained at

the Academy in the techniques of masking her thoughts. (Nearly all people have a certain latent Psi aptitude or ability, though there were some notable exceptions – Judge Dredd was infamous at the Academy for having been rated double-zero for Psi sensitivity.) The addition of the implant gave Miller a Psi 'mask' behind which to shelter her own persona, making detection nearly impossible.

After this complex operation was achieved, it was time for the physical 'make-over' to match Miller's looks to her new identity. That was where the fun began. Vanity was frowned upon within the Justice Department – there was an entire section about the perils of vanity in volume two of *Dredd's Comportment*, one of the set texts at the Academy. (Indeed, there was a whole chapter about why facial hair should be discouraged, something which had always intrigued Miller.)

Miller had always had beautiful strawberry blonde hair and been quite fond of it. But when she awoke from a coma after the incident involving the Nelson Rockefeller Orbital Satellite, she discovered her hair had turned shock white almost overnight. Now she was getting a quite legitimate opportunity to experiment with her appearance.

A session in a face-change machine remoulded Miller's face more in the image of her subject. The jawline became a little wider, the nose smaller, more finely shaped, her cheekbones a bit more prominent. Special 'permanent' contact lenses that did not require daily removal for cleaning turned her eyes from a warm hazel to ice blue. Last to change was her hair, cut back to an old-fashioned, functional pageboy bob, and dyed wild, brassy metallic red.

'Hence the alias Cherry,' Miller said to herself, examining the transformation in a full-length three-way mirror. It was a distinctly odd experience, looking at her face and seeing somebody else's features there, like one of those weird dreams she sometimes got while under the sleep machine, as if she could feel her mind drifting out of her body. Miller turned to the Wally Squad's 'dresser', Spiro Welham, who had been seconded from the fashion industry to supervise the transformation of Judges into utterly convincing ordinary citizens. 'What next?'

'Time to get you some decent clothes,' smiled Spiro. 'If you want to imitate a sex-bomb assassin, you have to be a killer dresser. Get out of that uniform, for a start.'

Miller pulled off her boots, then slid the long zip on the front of her leathereen tunic right down to the crotch, then shrugged her shoulders out before sliding the heavy, kevlar-reinforced bodysuit off. Spiro had disappeared from the tiny underground changing room into the cavernous wardrobe chamber that led off it, but his querulous voice boomed through.

'And the underwear too, please. You can hardly keep wearing standard issue Justice Department u-fronts now, can you?'

Miller guessed he was right and slipped off her bra and pants with quick, economical movements. Suddenly she felt self-conscious – not because of her physical nudity, but from the psychological nudity of being without her uniform with its reassuring feeling of authority and command and safety. She folded her arms awkwardly across her bare breasts and waited to see what Spiro would offer her to wear.

'Where's my father? What happened to da Don?' demanded Don Uggi IV, brushing away the hand of a female ape trying to clean a blood-clotted wound on his scalp. Around him in the Don's lushly furnished private office stood a silent collection of battered and bruised ape gang members – the survivors of the attack at Funeral Row. Finally, one of the lieutenants stepped forward to speak.

'Da Judges got him. I saw dem take him away in a pat-wagon,' said Tommy 'Gun' Topolinni, so named for his favouring the squat antique machine gun as his main weapon in a shoot-out.

'Den why da hell didn't ya stop dem?' demanded the angry young ape, banging a fist on the ornate real wood desk in front of him and jumping to his feet. The survivors of the ambush had struggled back to the family headquarters and were now gathered in the Don's office, coming to terms with their rout at the hands of the She Devils.

'Coz dose bitches were tryin' ta kill us! I couldn't get ta him!' protested Tommy nervously as the juve ape approached him.

'Issat so?' fumed Don Uggi IV, lashing out with his fist, smashing Tommy to the floor. 'Well it ain't good enuff!' He glared round at the others. 'Ya hear me, you bums? It ain't good enough. We're gonna get da Don back and make da Judges pay for dis! But until we do, I'm the new Don – anybody got a problem wit' dat?'

Silence. The new Don nodded at their agreement, going back to his seat. 'All right, go get yaselves cleaned up. I got me some thinkin' ta do!'

The motley group of lieutenants and female apes shuffled out of the office, leaving the new Don alone with his thoughts, one hand fingering the two keys on the chain around his neck.

Midnight in Sector 4 and a scream cries out in a Justice Department building. Two Judge-warders march down a corridor, leading a shambling figure in front of them. The warders are steadfast, firm, upright, but the individual they are escorting is a broken man, his eyes bloodshot, black rings marking the skin beneath them, his hair greying and almost frazzled. The skin on his face is sallow and grey, deprived of exposure to sunlight for so long in this place. A white gown hangs on his shuffling body. Ahead stands an open doorway.

The inmate sees the doorway, recognises it and screams

again. The warders grab one of his arms each, forcing him forwards towards the doorway. They step inside.

By contrast with the grey corridor outside, this room is overwhelmingly white, bright, light with dazzling brilliance. In the centre sits a chair, but not designed for comfort or rest or ease. The back is stiff and upright, the seat riddled with drainage holes to take away any human waste the user's body might purge during the ordeal to come. Both the arms and legs of the chair are heavy, solid, with thick leathereen restraining straps hanging from them, ready to clasp and hold the subject, giving total restraint and immovability.

Beside the chair stands a figure in the uniform of a Tek-Judge. Todd Greel smiles and there is something about the look in his eyes. In his hands is a comp-unit, details scrolling across the tiny screen – data, facts, information. Greel walks towards the captive.

'Ah, Stich . . . Sit down, make yourself comfortable.'

The warders shove the whimpering Desmon Stich into the chair, bind him tightly with the straps, pulling them just that fraction too tight, making sure it hurts. Greel strolls around the white-tiled examination room, the heels of his boots clip-clopping on the floor.

'I want to talk about Dredd.'

'I-I've told you everything, stammers Stich, desperate to appease, to avoid another session in hell, another long night of questions and pain and misery and hurting, oh the hurting.

'We've reason to believe you're not giving us the full story.'

Greel stopped, gestures to a white-coated Med-Judge who has been standing quietly in a corner. The medic produces a hypodermic needle from the pocket of his laboratory coat. Of course, the old-fashioned hypodermic has long been superceded for medical purposes with air needles that painlessly do the same job. But for interrogation purposes, the stainless steel needle still has a certain terrifying charm.

'So we're going to try something a little more powerful this time.'

Greel regards the sad, pathetic blubbering face of his captive for a moment before nodding at the Med-Judge. The white-coated doctor moves towards Stich, pushing the plunger of the hypodermic so a small jet of liquid squirts into the air.

Greel smiles again.

'Not bad, not bad, if I say so myself!' announced Spiro gleefully. He nudged Miller towards a set of full-length, three-way mirrors. 'Take a look at yourself, my dear, I think you'll be pleasantly surprised.'

'Sweet Jovus!' gasped the Judge when she got a good look at herself. 'I look like one of those women who walk the Slab!'

Miller was clad entirely in red and black. On her feet were a pair of stiletto-heeled black ankle-boots of finest leathereen, awash with buckles. Her long legs were wrapped in sheer red stockings, attached to a very visible scorching-red suspender belt. The stockings disappeared up beneath a tight black leathereen mini-skirt so short, Miller thought it had been a waistbelt when Spiro first handed it to her to try on. Instead, around her waist were slung twin utility belts, each laden with pouches full of bullets, mini-bombs and other essential assassin's equipment.

A red lace body stretched over her torso, with a red silk bra strapped over the top of it. The ensemble was completed with a black leathereen peaked cap and a collection of heavy red bangles on both arms.

'Spiro, why am I wearing the bra outside the body stocking? It's got no practical use there whatsoever,' Miller protested.

'My dear, that's the whole point! It's for shock value, for visual impact, not to keep your breasts in place.' Spiro rolled his eyes at the ceiling in mock-horror at her lack of fashion sense. 'You're meant to be a She Devil remember, not a nun!'

Miller checked the contents of the twin waist-belts and slotted a las-knife into the sheath strapped to her right thigh. Next she tried walking towards the full-length three-way mirrors again, and nearly sprained both ankles. 'Could I at least get some boots with a heel I can run in?' she asked plaintively.

Spiro relented and produced a pair of thigh-high shiny black rubbereen boots. 'Of course it ruins the total look . . .'

'Yeah, but at least I can walk now! Well, She Devils, here I come . . .'

Tek-Judge Ajibayo Akinsiku ran down the dark corridor, his mind racing. The leader of the Prometheus Project was back and demanding his presence. It didn't do to keep the leader waiting; he had a foul temper. And since that incident where the leader threatened to have him killed when Akinsiku tried to protect Magnus, the black Tek-Judge was genuinely frightened by the leader's rages.

Grud, why did I ever let myself get involved in this madness? he thought desperately. Then again, it was not like he'd been given a choice at the time. He had simply been seconded on permanent assignment to an offshoot of the Mechanismo programme. The order came from the highest authority in Tek-Division, so he could hardly flout it.

At first Akinsiku had been excited to work on the Prometheus Project. The task was challenging and if successful, it would change the face of all future wars, save millions of lives, prevent tragedies like Necropolis or Judgement Day ever happening again. But soon doubts began to nag at him. Could the end justify the means, especially when the means involved the slaughter of human beings like rats in a laboratory.

Those doubts had turned into stark terror when he saw the latest prototype and its brutal handiwork. Feeding time for the monster they were trying to create was a buffet of human brains, stomach-wrenching and soul-destroying. Sweet Jovus, if he ever got out of this underground hell-hole, he'd make sure the world knew about the sick experiments at the heart of the Prometheus Project.

As he got closer to the mezzanine floor where Magnus floated in his tank, Akinsiku could just hear a raised voice ahead of him. The leader and Magnus were arguing again, but the Tek-Judge could only hear the leader's side of the conflict, because Magnus was only able to communicate telepathically with one person at a time.

'I don't care what you think is right or wrong, you'll do what I say!'

A pause. Akinsiku presumed Magnus was replying to the leader.

'He screwed up, so he's got to pay the price and that's it!'

The Tek-Judge made sure he created a lot of noise as he entered the chamber by a side-door, not wanting the leader to realise he had heard part of the conversation.

'Ah! Tek-Judge Akinsiku! I've got some bad news,' smiled the leader, approaching the new arrival. 'It seems the Judges have found about your releasing our last guinea pig from the Dead Centre.'

'But you picked out the test subject yourself,' protested Akinsiku. 'You told me he wouldn't be harmed, that the test would be aborted before anybody got hurt, then they wouldn't be able to trace it back here.'

'An unfortunate accident, which no-one is blaming you for. But this slip-up at the iso-block definitely is your fault. I'm afraid you'll have to leave the project.'

The Tek-Judge's mind raced. What did the leader mean, leave the project? In a body bag, that's the only way I'll get out of here. 'Oh? Er, where will I go?'

'Well, I've arranged to have you transferred back to your old sector house. They're expecting you back on station within the hour. There will be an h-wagon to pick you up a klick to the south of here in about 10 minutes. I would have had them come here to get you, but you know how it is – security and all.' The leader chuckled at his own joke.

Akinsiku couldn't believe his good fortune – he was getting out of here, and alive! 'I'll go and collect my things from the sleeping quarters,' he ventured, turning to go.

'No need, I've already had them sent on – they'll be waiting for your arrival.'

'Oh, thanks. Well, I better get going.' Akinsiku looked at Magnus for the last time. 'Goodbye Magnus. Good luck with the next series of tests,' he said, but got no reply from the sad-faced mutant. Instead the leader chipped in again.

'Yes, we hope to start another set very soon. Now get going or you'll miss that h-wagon and have to walk back to the sector house. And don't forget – not a word of the work you've seen here to anyone.'

'No, sir, of course not.' Akinsiku saluted and nearly sprinted for the door. Within minutes he was emerging onto the surface above the secret research centre and began striding quickly towards the pick-up zone. The Tek-Judge didn't notice the old woman hiding in the rubble that had once been her home. She followed him from a safe distance . . .

'This is murder!' Magnus was shaking his head, his whole body vibrating with anger as it floated in the green suspension liquid.

'I don't care what you think, freak,' spat back the leader. 'Akinsiku screwed up, he placed this project in jeopardy. The least he can do is make up for that by providing us with another subject for testing. Now release the prototype – or I'll feed you to what's back there in the cage myself!'

Magnus shook with rage but could see no alternative. At least as he was in partial control of the prototype, he might be able to direct it away from the human sacrifice that was being put in its path.

Grud, forgive me, he thought and reached out with his mind . . .

Akinsiku ran around the corner and stopped. He was exactly a klick south of the project headquarters, but where was the h-wagon? Then he heard a voice in his head: 'Ajibayo, this is Magnus . . . run for your life, it's a trap – '

Then the Tek-Judge felt the slightest gust of wind and he was lying on the ground. When he looked down to see why he had fallen, his left leg was missing, just blood gushing out onto the ground. Ajibayo Akinsiku looked up as the monster loomed over him, allowing itself to become partially visible as it reared up.

'Oh stomm,' muttered the Tek-Judge and screamed.

you slash downwards with talons, slicing and clawing, tearing apart skin and bone and flesh, the blood warm and soothing as it splashes over you like hot rain on a summer's day. you flick out a tentacle and its razor-sharp edge digs into the helmet, pulling it away. next the scalp is torn off, exposing the sweetmeats of the cranium, the medulla –

Magnus strained but the creature was becoming harder and harder to control, straining against him all the time. Now the mutant telepath was merely a passenger to its carnage, an unwilling spectator to its horrific lust for blood and human brains. He felt sick, wretching green bile up in the heavy, viscous solution surrounding himself . . .

Genya Berger had been on her way home when the door appeared in the flat rockcrete ground before her. She had thrown herself behind some rubble and been amazed to see a Judge emerge from the doorway. He stood up, looked around to get his bearings and began striding briskly south, heading for the border between the forbidden fall-out zone and the rest of the city. The old-faced woman followed him, curiosity getting the better of her.

But the Judge moved too fast for her and she lost him after a few minutes. Genya was about to give up and go back to have another look at the doorway that had appeared out of nowhere when she heard a scream from ahead. She rounded a corner in time to witness the Judge lying on the ground in pieces and an indistinct *something* standing over him. It seemed to shimmer against the background, almost blending in but for splashes of red – the Judge's blood, Genya realised.

She could not stifle a gasp of horror as the creature scooped the Judge's brain out of his head and began to wolf it down, blood dripping from its mouth. At the sound of her gasp the monster stopped and turned to look at her. Genya wanted to run, to hide herself away but she felt rooted to the spot. Suddenly, she wanted to live after all.

'Oh Grud, oh Grud, oh Grud' she prayed . . .

you sense another treat and advance towards it. the prey does not move, it just stands, shaking. you reach forward to smash it to the ground, to deliver the paralysing blow before you savour the sticky, salty, red-stained treats inside but something holds you back. there is something familiar about this, something you don't understand –

Magnus reached out with his mind and touched the thoughts of the old-faced woman and was shocked. Involuntarily he used the prototype to speak for him –

Genya wondered why she wasn't dead yet. She opened her eyes to see the monster towering over her. The gaping mouth opened, revealed rows and rows of blood-stained teeth like sharp metal. The breath was foul, rancid, the smell of rotting flesh. But then came a word she never believed she would hear.

'mother'

* * *

you can barely contain the beast, its urge to strike to kill.
return to base, you command, return to base and somehow
exert enough authority to make it turn away from the living
feast

Moments later, the monster returned to its cage beneath the ground.

Magnus opened his eyes and looked at the project leader. 'It is done,' he spoke in the leader's mind. 'Tek-Judge Ajibayo Akinsiku is dead.'

'Excellent,' smiled the leader, rubbing his hands together gleefully. 'Nobody will ever find his remains in the radioactive zone outside the base – the wild animals will eat them in a day or so. One more test, maybe two, then we can present our results and get the go-ahead for full production.'

'But I told you, the prototype is becoming harder to control, not easier. Soon it shall be totally independent,' pleaded Magnus.

'A minor set-back, nothing to delay our plans. And I will take the next test personally, using the new portable control slave relay. Keep up the good work, Magnus!'

Once the leader had gone, the mutant was able to relax his thoughts properly. Magnus knew his usefulness was rapidly coming to an end. Once the leader could control the project's end product himself, he would kill the mutant, just like Akinsiku had been sacrificed. Time was running out.

Magnus reached out again, trying to touch the mind of the woman he had just encountered, the mother he never knew he had – until now . . .

The h-wagon was returning from a routine patrol of Mega-City One's northern borders and so still had its sensor array trained at the ground below as it passed over the fall-out-riddled forbidden zone encompassing Sector 333. The monitor Judge on duty was running a diagnostic on all the systems when they picked up the tracer blip.

173

'What the drokk was that?' She ran the scan of the ground beneath the flying vehicle again, got the same response and contacted the pilot on her helmet-com. 'I know it shouldn't be there, but we're picking up a Judge's distress beacon down below in Sector 333.'

'What the hell? That's the dead zone, no Judge should be patrolling that area!'

'I know – hardly suprising the signal wasn't picked up before, the ground level radiation would damp it right down,' said the monitoring Judge. 'We better take a look anyway.'

The channel-breaker had cost Whiti Vitaliev a small fortune in creds on the black market, but it would be worth every cred if it helped him track down the Sector 66 Slasher and grab the glory. Unfortunately, right now all it was giving him was grief.

'Work, you stupid piece of stomm!' he cried and smashed it a hefty blow with his fist. To his amazement the receiver burst into life, with a noisy cacophony of conflicting channels shouting over each other. The enterprising reporter carefully adjusted the controls, gradually streaming out the extraneous chatter from radio and tri-D broadcasts, homing in on the signal he wanted: the Justice Department's channel for Judges only.

Of course, owning equipment capable of intercepting department transmissions was highly illegal, let alone using them. And the department liked to change the scrambler codes at least once a week to frustrate the efforts of perps listening in to aid their criminal activities. But Whiti had paid good money for the receiver and this week's code and he didn't plan using it for any criminal activity – he just wanted a scoop.

The journalist almost missed the broadcast that would change his life, simply because he was only listening for messages in Sector 66. So he sat through the transmission from the h-wagon impatiently, until the words 'brains for dessert' caught his attention.

'I repeat, we have discovered what appears to be the body of a dead Judge in the fall-out zone, old Sector 333. There ain't a lot left to identify him, but the uniform indicates he was a Tek-Judge. And get this, Control: whatever killed him, it had his brains for dessert.'

'Roj that. What's your ETA?'

'About twenty minutes. We've scraped up what we can of this poor sucker and we're bringing it back with us. H-Wagon THX 1138 out.'

Whiti switched off the receiver. It made no sense, the Sector 66 Slasher only struck in Sector 66 – it was the whole reason he'd created the nickname for it. If the alien predator started travelling around for its kills and thrills, it would sure put a dent in his story . . .

Unless there was more than one alien predator, Whiti realised. What a story that would make! And he'd be the one to break it! All he had to do was get up north to the dead zone and start searching Sector 333. He'd need to get a radiation cloak and some special medication to stave off the effects of the deadly fall-out that still lingered in the sector, but the black market would soon provide him what he needed. Ah, the joys of a free market economy, thought Whiti happily!

In the examination room, Desmon Stich blinked but his eyes didn't see the white-tiled room around him. In his mind's eye he was back in the sewers again, back in the past, nearly twelve months ago, when he saw his dream of an entire force of robo-judges destroyed by just two bullets.

'It wasn't the rogue mechanoid that destroyed the Mark II robo-judge. It was Dredd – Dredd did it! Then he tried to bully me into believing he wasn't responsible. It wasn't my fault, you can see that can't you? It wasn't my fault at all!'

Greel laid a comforting hand on Stich's shoulder.

'Don't worry, Stich, nobody is saying it was your fault. That's a very interesting story you've told us. If we got a

175

stenographer in here, do you think you could remember it all again for us, every single detail of what really happened?'

Stich nodded. 'I remember everything now. It was Dredd . . .'

TWELVE

Countdown to Destruction

The Atomic Wars: These were triggered by President Robert L. Booth in 2070, devastating much of North America, the Soviet states and Europe. The Mega-Cities survived, thanks to a new, experimental laser defence system, but the middle of North America was left a radioactive desert, commonly known as the Cursed Earth.

'Bad Bob' Booth was deposed and the Judges took over running of the three Mega-Cities. But Booth's Presidential Guard fought on in the Cursed Earth for another year, the so-called 'Battle of Armageddon' which cost the lives of more than a hundred thousand warriors.

Despite the nuclear holocaust caused by the Atomic Wars, total disarmament has never been totally achieved. Nor is it ever likely to, with the need for a nuclear deterrent still considered essential by most citi-states. Most frightening of all, when disarmament does take place, some unscrupulous governments sell their atomic devices to the highest bidder. Thus a number of highly dangerous twenty-first century (and even some twentieth century) atomic weapons are still in the hands of private groups . . .

Extract from *The Benefits of War Through History*
Professor Emil Shuffhauser, 2110 AD

Judge Lynn Miller drew a deep breath, adjusted her suspender straps and stepped into the lobby of the Bet Lynch Twin Towers Hotel. She strode confidently up to the reception desk and addressed the concierge droid, all the while chewing some synthi-gum – cherry flavour, of course.

'The name's Cherry. I've got an appointment with your guests in the penthouse suite.'

'Really?' The droid raised an eyebrow archly and interfaced with the communications network. Miller calculated the emotion snobbery implant plus the technology to make it so subtly evident on a droid which probably set back the owners of the hotel at least thirty thousand creds. She cast an eye around the lobby which exuded an equally expensive impression of opulence and deep pockets in the decorating department. For Grud's sake, they even had real trees!

'Ahem.'

Miller turned back to the droid.

'You may go up. Please use the turbo-lift at the far end of the lobby, it will take you directly to your destination.'

'Thanks,' smiled Miller and popped a huge bubble of gum noisily as she strolled casually across the lobby, very aware her every move was being monitored on a range of security scanners. She added an extra wiggle to the sideways movements of her hips, just for good measure – no telling who was watching. The door of the turbo-lift was already open and awaiting her. She stepped in and the doors slid silently shut behind her.

Miller reached out for a control pad but found none – the mirror walls were clean, almost pristine. Curiously the floor was made of a fine grille. Why go to so much trouble to make the walls so elegant, then ruin the effect with an ugly grill for a floor, she wondered.

The answer came in moments as clouds of gas surged up through the floor, clawing at Miller's nose and mouth, biting at her throat, taking away her breath.

'Nerve gas,' she choked and started slumping to the floor. Her last thought before she passed out completely: I never thought I'd die wearing an ensemble like this . . .

Dredd had taken care not to be followed or monitored in any way. After making sure Don Uggi III was secure under Brighton's watchful eye in a private Holding Tank, the acting sector chief had logged off from active duty for two hours. He went to the motorpool in the basement area of the sector house and randomly selected a Lawmaster, leaving his own bike in its individual parking area.

Then he rode across a dozen sectors, using a variety of overzooms, skedways and venturing down to City Bottom several times, pausing to check if anyone was following him. He rode into the Slab, one of Mega-City One's most dangerous, run-down areas, full of underpasses, alleyways and shadows. Finally, he pulled into an underground pod-park and drove around until he found them.

The group were half standing, half hiding in a deserted corner of the basement level, their bikes away to one side, hidden from view of any casual observer. Dredd stilled the engine of his Lawmaster and dismounted, walking over to the gathering. He scanned the faces of those present, his lip curling with disapproval.

'When Judges start meeting like thieves in the night, I start getting worried,' Dredd muttered.

'It's McGruder,' replied Hershey. She had called the meeting, picked the venue, instigated all this but still felt uncomfortable with the secrecy. If there had been any other way, she would have been happy to take it, but the Chief Judge had forced this to happen. 'She has to go.'

Besides Hershey stood Shenker, head of Psi Division. The light cast by Dredd's Lawmaster glinted on the psychic's bald pate. 'The thing is, now that she's disbanded the Council of Five, there's no mechanism for voting her out.'

Next spoke Niles, head of the SJS and a giant of a man, tall, black and heavily muscled. His voice was angry, determined. 'As I see it, there's no alternative – we have to arrest her.'

'And then?' asked Dredd.

'And then we institute some measure of democratic reform, so the same situation can never arise,' replied Hershey. There was a snort of derision from Plaski, a hardened street Judge with a livid red scar down his face to prove it.

'Democracy? Are you out of your mind? It's the smack of firm leadership we need!' He hammered a fist into a hand for emphasis.

'Quite a little conspiracy.' Dredd's voice was scornful. 'You can't even agree amongst yourselves.'

Now Herriman stepped forward. Like Plaski, he was a long-serving street Judge but his speciality was hostage negotiations. 'Much can be said for both sides. It's an argument for another time, perhaps.' He looked at Dredd carfully. 'The thing is, Dredd, we need you with us.'

Hershey added her weight to the statement. 'Without your support the Department will never buy it.'

Dredd shook his head. 'The anwer's no.'

'But why?' demanded Hershey. 'You've said it yourself, she's insane! You've openly demanded her resignation!'

'According to the rules. She must resign. I won't be part of a coup,' insisted Dredd.

'Then there's no more to be said – for now,' stated Niles. The rest of the Judges began getting on their bikes, preparing to leave. Plaski did not disguise the disgust in his voice.

'I told you we were wasting our time!'

Before he left, Niles paused by Dredd and slipped him a scrap of paper. 'I wish you'd reconsider, Dredd.' The gathering broke up, all the Judges riding out of the basement except Dredd. He looked down at the scrap of paper in his hand. On it was a cryptic message: 10–20 SILENCE

Miller opened her eyes and winced. She tried to clasp a hand to her aching head but was unable to. Both her arms were strapped to the ornamental metal chair in which she was slumped, as were her legs and neck. Instead, she scanned the room as far as her bonds would allow, taking in the plush, purple surroundings.

It was a huge, open-plan space – the penthouse suite,

presumably. Sofas hovered just off the floor, real trees grew in massive ceramic pots and a massive cache of weapons and ammunition stood in the sunken centre of the suite. Along one wall were a bank of tri-D monitors, showing dozens of views of the city, the sector and the airspace extending around Bet Lynch. Two rubbereen-clad women sat before the monitors, keeping a close eye on approaching air traffic. Defense systems, thought Miller, careful to maintain her psi shields, keeping her new persona at the forefront of all her thinking.

Three women stood around her, all clad in identical shiny black, skin-tight rubbereen bodysuits. Each had their 'name' emblazoned on their left breast in bold red letters. 'Dune' was a black woman with close-cropped hair and wrap-around eyeshades. Next to her stood 'Cam-ille', a smaller woman of Hondo City descent with pene-trating eyes that seemed to stare into Miller's very thoughts. The third woman was 'Spice', whom Miller instantly recognised – it was Judy Scarotti, head of the Wally Squad for Sector 66. Now this would be a real test of the new persona . . .

'Quite a welcoming committee! Do you offer this reception to all your new recruits, or am I especially privileged?' asked Miller. Dune stepped forward and gave her a heavy, back-handed slap across the face, her long nails leaving scratch marks behind.

'I'll take that as a no, shall I?' persisted Miller.

Dune was about to strike her again when a voice rang out, full of fire and authority.

'Wait!'

Miller craned her neck to see the source of this timely intervention, but the speaker remained behind her, out of view.

'Why have you come here?' asked the unseen voice.

'I came for a job. My name's Cherr – '

'We know who you are!' interrupted the unseen voice. The identification taken from the original Cheryl 'Cherry' Lane was thrown into Miller's lap by Camille, who had

181

been clasping it behind her back. 'Well, what does it tell us?'

Camille stepped forward. 'The name is an alias, but the material belongs to this woman. She came here looking for a gang called the She Devils, she is on the run from the Judges here and in Brit-Cit. She seeks a sanctuary. And she is steeped in blood, she has killed many times.'

'Thank you. Dune?'

The She Devil psychic stepped back to be replaced by the menacing Dune. She produced Miller's utility belts, laser-knife and sheath.

'An interesting array of weapons, some foreign items. But mostly standard Justice Department issue.'

'I took most of that from a Judge I killed two days ago in – ' chipped in Miller but was cut off by another blow from Dune.

'Thank you, Dune. Spice?'

'According to department records a Cheryl Lane a.k.a. Cherry entered Mega-City One from Brit-Cit more than a week ago. Two days ago she shot a Judge but was captured and taken to the Holding Tanks at Sector 44. Apparently she escaped this morning, during a cube riot there.'

'Thank you, Spice.' Scarotti stepped back into line, but her eyes remained on Miller, a faint, quizzical look at their edges.

'Well, perhaps it's time I had a look at our mystery guest. Turn her round, please Dune.'

Dune swivelled Miller's chair around so she was facing the leader of the She Devils. Fury was sitting behind a heavy, ornamental desk, her delicate hands held up in a steeple before her face. Miller couldn't help gasping as she looked at the face of her captor. It wasn't the scarring across the nose and forehead, the tell-tale signs of reconstructive surgery on a face that had once had a breathing mask welded to its features – the brutal welding procedure was standard practice on the Judicial penal colony on

182

Saturn's moon of Titan. It was something far more shocking.

'My name is Fury and I am the leader of the She Devils. And unless you can tell me something I want to know in the next twenty seconds, I'll have you put back into the turbo-lift. But this time, we won't bother putting the floor in. So – any questions?'

Miller was still reeling, trying to get to grips with her situation. The leader of the She Devils was a girl, barely twelve years old!

Genya sat by the acid pool, amidst the rubble and carnage of Sector 33, trying to deny the incident had happened, trying to block it out of her mind. Not because of the horror of seeing the poor Judge torn limb from limb, though that was surely reason enough. No, it was the word the monster had spoken, the word projected into her mind by some unknown force, some unknown person she had always believed dead.

'mother . . .'

Tears rolled down her ashen, heavily lined face. It couldn't be true: her child couldn't be alive! The Judges had taken her baby away, aborted it and left her a drugged-out zombie, destroyed her life before it had even begun. And now, was this to be the final, cruel irony? That her child had survived, been kept alive while she wandered the skeds a mindless vegetable? And what did her child have to do with that thing, that monster she had witnessed? Genya shook her head, trying to shake the word out of her brain, trying to pretend it never happened, but it was no good, the word kept repeating itself, a sad refrain to a sad life.

'*mother*. . .'

But this time, the word was different, more urgent, probing, almost searching her out. Genya realised this was not her memory playing tricks on her – this was her child calling out to her, speaking directly into her mind. Her child was talking to her. But how could she talk back?

'Just speak normally . . . I can hear your thoughts . . .' replied the voice in Genya's head, the words soft, as if warmly spoken.

'Who – who are you?' She said out loud, hesitantly, looking around herself, feeling not a little stupid talking into thin air. Then again, having been crazy all these years, at least her actions shouldn't seem out of character to anyone else! She didn't notice that she was being observed.

'I'm your son, I'm a telepath . . . I can speak into people's minds, sense their presence . . .'

'But how did you find me? How did you recognise me?' asked Genya, still unsure, uncertain. Perhaps this was just another form of madness, some new insanity to plague her in her final days.

'You're not crazy . . . I was inside the mind of that – creature – you saw earlier . . . I reached out into your mind and I just knew who you were . . .' The voice faltered. 'You've had a very sad life and it's mostly my fault . . . I'm sorry for all the pain you've suffered . . .'

Genya smiled. 'Carrying you for the seven months that I did was the happiest time of my life. It was the Judges who ruined my life, when they took you away from me. They should never have done that.' Genya made a decision and stood up. 'Where are you? Are you close?'

'Yes, but you cannot come here, it is too dangerous . . .' said the voice hurriedly, worry evident in its gentle tones.

'Well, can you come to me? I'm not as agile as I used to be.'

'That's impossible . . . I'm a mutant, as much a child of the fall-out from the war as I am your child . . . It was the radiation that made me what I am – a freak . . .' replied the voice sadly.

'That settles it, I'm coming to you,' stated Genya firmly. 'I came home to Sector 333 to die, but I refuse to do that before I see my child at least once. You're all that remains of the only person I ever loved.'

'I know . . .' said the voice hesitantly. 'All right, I'll guide you to me, but you must be careful . . . Coming here is almost certain death . . .'

'My child, I've been living on borrowed time since the bombs fell twelve years ago. Lead on!' Genya set off, almost a spring in her step. Finally, she had a reason to go on. She didn't see the lone figure following her from a discreet distance.

'It all happened in the old sewer system. I had escaped from the psycho-cubes and had gone down there, looking for Number 5. That was one of the original Mechanismo robo-judges. When we pulled the first batch of robo-judges back in for repairs and improvements after the initial field testing went awry, something went wrong with Number 5. Although it was damaged, it wasn't decommissioned properly. It was able to restart itself and escaped down into the sewers. It had never been found and I became obsessive about its disappearance. Eventually I had a breakdown, and was committed to the psycho-cubes. But I was able to escape and go searching for Number 5.'

The voice was quiet, calm, Desmon Stich could see the events being slowly replayed in his mind, like an old vid-slug. The truth drug had brought it all back to him. Now he slowly described the events of that fateful day.

Behind him stood Greel, making sure Stich's testimony was being fully documented. This was the evidence he'd been trying to get out of Stich for weeks. This was the smoking gun that would get rid of that interfering fool Dredd once and for all! Then the new series of field tests could be made public, the secret project revealed at last.

No more secrecy, no having to creep around to achieve his goals. Greel's brain-child could go into production within weeks, days even. Then he would be proved right after all, then he would be vindicated. And all those who had died getting the project so far wouldn't have died in vain. The ends did justify the means, he truly believed that.

Stich's voice continued with his story, bringing the head of Tek Division out of his private thoughts.

'It was while I was down in the sewers that I first saw the new, improved Mark II Mechanismo. In my deranged state, I thought – '

'Stop!' shouted Greel. 'Stenographer, scroll back and replace the word deranged with, ah, "confused" please. Yes, that sounds better.' He laid a comforting hand on Stich's shoulder. 'All right, Desmon, carry on.'

'I thought it was Number 5 and followed it down the sewer system, but it was too fast, it got away from me. I heard voices from ahead of me. One of them was Judge Dredd, he ordered the Mark II robot to hold it's fire. But it ignored him and terminated Number 5 with an armour piercing bullet. I was just in time to see that happen. I ran up to get a better look. It was definitely Number 5 lying in the sludge, completely destroyed.

'Dredd questioned the Mark II, he wanted to know why it hadn't held its fire when ordered to do so. It said the order was invalid, the Chief Judge's instructions to terminate Number 5 on sight took priority. Then Dredd pointed his Lawgiver at the Mark II robot's chest, point-blank. He said the robot left him no altenative, that the Mark II was no Judge in his book and he fired! The Mark II was destroyed . . .'

Stich's voice ground to a halt, a tear rolling gently down one cheek.

'Keep going, Desmon, you can do it,' urged Greel. Stich drew a deep breath and continued.

'It was then that Dredd deliberately tried to trick me. He told me he hadn't shot the Mark II robot, but that Number 5 had pulled the trigger. He escorted me back to the psycho-cubes, all the way pushing his version of the story. By the time I got back to my cube, I couldn't properly remember what had happened. But I can now . . .'

Greel leaned forward to ask another question. 'So what you're saying is that it was Judge Dredd who destroyed the Mark II robo-judge, destroyed official Justice Department property. Then he coerced you into believing his version of events – is that right?'

'Yes, yes that's it,' nodded Stich.

'Very good, Desmon,' smirked Greel. 'Very good indeed!'

'Have you ever thought about giving up crime?'

'What?'

'I said, have you ever thought about giving up crime,' repeated Brighton. 'It's just it doesn't seem to make you very happy. All these killings, the gang wars, humans always constantly picking on you because you're different. Wouldn't you rather go somewhere else, somewhere you'd get a little respect for once?'

'Respect! The only respect I get is from other apes. You skinfaces – you don't know what it's like for us.' Don Uggi III was pacing the floor of his cell in a private Holding Tank beneath Sector House 66, away from the standard confinement areas. The area was tiled in gleaming white yet still retained the depressing presence of a place of confinement, that innate sense of hopelessness. 'Why, we's been slaves and pets and guinea pigs in your experiments for centuries. Now we's finally gets us a piece of da action, des damn dames come and massacre us!'

Brighton was sat outside, following his orders from Dredd to maintain a strict watch over the Don, to prevent any more trouble. Dredd himself had disappeared nearly an hour ago, but Brighton was happy for a little peace and quiet after the carnage earlier. 'We estimate that more than half your lieutenants were killed in the shoot-out at Funeral Row.'

'See what I mean? Dat's typical. Youse lousy skinfaces have been exploitin' us apes since we were stolen from Pan-Africa, generations ago!'

'Really? I've been to Pan-Africa, on a Cadet exchange scheme three years ago. Incredible place,' remembered Brighton wistfully. 'Did you know that in the development areas, anyone with enough money can buy their own land and start their own nation?'

The Don stopped his pacing, he was interested now. 'What development areas? What money?'

'The one I went to was called the Congo Development Area. Amazing place,' confided Brighton, warming to his topic. 'For a million creds you can buy a valley. In fact – '

Judge Wallis burst in, her voice emitting a metallic croak from her artificial larynx. 'Brighton! You better come and see this message that's just come over the Crimeline.'

'Okay, but you stay here and guard the Don. Don't let anyone else back in here until I return – Dredd's orders.'

Wallis nodded and Brighton ran from the room, heading for the monitoring area near the front desk upstairs. Once there, he had one of the Judges on station replay the message for him. On the tri-D screen appeared the angry face of Don Uggi IV.

'Dis is da new Don of da Uggi family. We know you Judges have got Don Uggi da Third in custody at Sector House 66. Youse have got six hours ta release him, or else we launch our little surprise at youse.' He stepped aside to reveal the bomb on a control screen. Beside it was a countdown clock. The young ape jabbed at a button and the time limit began ticking away.

06:00:00; 05:59:59; 05:59:58 . . .

'Back during da Apocalypse War nearly all da Jungles in Mega-City got wiped out, but nobody came to help us. In fact, Judge Dredd moidered many of da survivors. So dis time, we got da bomb and we's gonna use it. Dat's all, skinfaces!'

The transmission cut out, leaving static behind. Brighton wondered where Dredd was – right now, he was needed here!

A roar like thunder, but close and growing ever louder echoed down the small side-sked. Dredd rode past a street sign on his borrowed Lawmaster, its name briefly illuminated by the headlights: STREET OF SILENCE. He parked by a large, blockhouse-like building and strode to its heavy metal door. Set into the wall beside it was a plaque naming the building's purpose and its street number: JUSTICE DEPT SECTOR DEPOT 10–20.

Dredd pushed a bell set into the wall and waited. After a few moments, a faint voice emitted from a speaker grille above the bell.

'This building is off limits.'

Dredd glared at a security scanner over the door. 'Off limits to me? Open the door!' he snarled. It slid open to reveal a long wide foyer with a Judge sitting behind a reception desk at the far end. Dredd strode towards the Judge, glancing around suspiciously. Behind the seated Judge a wide access door led into a warehouse area, where hundreds of metal shelves were stacked with Justice Department stores and equipment.

'Thought I saw a prowler,' exclaimed Dredd.

'In here? You jest!' retorted the desk Judge.

Dredd ignored him and strode into the stores area. 'All the same, I'll take a look around.'

While Dredd was searching the storage area, the desk Judge activated a vid-phone intercom system. A slightly overweight Tek-Judge appeared on the screen, adjusting his glasses. The desk Judge explained about the 'visitor'.

'Dredd! Wh-what does he want here?' asked the Tek-Judge.

'Search me. He's having a good snout round.'

'All right, I'll come up.'

Within a minute the Tek-Judge appeared from a side door and approached the intruder. 'Can I do something to assist you . . . ?'

Dredd recognised him. 'What's going on here, Quiggly?'

'I don't know what you mean.'

'Your man on the door wasn't going to open up. Kind of heavy security for a simple storage depot.'

'Sellek . . . he's new, I'm afraid,' agreed Quiggly. 'Takes his duties a bit too seriously.'

Dredd frowned at Quiggly. The Tek-Judge had been Desmon Stich's assistant on the Mechanismo project, before it was suspended following Dredd's report about the incident in the sewers.

'What are you doing here, Quiggly?'

'Demotion, my reward for failure. I believe I have you partly to thank for that,' replied the Tek-Judge sarcastically.

'We can all consider ourselves lucky,' said Dredd, missing the sarcasm. 'The last thing we need is robo-judges on the skeds.'

'That's a matter of opinion. Now, I'm sure you have much more important things to be doing . . .'

Dredd left reluctantly, watched carefully by Quiggly and Sellek. As soon as the senior Judge was gone, Quiggly activated the vid-phone. 'Greel better know about this . . .'

Miller looked over the edge of the sloping roof beneath her feet and gulped. She had never had a great head for heights and being atop a hundred-storey high building as the winds whipped around her without anything to hold on to wasn't making her feel any better.

When Fury had offered her twenty seconds to come up with some interesting information or a very quick trip to the bottom of the turbo-lift shaft, Miller's mind had raced through the alternatives before she blurted out the only thing she could think of.

'One of your She Devils is actually a Judge in disguise!'

Fury had just laughed, the rest of the gang joining in the merriment. 'Is that the best you can do?'

Miller had persisted. 'Spice is actually a Wally Squad Judge called Judy Scarotti.'

'I'm sorry, but we're well aware of Spice's true identity. I recruited her myself two months ago. She supplies all our best Justice Department weaponry and information,' smiled the child. She gestured to the gang members to take 'Cherry' away. 'It looks like this is goodbye . . .'

Miller was unstrapped and dragged by Camille and Dune across the suite towards the turbo-lift doors, which were already standing open, just blackness, no lift waiting for anyone who passed through the doors. 'But did she tell you that Dredd has discovered about her little sugar habit and how she's selling weapons to pay for that habit? I bet she also didn't tell you that there's a warrant out for her immediate arrest and that she can never leave this building safely! Well?'

Fury held up a hand to stay Miller's execution and turned to Scarotti. 'Well, Spice, anything you want to say to this?'

'Er, no, she's bluffing, I mean how could she know . . .'

'I overheard it while I was in the Holding Tanks at Sector 44. The Judges there had just been sent your ID details,' shouted Miller.

'Hmm. Decisions, decisions,' mused Fury. Finally, she gestured for Miller to be pulled back from the turbo-lift. 'I have a better idea. Since we can't easily choose between the two of you, I think we'll have a little contest to resolve this dilemma. The winner gets to stay on as a fully fledged member of the She Devils. And as for the loser . . .'

Five minutes later Miller and Scarotti were shoved out onto the sloping glass roof of the penthouse, tied together at the wrist with a scrap of cloth. The skylight access was locked behind them. Fury's voice burst out from a speaker grille set into the accessway.

'A fight to the death. The only rule is – there are no rules!'

Miller was about to protest when Scarotti headbutted her full in the face. Miller crumpled to the roof and began sliding towards the edge, dragging her opponent down with her. Just before they reached the edge, Miller managed to brace herself and caught Scarotti with a heavy forearm to the stomach as the other woman drew level with her. Miller followed it up with a knee to the groin and a two-thumbed eye-gouge that threatened to blind her foe.

Scarotti scratched at Miller's face and clothing, ripping great holes in the material of her top. The fighting was desperate, close-quarters ripping and clawing, with no room for fancy moves. The battle lasted a full minute before Miller sensed an opening and managed a chop to Scarotti's throat, severely bruising the windpipe.

Scarotti – She Devil Spice – whirled her arms and caught Miller in the face and off balance, sending her tumbling over. She teetered on the edge of the roof and couldn't help looking over, the city spiralling away down below her dizzyingly. Miller knew that Scarotti must be desperate for a fix of sugar and that desperation was giving her opponent a raw edge. Miller needed to make Judy angry, force a mistake out of her.

'Hey, Judy, it's me – Miller, Lynn Miller. Don't you recognise me?'

Scarotti was dumbstruck then quickly furious. 'I knew there was something familiar about your voice – what are you doing here, slitch?'

'Dredd sent me, I'm taking the She Devils down.'

'Yeah? Well the only thing going down here is you – about a hundred storeys!' spat Scarotti and threw herself at Miller. The younger Judge sidestepped the charge and Scarotti went flying over the parapet – taking Miller with her!

Miller managed to grab at the edge of the roof as she was dragged over, and her fingers held on for all their worth. But the wind howled about the edge of the building, bouncing her against its side and Scarotti was heavy, dragging her down towards a mutual death on the pedway below – street pizza. There was only one chance . . .

Miller lashed out with her heavy boots (thank Grud she'd insisted on these) and began kicking Scarotti, delivering heavy blows, one after another, kicking the other woman unconscious. Then, she twisted and strained her

192

wrist around until it was rubbed raw, red and bloody by the material. But, finally, blessedly, it slipped from her wrist and Judy Scarotti fell, turning over and over as she tumbled through the air . . .

Miller heaved herself up onto the roof and crawled over to the skylight accessway. Fury opened it and Miller fell through onto the floor of the penthouse suite. She looked up at the leader of the gang.

'Well, have I passed the initiation?'

'Welcome to the She Devils!'

Extract from the private journal of Judge Laverne Castillo:

The Chief Judge was raving again today. She seems convinced there's a conspiracy against her. I haven't had a chance to talk to Judge Hershey since our first 'discussion' but I got the impression then that McGruder might be right. To be honest, I don't know who is right and who is wrong in this situation.

I mean, yes, the Chief Judge is unstable but she is lucid and agile thinking more than ninety per cent of the time. It's just occasionally her brain seems to go darting off on weird tangents, or keep picking obsessively at the same point in a discussion over and over again. Is that enough reason to stage a coup and drive her out?

Surely she deserves more respect than that. Also, she is the Chief Judge, the one person with ultimate responsibility over this city. Without her, things could well fall apart, it's hard to tell. Right now, I don't like to think what's going to happen in the next few days, especially after the conversation I overheard earlier . . .

McGruder was talking to that creep Greel again, this time on the vid-phone. It was hard to hear what he was saying to the Chief Judge, some of it didn't seem to make sense. There was something about Judge Dredd and Silence which seemed to worry McGruder.

But Greel was as smug as ever, saying that she needn't worry. Apparently the drug they've been using on Stich has worked. Stich has some very interesting things to say about what happened in the sewers. Greel said Dredd was not the blue-eyed boy everyone believes.

Could he mean that Judge Dredd is corrupt? I can't believe that! Dredd is the most honest Judge in the city, everybody knows that. He's a legend at the Academy. Why, if Judge Dredd could be corrupt, there's no hope for any of us!

It's Judge Greel that I'm not so sure about . . .

THIRTEEN

Mother and Child

The Inferno Incident: In 2115 there was a rebellion at the Judicial penal colony of the moon Titan. The revolt was led by ex-Judge Grice, who had been sent to the colony for organising a conspiracy to assassinate Judge Dredd in the run-up to the Democracy Referendum. Grice and his fellow inmates destroyed their section of the penal colony and set off for Earth and revenge, taking with them a deadly experimental chemical weapon called the Meat Virus.

The rebels launched a stunning attack on Mega-City One, using their deep knowledge of the defences and the Meat Virus to seize control of the city. Dredd was able to lead a resistance force against Grice and his crazed cohorts and defeat them, but only just. At the time it was believed all the rebel Judges were either recaptured or killed, but a few – less than five, it is now understood – escaped in the confusion of the final battle. They used stolen Justice Department technology to remove the respiration masks (which are welded onto the faces of all inmates of Titan so they can work in the near-vacuum-level atmosphere), then slipped away into the hundreds of millions of citizens to create secret new identities and new lives for themselves . . .

Extract from *Justice Department Case Histories*
Volume 13 (2116 update)

In the secret control chamber, Don Uggi IV watched the countdown tick away on the wall monitor.
04.09.01, 04.09.00, 04.08.59 . . .

Nearly two hours had passed since his ultimatum was

... directly to Sector House 66 but still no reply
... that murderer, Dredd. The new Don fumed silently,
sorely tempted to abandon the countdown and simply
launch the missile. But his father had always prided
himself being an ape of his word and the new Don was
trying to follow his father's lead. So he resisted temptation
and kept the activation keys for the firing sequence on the
chain around his neck – for now . . .

Whiti Vitaliev clutched his radorak tighter around him
and continued his pursuit of the eldster. He had stumbled
around the ruins of Sector 333 for nearly an hour before
he had heard a lone voice, holding a very disjointed
conversation. He traced it to an old woman, sitting on a
pile of rubble, talking to herself.

Whiti had nearly walked away when a particular word
caught his ear: 'creature'. That got his attention. Could
this crazy old crock know something about the monster,
this new alien predator? When she started walking, still
nattering away to herself, occasionally pausing as if awaiting new directions, he had followed (hover-cam floating
along behind him), anxious not to lose sight of the eldster.
If she could lead him to the alien's lair, it would give him
the scoop of the century.

The roving reporter rounded a corner and was gripped
with panic – she had disappeared. Then he spotted a door
slowly closing in a rockcrete wall and ran towards it, just
squeezing through before it slammed shut. Whiti was
plunged into darkness and wisely stood still, waiting for
his eyes to adjust to the lighting in this buried entrance.
He heard a dull tapping noise behind him and swore
under his breath. The hover-cam had been too slow and
was now stuck outside the secret doorway. With no
obvious way of opening it, the hover-cam would have to
stay out there for the moment.

Whiti groped his way forward towards a distant light,
the sound of the eldster's footfalls echoing in the darkness
ahead of him. He had a nagging feeling he was on to

something big, but without the hover-cam to record it, who would ever believe him? After a few minutes he emerged into the half-light of a small corridor, the old woman still just visible ahead of him. For an old crock she showed quite a turn of speed when it suited her, thought Whiti.

'Where the drokk is Dredd? Doesn't anybody know?' Brighton looked round at the other Judges assembled in the sector chief's office.

Symes shrugged. 'He logged off from active duty for two hours, but that was nearly four hours ago. Since then he's maintained radio silence. We can't pick him up on any of our eye-in-the-sky cameras in this sector and I don't want to go asking Control if they can find our sector chief for us – we've already lost one this week!'

Brighton nodded his agreement. Judge Dredd was very much his own man, and had proved that in his many years on the street. If Dredd logged off from active duty, then he probably had a damn good reason. Brighton just wished he knew what it was. Time for somebody to make a decision, anyway . . .

'Well, with Dredd gone and Miller off injured, somebody better take charge. Where's Wallis? She's the next most senior Judge on station. Has anyone seen Wallis?'

More silence. Brighton rolled his eyes heavenwards.

'Grud, give me strength!' he muttered under his breath. 'All right, we've got just over four hours till the deadline runs out. I'll go see if I can get any sense out of Don Uggi downstairs, everybody else return to normal duties and stay alert. Grud knows, we don't need any more excitement.'

Brighton strode from the office and headed down to the Holding Tanks via the turbo-lift. Where the hell was Dredd, anyway?

Among the shadows inside the darkened Justice Department service depot on Silence, Quiggly operated a hidden mechanism on a storage rack. The wall slid away to reveal a wide ramp – big enough to drive a small hover-van down – sloping away down into darkness. The furtive Tek-Judge slipped inside and the wall began to close again behind him. Just before it slid completely shut, Dredd squeezed through the rapidly disappearing crack and cautiously followed Quiggly down to the hidden level below. The unwanted intruder had waited outside the depot for more than an hour before being able to use the arrival of a delivery to slip back inside again unnoticed.

Quiggly walked along a corridor and then through a doorway into a large chamber. Dredd followed soundlessly behind him, taking care to keep low and casting a shadow on any of the frosted glass windows set into the wall of the chamber. Finally, he peered through the clear glasseen set into the doorway Quiggly had just entered.

'Drokk!' gasped Dredd at the contents of the large chamber.

Inside were a row of robo-judges. They were of a similar design to the first two versions produced by the Mechanismo programme, but the helmets had been reconfigured, making them look human, and a lot more sinister in the process. Instead of gunmetal grey, the robots were now gleaming black, with tiled metal body armour in place of moulded metal panels. The previous versions had been numbered, these now had a 'name' badge moulded into their left shoulder. Dredd could see the names of the three nearest him: Jefferson, Roosevelt, Tito.

The new-look robo-judges were undergoing weapons testing, supervised by Quiggly and an assistant that Dredd did not recognise, another Tek-Judge. The intruder strained to hear their conversation over the gunfire of the robo-judges.

'Greel wants the programme accelerated. Final trial Thursday,' said Quiggly to his assistant's obvious surprise and dismay.

'Thursday? That's unreasonable! We'll never have them

ready!' The assistant turned to the robo-judges. 'Cease firing!' The targets automatically glided across the room towards the two Tek-Judges, who examined the results.

'Targets were spinning at 500 rpm. One hundred per cent accuracy,' said the assistant.

'Very impressive,' growled a distinctive voice from the doorway. Quiggly whirled to look at the unwelcome visitor.

'Dredd!'

'They make us poor old human Judges seem totally inadequate,' said Dredd, a hint of mockery in his tone. 'Looks like they've had an update too.'

The assistant failed to catch Dredd's real meaning. 'The Mark IIA – we've made quite a number of improvements, I'm sure you'll – '

'Be quiet, Somes!' commanded Quiggly. 'There's no point trying to reason with him.'

Dredd stepped close to Quiggly, towering over the smaller man. 'Last I heard, the Mechanismo project was officially suspended, Quiggly.'

'I take my orders from the Chief Judge,' replied the Tek-Judge.

'And I thought she'd dropped the whole idea,' muttered Dredd, shaking his head. 'I should have known better. Plotting away in secret . . .'

'That's the way it's going to stay!'

Dredd turned to leave. 'Don't count on it.'

'Damn you, Dredd!' Quiggly's face flushed with anger. 'You've done enough to damage my career! Thanks to you we had to spend months redesigning the Mark IIA – totally unnecessary in my view. There was nothing wrong with them, and I won't let you destroy things again.' He beckoned to two of the robots. 'Jefferson, Tito – active!'

Quiggly gestured at Dredd. 'Intruder on the premises – eliminate him.' The two robots swivelling to examine their target.

'Have you lost your mind, Quiggly?' demanded Dredd, backing towards some workbenches behind himself.

'I'm perfectly within my rights! You've no business here!'

One of the robo-judges spoke. 'Please confirm order to terminate.'

'Kill him!' shouted Quiggly and the robots began firing at Dredd, who dived for the cover of the benches. Behind Quiggly, Somes was cowering in fear.

'Arthur – I-I think you're over-reacting,' stammered Somes. 'You can't do this!'

'He has to be silenced,' replied Quiggly grimly.

Dredd moved along behind the workbenches, using them as cover from the robo-judges while edging his way closer to Quiggly and Somes. He tried shouting an order for the robots to cease firing, but the hail of bullets continued unabated.

'It's no good appealing to their sense of right and wrong, Dredd,' called out Quiggly, 'we haven't programmed that in yet. They obey only me and Somes.'

'Another good reason to scrap the damn things!' shouted Dredd, moving ever closer to the Tek-Judges. 'If it can be programmed in, it can be programmed out.'

'Not if they're kept under proper supervision.'

'By people like you? Give me a break!' Dredd fired off several armour piercing and hi-ex rounds, disabling one of the robo-judges.

'What's the matter with you?' Quiggly demanded of his creations. 'Kill him – now!'

As the last of his cover was blown away, Dredd pushed a section of high shelving on top of the other attacker robot and launched himself at Quiggly. He caught the Tek-Judge by surprise and knocked him over. Dredd quickly pulled Quiggly up, making the Tek-Judge a human shield against the robo-judges. He jammed his Lawgiver in Quiggly's face.

'If I die, you die! Now, call them off,' hissed Dredd.

'C-cease firing, stand down,' stammered Quiggly. The robo-judges whirred to a halt, becoming like statues again. Dredd clamped a gauntlet-clad hand over the Tek-Judge's mouth.

'You're doing heavy time for this, Quiggly!'

Somes hovered nervously in the background. 'Y-You understand, I'm not to blame! I didn't do anything!'

'Exactly!' barked back Dredd. 'You stood by and did nothing while Quiggly broke the Law! That puts you in the frame too. Now, move it! And one word to those robots, and your brains hit the ceiling.'

The Don was dozing in his private cell, watched over by a weary Brighton. Any minute now the young Judge hoped to nip off for a quick ten minutes in a sleep machine, to replenish his strength. He looked forward to the day when he was given his own conapt to go home to on those infrequent days off . . . A message on his helmet-com jolted him back to reality.

'Brighton? This is Symes. You know you requested updates if anything interesting happened on that tracer you put on the reporter?'

'Yes?'

'Well, he's gone up into the northern sectors.'

'So?'

'The old northern sectors, that were bombed out in the Apocalypse War, the forbidden zone. He's been up there nearly two hours. All the residual radiation is making tracking hard, but we've got him fixed in Sector 333,' reported Symes.

'Roj that. Keep a constant monitor on his location, in case we lose the signal altogether. Thanks.'

Up in the monitoring department of the sector house, Symes couldn't help smiling. Brighton had to be the most polite Judge on the force, it was almost quaint. Most street Judges would barely give a desk Judge like Symes the time of day, but Brighton was different.

'Drokk! We've lost him!' cursed Symes, staring at a blank monitor screen in Sector House 66. 'Get me a triangulated fix on the last known co-ordinates of that tracer unit!' he yelled.

'That's a Roj!' responded one of the monitor Judges briskly.

'And somebody tell Brighton; he'll want to know too.'

'You passed the initiation well, Cherry. Now I imagine you have some questions you want to ask?' Fury smiled, her young face almost cherubic, but her cold, flinty eyes full of evil and cynicism. Miller suppressed a shudder and maintained the Cherry persona at the front of her thoughts, keeping her Psi-damping techniques to the fore. The leader of the She Devils was back behind her huge desk, but this time Miller was sitting unrestrained in the chair before it.

'Well, there's the obvious question: how can someone who looks so young be in charge of the fastest growing gang in this sector?'

'Simple,' replied Fury, flourishing a sheet of medicinal tabs. 'Pure, uncut stookie. Not only does it stop the ageing process, in its purest form it actually reverses that process. I keep myself at a physical age of 12 simply for convenience's sake – the Judges would never believe someone of my age could command the She Devils. Just another disguise, really.'

'Then there's the scars on your face. They look like – ' began Miller.

'Like I've had a Titan breathing mask removed – I have. I used to be a Judge, a damn good one, until I had an accident one day. But the Department didn't see it that way, so I ended up on Titan. When Grice led the breakout, I hitched a ride back to here. Thanks to some new surgery techniques, the stookie and a few old friends within the Department, I was able to get a new start. But this time, instead of pretending to lead a gang called the She Devils, I decided to do it for real. Using the She Devils name keeps the Department – and all the other gangs – guessing. Anything else?'

'Why target the ape gangs? I hear you lost nearly half your team during the massacre on Funeral Row,' ventured Miller, anxious not to press for too much information too soon. Deep down she knew her cover wouldn't last long – as soon as the gang organised its next hit, she would be obliged to turn the tables on it.

'Don Uggi's family are the strongest of the ape gangs. Wipe them out and the rest will fall. They control a lot of turf, which I intend to make mine.' Fury toyed with a machine-pistol laying atop her desk, her brow furrowed with worry. 'You ask a lot of questions, Cherry. Perhaps too many . . .'

'I just like to know where I stand. No point tying myself to a bunch of losers now, is there?' smiled Miller sweetly.

Fury's attention was distracted by a call from one of the gang members on monitor duty. 'Vox is on her way up!'

'Good! Now we can catch up on how our friends at the Justice Department are getting on,' smirked Fury. 'Poor dears, they seem to be overrun with problems at the moment. I wouldn't be surprised if there's a mutiny in the senior ranks soon!'

The turbo-lift doors opened behind Miller and a chill ran up her spine as a familiar, metallic voice spoke. 'Fury! I've just heard that Dredd has assigned someone from Sector House 66 to try and infiltrate us!'

Miller swivelled halfway round to get a look at the new arrival, taking care to keep one hand on the edge of Fury's desk. She looked at the gang member codenamed Vox – it was Wallis, the day desk Judge from Sector House 66, her Judge helmet clutched under one arm. Wallis's eyes examined the new member then widened in startled recognition. So much for the disguise, thought Miller. It might have fooled Scarotti who had only met her a few times, but Miller had partnered Wallis on the streets before her injury. When you work that closely with someone, you learn a lot about them. Miller had always wondered about Wallis' true allegiance to the Department after her shooting . . .

'Drokk! Miller! What are you doing here?' As Wallis realised who the infiltrator was, 'Cherry' grabbed the machine pistol off Fury's desk and began firing. The first bullet blew the artificial voice-box through the back of Wallis' throat. The second ripped off her left ear, the third exploded inside her brain.

Miller was already rolling across the floor, strafing the rest of the gang members with bullets from the machine pistol as Wallis's body fell backwards into the turbo-lift, jamming the doors open. Most of Miller's rounds were wide of the mark but a few found their targets. The two She Devils on monitor duty both caught body shots, other bullets exploded into the sophisticated security system, disabling it in seconds.

Miller turned to see Fury duck behind her desk and kept turning as Dune and Camille burst from one of the bedrooms, guns blazing. A leg-shot downed the psychic while Dune unleashed a full magazine at Miller before the top of her head came off, painting the glasseen ceiling-to-floor window behind her with a scarlet mess of blood and brains and bone.

Miller threw herself into the jammed turbo-lift, using the half-open doors as cover. She flicked the empty cartridge out of the machine pistol and pulled another from her waist belts, jamming it into the weapon before squinting round the doors as they juddered back and forth, bashing against the remains of Wallis. Friends in the Department, Miller remembered Fury saying. I wonder how many other Judges in Sector House 66 are rotten? It hardly bore thinking about.

Out in the main area of the suite, the air was thick with smoke from the burning circuitry of the security system. The overhead smoke alarms were triggered and water started pouring out of the overhead sprinkler system, making vision even more difficult.

Miller heard a moan from Camille and sent half a magazine speeding her way. There was a scream of pain, then a satisfying silence. But Miller didn't see through the

204

smoke and indoor rainstorm that one of the She Devils by the security system was still just alive. A hand crept over to a control for the turbo-lift system and, with a final, desperate jab, punched a control pad. Toxic green gas began billowing up around Miller.

'Stomm! The nerve gas!' she spluttered and grabbed Wallis's helmet from beside her body, jamming it on her own head and pulling the respirator down over her face.

Behind the desk, Fury had reached into one of the doors and pulled out a Lawgiver and a box of ammunition. Now she was carefully slotting the bullets into the cartridge of her weapon. 'Miller! Is that your name? You were pretty smooth, Miller. But it doesn't matter what you do here today. You know why? Because I got friends in the Department, lots of friends, and if you kill me, they'll make sure you never see the end of next week. You know why? Because I supply stookie to them all, and without me, they're all as good as dead anyway!'

Miller didn't reply, she just waited to see what the She Devils would throw at her next. By her estimate, there were only two or three left alive, and Fury was the only one without heavy injuries. I might even have a chance of getting out of here alive, thought Miller wistfully.

'But how about I offer you a deal,' continued Fury. 'Leave now and we'll call it quits. This whole suite is gonna blow soon anyway, there's an auto destruct built into the security system if it's interfered with. I could just disappear, and as far as the Department is concerned, I died in the explosion. How does that sound?'

'No deals!' shouted Miller through her respirator.

Fury leaned over the top of the desk and took careful aim at the interior of the turbo-lift. 'Well, try this for size then, bitch – ricochet!' She fired round after round into the turbo-lift.

Inside the lift, the bullets bounced around the walls, floor and ceiling until they found a soft target. Miller grabbed at Wallis's body, desperately trying to use it as a shield but at least half a dozen rounds thudded into her body, stabbing into her chest, arms and legs. She cried out in pain as blood began pouring from her wounds.

Miller grabbed at the pouches on her belt, flicking them open so the contents clattered onto the metal floor of the lift. Her eyes lit upon three special bullets, each emblazoned with a red 'H' on their side. She slotted them into her machine pistol and aimed out through the doors, towards the desk.

'Hotshot!' She pulled the trigger – once, twice, three times. The heat-seeker bullets flew out across the room, over the top of the desk then zoomed down and straight into Fury, who threw up a forlorn arm to protect herself.

Miller lay on the floor of the turbo-lift, bleeding heavily, her limbs jerking a little as shock started to set in. So cold, so cold. Can't let myself . . . blackness.

Dredd stormed into his private office at Sector House 66 and slammed the door after him. He punched up Hershey's callsign on the vid-phone and eventually got a bleary-eyed reply.

'Sweet Jovus, Dredd, do you know what time it is?'

'Save it. I've just arrested Tek-Judges Quiggly and Somes for trying to kill me, using Mark IIA robo-judges as their weapon.'

That woke Hershey up. 'What? Mark IIA robots?'

'Seems McGruder authorised a secret re-design. I found the test location from a note Niles slipped me at the meeting.'

'Drokking hell! Now what?'

'I've requested an urgent meeting with McGruder. Contact the others – she's gone too far this time!'

. . . can't pass out. Oh stomm, thought Miller. How long have I been lying here? She looked around her. In the suite the sprinklers were still dripping, indicating they had only just cut out. About five minutes then, thought Miller, auto sprinkler systems stay on for about five minutes.

Two words drifted to the front of her mind: auto-destruct sequence.

'Drokk! I better get out of here!' She tried to prop herself up but both arms gave way underneath her. Instead she kicked at the corpse of Wallis, gradually pushing out through the lift doors into the penthouse suite. At last, they closed and the lift began to descend.

'Thank Grud, thank Grud,' Miller repeated, over and over again.

It was just after the turbo-lift reached the thirtieth floor on its descent that the penthouse suite of the Bet Lynch Twin Towers Hotel exploded, cutting all power to the turbo-lift control shaft. The lift fell the rest of the way, rapidly accelerating towards the ground floor . . .

Extract from the private journal of Judge Laverne Castillo:

Looks like the stomm is hitting the fan. I've just been to deliver a message to the Chief Judge. It seems Dredd discovered the secret testing laboratory for the new Mark IIA Mechanismo robo-judges. Apparently the two Tek-Judges running tests on the robots, Quiggly and Somes, went a bit crazy and tried to kill Dredd. Now Dredd has requested a meeting with the Chief Judge, but she seemed unworried.

She said there was nothing illegal about the testing of the new designs for the robo-judges. She said it had been kept under wraps simply to prevent incidents like the one with Quiggly and Somes, the pair had just foolishly over-reacted. McGruder told me to go ahead and arrange the meeting but she wants it delayed for a few hours, because she's preparing to go on a short tour of some of the Justice Department's deep space colonies, starting with the Tenth Planet, Hestia. She only told me tonight that I would be accompanying her! My first deep space assignment. (Why do I feel such a strong sense of foreboding at what should be the most exciting journey of my life?) In fact, I believe she is simply stalling to allow time for some more 'evidence' of her own to be gathered.

I contacted Sector House 66 and left the message for

Dredd. I also left a message in Judge Hershey's office for her. I suspect this meeting, when it does happen, could endanger the future of the whole Justice system. The Chief Judge is convinced there is a conspiracy against her and I'm beginning to believe her. Not a bad conspiracy, but there is definitely a lot of plotting going on, senior Judges whose only goal is meant to be maintaining the Law are all fighting for the chance to sit in the big chair. Right now, I'm drokking worried.

Genya Berger looked at her son and cried. He floated before her in his massive globe-shaped tank, suspended in green fluid, his eyes transfixed by her, the mother he'd never known.

'I don't know what to say . . .' he murmured into her mind.

'We don't have to say anything – we're together now,' replied Genya. She reached over the balcony rail of the mezzanine floor to touch the side of the tank. 'It's warm!'

'Yes, when I was born they discovered I would die if exposed to open air, because of an allergic mutation in my skin . . . so they put me underwater with a breathing apparatus at first . . . After a few years the Tek-Judges developed this green solution that I can breath, it gives me the air I need without burning my skin, liquid oxygen they call it . . .'

'That monster – what was it I saw?'

Magnus hung his head, ashamed. 'I have special talents, I can do things that normal people can't . . . They forced me to help them create monsters like that, to be used as weapons . . . If I didn't, they said they would take me out of the liquid oxygen and leave me to die . . . I was scared . . .'

Genya was angry. 'They took you away from me, they treat you like some kind of freak, and then they exploit you. Is there no justice?'

'No, I don't think there is!' Whiti Vitaliev stepped out

of the shadows. He didn't notice a red beam of light as he stepped through it.

'My name's Whiti Vitaliev and I'm a reporter for tri-D 27, perhaps you've seen my show? I wonder if you'd like to answer a few questions? Now, I heard you mention something about a monster. I've been investigating a case called the Sector 66 Slasher, perhaps you've heard of it, it's been all over the tri-D broadcasts for days. No? Well, anyway – '

Magnus cut him off. 'The alarm . . . you've set off the alarm . . .'

Elsewhere in the underground complex, alarms were wailing. The leader of the Prometheus Project looked up at a tri-D monitor and saw the two strangers standing in the mezzanine.

'What the drokk? How did they get in there?'

He leapt up from his seat and was about to run from the room when he checked himself. 'No, wait. Now would be the perfect time to test that slave relay unit!' He returned to his desk and strapped the remote control unit to his utility belt, before slipping the goggles over his eyes. Now he could see what the prototype could see, now he could control its movements, now he was the true controller of the Prometheus Project!

'Open the internal door on the centre cage,' he commanded.

the bars slide down into the floor and you step out into a dark chamber. you smell blood and sweat and fear in the air. feasting time . . .

'You must leave, it's too dangerous for you,' Magnus told Genya, then Whiti. 'The project leader has released the monster . . . I cannot control it anymore, please go . . .'

Whiti didn't need to be told twice. He was already running from the chamber, heading back to the secret entrance. But Genya didn't move.

209

'I'm old beyond my years,' she said sadly. 'If I die, then I die – but I want to be near you for as long as I can.'

surge forward and you see the prey. it runs before you but your legs are faster, stronger, they beat down on the floor, sending thunderous jolts down the corridor ahead of you. the prey screams and falls and then you're upon it, tearing at its flesh with your talons, pulling away the garments that cover its tastiest parts. bloodlust surges through you . . .

The leader of the Prometheus Project licked his lips, savouring the thrill of his first kill . . .

Whiti Vitaliev died screaming. Outside the entrance-way, his hover-cam slumped to the ground. When the heartbeat of its owner stopped, so did the remote control bonding device. As Whiti died, so did his camera . . .

Magnus felt Whiti's death cry, no matter how hard he tried to block it out. He looked down at his mother and shook his head.

Genya smelt a foul stench as the creature entered the chamber. She turned to face it, the shimmering beast towering over her. 'Goodbye, my son,' she whispered as the talons slashed down through the air towards her frail body.

'Noooooooooooooooo!' screamed Magnus.

FOURTEEN

Trouble Times Three

Psionic Modem: An exciting new development in the
world of compu-technology is this device which enables a
Psi talent to download material directly from their own
mind into a permanent file. It is hoped the psionic modem
will revolutionise both the recording of historical data and
analysis, thus building up an invaluable archive of the
thoughts and experiences of the great Psis of our time, but
also eventually lead to a link with artificial intelligence
technology, enabling far greater interface between the
human mind and the synthetic consciousness. The inven-
tion of the device is credited to an as yet unnamed Tek-
Judge. Unfortunately, there has only been one recorded
instance of mind and machine coming together to create
this new device, and it was apparently destroyed immediately afterwards . . .

> Extract from *Psi and Science – An Investigation*
> Professor Phillip Marius (revised edition, due for
> publication 2117)

'The top five floors of Bet Lynch Twin Towers Hotel were
destroyed by the series of explosions. The penthouse suite
where we believe Miller was with the She Devils is
completely gone. Right now construction robots are sift-
ing through the rubble, but they aren't holding out much
hope of finding anybody alive from the top half of the
building. Casualties estimated at a little over two
thousand.'

Brighton was updating Dredd on what had happened in
his absence. The acting sector chief interrupted with a

211

question. 'What happened to our roving reporter, the irritating Vitaliev? I notice the media vultures have disappeared from outside . . .'

'So has he. Our tracking device has stopped working. Last position noted was in the fall-out zone of the old North, Sector 333.'

'He can cause someone else some trouble up there. That should end this Sector 66 Slasher hysteria at least,' muttered Dredd, before nodding for Brighton to continue.

'Don Uggi IV has given us six hours to release his father or else he will launch a nuclear warhead at this sector house. We've now got just over two and a half hours until the deadline. Of course, with the She Devils apparently eliminated, we could simply release him and solve the problem,' suggested Brighton.

'The Justice Department doesn't make deals,' grunted Dredd.

'Even if we did release him, there's no guarantee the ape gang wouldn't use the warhead as a threat again. Plus there seems to be a lot of hatred for you personally amongst the apes. They might launch the nuke anyway – regardless of the consequences – just to kill you.'

'Seems to be my week for it,' Dredd grumbled.

'There is another possibility,' ventured Brighton. 'I've been talking to Don Uggi III and he seems quite interested in something I mentioned. I told him about – '

Brighton was cut short by Dredd's tri-D vid-unit which suddenly began projecting into the air above his desk. Masses of data, diagrams and other information scrolled across the holographic image at an incredible speed, Dredd's comp-unit struggling to absorb all the information it was being fed, seemingly from out of thin air.

'What the drokk?' exclaimed Dredd. After a full minute, the machine outputted an info-wafer. Then Dredd held a hand to the side of his head, cocking it slightly to one side, as if listening to something. He looked up at Brighton.

'It seems we have a traitor or two in our midst. You better leave the room while I examine this material.'

Brighton was baffled but thought it best not to raise any objection – Dredd wasn't known to take junior Judges questioning his decisions too well, no matter how odd those decisions might appear.

When Brighton had gone, Dredd examined the wafer's contents on his monitor screen. The wafer was loaded with information about the Prometheus Project, a secret research off-shoot from the 'suspended' Mechanismo programme. The project's aim was to create a viable new bio-weapon that could complement the robo-judges. The creatures produced would be dispensable warriors, but nearly invincible in battle – the perfect cannon fodder in a brutal, costly conflict like the zombie warfare of Judgement Day.

But the methods and means by which the project had been run and tested were at best highly dubious, and at worst a gross breach of the criminal code. The most disturbing aspect was the name of the Judge in charge of the project. Dredd called Brighton back into the office.

'Trouble's coming. We haven't got long before it arrives. What was your idea for dealing with the ape gangs?'

Brighton explained his loose plan, elements of it coming together as he explained it out loud to Dredd. The senior Judge nodded.

'It could work. Pitch it to Judge Hershey at Justice Central, tell her you've got my backing. If she approves, then go ahead with it. Got that?'

'Yes, sir!' Brighton positively beamed with delight.

'Now wipe the grin off your face and get every Judge in the sector house ready for a special briefing – do it!'

The traitor tore off his goggles as Magnus's psychic scream tore through his brain. Clasping the slave relay unit to his side, he began to run through the underground complex, heading for the mezzanine.

He arrived in time to see the creature licking the blood from its claws. All that remained of Genya Berger was a pile of broken bones and torn skin and blood-soaked clothing, thrown to one side in the feeding frenzy of the creature. For the moment, the monster was sated.

The leader smiled at Magnus. 'Friend of yours, was she?'

'She was my mother . . .' replied the mutant with surprising calm.

'Really? How sad,' smirked the leader. 'Well, I'm sorry to say this, Magnus, but you've outlived your usefulness to this project. The slave relay unit is a complete success. Armed with these an operative would be able to control one of our creations from a range of up to three klicks. I believe the field testing is complete now, and I shall be recommending we begin mass production of the prototype within the next month. Maybe even sooner. How does that make you feel, hmm?'

'You're too late . . .' said Magnus.

A flicker of doubt crossed the leader's face. 'What do you mean?'

'I just emptied all the available data on the Prometheus Project out of the compu-net . . . transferred it to an info wafer in a sector house in another part of the city . . .'

'How? Why?' demanded the disbelieving Judge.

'Remember the psionic modem we were trying to develop . . . it works . . . As for why, you're about to kill me anyway . . . Before I die, I wanted to make sure the horror show freak we've created dies with me . . .' said Magnus telepathically, a quiet satisfaction evident in his tones.

'When the Judges discover what you've done here, how many have died so that you can play Grud . . . I don't think you'll have much of a future either . . . Especially considering whom I gave the information too . . . He's hardly a fan of the Mechanismo programme . . . let alone this . . .'

'Dredd!' spat the leader, quite aghast.

'Appropriate, really . . . I could hardly trust anyone else, your friends are too highly placed in the Department . . . The information you want is held in Sector House 66 . . .'

Magnus moved a little closer to his hated enemy, wanting to see the look in his leader's eyes as the whole evil project fell apart.

'Without that info-wafer, you'll never be able to recreate this nightmare, let alone go into mass production . . . You won't dare destroy the wafer, it's your only hope . . . but while Dredd has it, the wafer is the very evidence that will destroy you . . . Don't worry, I've warned them you'll be coming, along with your hideous creation . . .'

The Tek-Judge slipped the goggles back over his head and activated the slave relay unit, sending the monster back to its cage. Then he drew his Lawgiver and aimed at the floating mutant. The first bullet shattered the glasseen globe, which began spewing its green contents out onto the mezzanine floor. The second bullet buried itself deep in Magnus's brain. He died instantly, but the leader of the Prometheus Project kept pumping bullets into the corpse.

Finally, he turned and walked away, holding the slave relay unit in both hands. Despite Magnus's sabotage attempt, the leader still had a trick or three up his sleeve. With this unit, he could control the product of all their hard work. And he also knew something that Magnus didn't, a secret he'd deliberately withheld from the mutant. A deadly secret that could prove decisive in the hours ahead . . .

The man in the Tek-Judge uniform started running for the special hangar at the other end of the research complex. It was time to get the drop-ship out of storage again – he would be needing it for one last trip, one final field test. Thinking about it, perhaps the malignant mutant had done him a favour! Dredd would make a worthy opponent for the creature – the ultimate foe, in fact . . .

* * *

The construction droid tore away at the battered remains of Bet Lynch Twin Towers. The two, titanic peaks had been devastated by the explosion. Now they were a broken relic of their former glory and would have to be torn down completely and rebuilt from scratch.

As the massive metal arms dragged tonne after tonne of twisted metal and rockcrete away, delicate sensors housed in protective casings at the front of the arms kept scanning for any possible lifesigns.

A klaxon wailed and the digging halted immediately. The robot foreman moved in to examine the readings. 'Probably just another warm corpse,' it muttered grumpily, thanks to an esoteric emotive chip someone had once donated to its circuit boards. The droid stepped in front of the massive digging arms and examined the rubble directly ahead, but could see nothing. It was about to call for work to resume when a strange sound emerged from the rubble.

'Huhhh . . .'

The robot's highly sensitive hearing pods twitched, hunting, searching for the slightest murmur.

'Huhhh,' came the noise again, distinctly humanoid too, the droid decided. Listening beyond that, it almost felt it could sense a heartbeat – faint, irregular, but definitely a heartbeat. The robot looked back over its shoulder to the droids behind it.

'Better call a med-wagon, we got a live one here!'

At the ape gang headquarters, the countdown continued: 02.07.38, 02.07.37, 02.07.36, 02.07.35 . . .

'Who?' Hershey was in her office striving to pull together a delegation of senior Judges in time for the meeting with McGruder, but an endless series of calls had only managed to contact half the badges she was after. So taking calls from some unknown young Judge was not high on her list of priorities at that moment.

'Brighton, ma'am. Judge Kevin Brighton. I'm assigned

to Sector House 66. My sector chief, Judge Dredd, suggested I call you,' explained the nervous caller on his vid-phone.

'Dredd, eh? All right, go ahead.'

'We're having problems with a local ape gang. They've got hold of an old nuclear warhead and are threatening to launch it at us.'

'So? Surely that's a local problem.' Hershey's tone did its best to indicate she had much bigger fish to fry.

'Yes, but I've got a possible solution that could prevent both this and similar situations in other sectors in future. But it needs your approval,' added Brighton cautiously, before explaining the idea.

Hershey gave it some quick thought before replying. 'Sounds feasible. When do you need the announcement by?'

'Within the next sixty minutes, if possible. We're running out of – '

'Yes, yes, all right, I'll see to it. Hershey out.' She quickly made a new call, to the media liaison section. 'We need a public announcement made across all the tri-D channels we can muster and we need it within the next 60 minutes! Here's the details . . .'

Deep in the heart of the Halls of Justice, a highly skilled team of Judges monitor all air traffic in the skies of Mega-City One. Considering the proliferation of skysurfers, hover-cars and other flying vehicles, this is a massive job, requiring very sophisticated technology. Automatic systems handle all but seven per cent of the total air traffic, which require human control. That seven per cent alone require nearly 30 Judges to be on station at any time of the day or night.

Among the seven per cent of items handled are unscheduled flights by Justice Department registered vehicles. All department vehicles have an electronic fingerprint beacon, which allows them to be recognised by the vast array of official sensor devices focused on the skies of the Big Meg. It was such a beacon that Tek-Judge Deighan detected on his scope as dusk fell outside.

'Strange,' he muttered to himself. There was nothing unusual about the aircraft, it was a standard Justice Department drop-ship, registered to the Research subdivision. There were dozens of these in the skies all the time. The strange part was it had appeared from over the forbidden fall-out zone to the north of the city, where no such aircraft were permitted to land. Deighan opened a channel.

'Justice Department drop-ship DNE 052, this is Control. What is you destination and purpose of flight?' he asked.

Aboard the drop-ship, the pilot cursed himself for forgetting to activate the 'cloak' that would have masked the flight's presence on the sensors.

'Control, this is DNE 052. We're just returning to Sector 66 after a malfunction forced us down in Sector 333. We were unable to call for assistance, signals jammed by localised radiation blackspot, but we've managed to make running repairs and are returning to base,' he replied, hastily trying to second guess Control. There was a long pause before the reply crackled back.

'Roj that. Don't forget to run full decontam procedures on arrival.'

'That's a Roj. DNE 052 out.'

The pilot waited but there was no come back, Control must have swallowed his story. Good! He plotted in an approach course for Sector 66. He would have to drop his cargo close to the sector house before actually landing in the artificial park close by. Dredd and the rest of the fools there might think they were ready, but he had some surprises waiting for them.

Back in the hold of the drop-ship, something shifted in its cage and snarled. It was hungry again.

Halfway round the world in Pan-Africa, it was early in the morning and Judge Kwame Assengai was furious. He

218

had been dreaming of lions running and wind blowing through the grass and then the green grass had turned into long, flowing black hair, just like the hair of –

That was when the vid-phone rang, jolting him awake. He had activated the screen and done his best to rub the sleep out of his eyes. When the source of the incoming call scrolled up the screen he just groaned. Who was calling from Mega-City One at this time of the night? So the first words out of his lips to the expectant face at the other end of the line were hardly the best of greetings.

'Don't you know what the time is here?' Assengai demanded.

'I-I'm sorry, I know it must be quite late – '

'Quite late? Quite early, you mean! What the hell do you want?'

Judge Kevin Brighton had turned crimson with embarrassment.

'I am sorry, but this is quite urgent. You might remember me, Judge Brighton? I was in Pan-Africa on a Cadet exchange scheme about three years ago. I went on patrol with you in the Congo Development Area.'

Assengai put aside his anger and forced himself to think back. Yes, he did remember Brighton – fresh-faced, friendly, cheerful to a fault. Now it seemed the Cadet was a full Judge.

'Yes, I remember you, Brighton. What do you want?'

'In the Congo Development Area, anyone with enough money can buy land and set up their own community, even their own state – is that still true?' asked the Mega-City One Judge.

'Yes, yes. Why do you ask?'

'Does it matter if those with the money aren't actually human?'

'No. If my boots had enough money, they could buy some land in the CDA!'

'Good! We might be sending you some new settlers,' smiled Brighton. 'Sorry, but I've got to go. We're having a small crisis here – bye!'

'Wait! What new settlers?' asked Assengai but it was too late, his caller had gone. The Pan-African Judge deactivated his vid-phone and rolled back over in bed, snuggling up close to the other occupant.

'Who was on the vid-phone?' asked the bed-fellow sleepily.

'Nobody important. Go back to sleep,' replied Assengai and closed his eyes. He was starting a new mission in the morning and he wanted some more sleep before he had to get up.

Dredd had gathered all the Judges in Sector House 66 together in the briefing room. There were 32, less than half the sector's full complement. The rest were out on patrol and unable to get back in time, or on permanent assignment to other duties, such as Wally Squad members deep undercover. Out of the 32, more than half were not Street Judges, most being drawn from specialist divisions like the Meds, the Teks and the Psis. Some of the others were on permanent station in the sector house because of disabilities which kept them off the streets, such as Symes. Some were tied up with maintaining essential services, such as the monitor Judges in the sector house's Control sub-station.

'Put simply, we're in deep stomm. Symes, would you give them the full briefing?' Dredd turned the meeting over to the night desk Judge, who stepped forward to address the gathered Lawkeepers.

'This sector house is about to be attacked by the creature known as the Sector 66 Slasher. It is not an alien predator as we had been led to believe but in fact a genetically-engineered bio-weapon. As you already know, this monster has killed at least half a dozen citizens, including our former sector chief, Eammon Kozwall.'

That brought a murmur of anger and recognition from the gathering. Symes held a hand for silence before continuing.

'The creature is quite deadly – a killing machine. We

220

know it has the ability to make itself virtually invisible, both visually and by Psi detection. It was attacked on the Wasteland by a perp armed with a department issue Widowmaker 3000 and the perp lost – badly.'

One of the assembled Judges asked the obvious question. 'Why don't we call for back-up?'

Dredd stepped forward. 'We have but it could be hours getting here. There's a full scale block war going on at the moment, spread over three of the adjoining sectors. All local resources are committed to that. Right now, we're on our own. I want barricades at all entrances and infrared nightscopes issued to everyone. From this moment on, nobody gets in or out of this sector house without my personal approval. Move out!'

'Let me see if I'm hearin' ya straight, kid. You're offerin' us a piece of da action – in da Congo?' Downstairs in the Holding Tanks area, Don Uggi III got out of his seat and approached the door of his cell, to get a better look at Brighton's face. 'What kinda crazy business is dis?'

'It's not crazy, it makes perfect sense,' insisted the young Judge, rubbing a hand through his tousled hair. 'Look, before, you were telling me how you only get respect from other apes, right?'

The old Don nodded his agreement, grudgingly.

'You told me how you'd been slaves, turned into talking freaks by humans. When you finally get some control of your lives, the She Devils turn up and slaughter your mother, your aunt and half your lieutenants. Am I right so far?'

'Ya ain't tellin' me nothin' I don't already know, kid!'

'Well, how about dis – I mean this . . . You told me that your ancestors came from Pan-Africa, generations ago, stolen for evil experimentation. I'm offering you a chance to go back there, get away from all this killing and revenge and hatred. Get away from the skinfaces that have made your lives a misery. Go there, buy yourself as much land as you want, set up your own community –

drokk, even your own country, if you want to! What do you say?'

The Don shook his head. 'You Judges will never let us do it!'

'Why not? We can only gain by this. You're as much a thorn in our side as we are in yours. And I've had this offer approved by the top brass at the Department!'

'It's kosher?'

'It's a genuine offer, if that's what you mean, yes.'

The Don rolled the rim of his battered black trilby hat around in his hands. 'Ya forgot somethin' – da money! Where do we get da creds for alla dis?'

Brighton held up a finger. 'Ah! I was wondering when you'd mention that!' He deactivated the electronic lock on the Don's cell and the door slid aside to let the ape out. 'If you'll follow me . . .'

The Don hesitated for a moment, then stepped cautiously outside and followed Brighton out of the confinement area.

Two minutes later, they were allowed out of the motorpool in a hover-pod, the doors sealed shut behind them. Brighton didn't like to leave his fellow Judges at a time like this, but unless his mission succeeded, there might not be a sector house to come back to. Brighton and the Don were the last to leave Sector House 66 before the attack came . . .

To the west of the sector house, the drop-ship hovered close to the ground. Two doors opened beneath the cargo bay and something dropped to the hard rockcrete surface below. Instantly it's shape began to shimmer and disappear, its colouring changing to merge into the surfaces around it. Within a second, the creature was virtually invisible. It crept away through the darkening skedways as night fell on Sector 66 . . .

At the ape gang headquarters, the count-down continued relentlessly on. 01.09.41; 01.09.40; 01.09.39 . . .

* * *

The patient woke up with a start. She tried to sit up but the pain lancing across her body quickly persuaded her against the idea. Instead she opened her eyes to look around herself. The room was clean, white and smelled of disinfectant – she was in a med-unit.

A robo-doc leaned over her, his metal face blank and smooth, but for two gleaming red sensor 'eyes' and a thin, rectangular metal grille for a mouth. Its head tilted to one side as it regarded the patient.

'How do you feel? the mechanoid medic asked.

'Like I've just been run over by an h-wagon. What happened?'

'You're very lucky to be alive. You were pulled out of the wreckage of the Bet Lynch Twin Towers Hotel disaster. Hardly anybody else got out alive. Can you remember anything, your name?'

The patient shook her head. 'I can't seem to remember . . . anything.' She ran bandaged hands over her face. 'A mirror! Have you got a mirror?'

The robo-doc handed her a small, reflecting slate. The patient stared into it, pulling at her features.

'My face – this isn't my face!' she whispered.

'Are you saying someone has altered your face?'

Then she saw the hair and it all came flooding back. The patient looked up at the robo-doc happily.

'I remember now – my name is Lynn Miller, Judge Lynn Miller!'

'You're watching tri-D 23, the only news channel that ain't a snooze channel! My name's Candy O'Hara.'

'And I'm Chip Blake. The headlines: Block War breaks out in Sector 64, 65 and 69, thousands feared dead already. One of Mega-City One's most controversial buildings, the Bet Lynch Twin Towers Hotel, exploded today, killing more than two thousand guests – cause: unknown. And top tri-D fashion consultant, Spiro Welham, forecasts flares will be fashionable again tomorrow, but only between the hours of twelve and two, Candy?'

'Thanks, Chip! Now, back to our main story. The Judges have announced an intriguing new amnesty policy – money for munitions! That's right, the Justice Department has just announced it is offering cash incentives to anyone who turns in either guns or ammo to their local sector house. Among the tariffs mentioned: one cred for every bullet you bring in, twenty creds for a handgun and up to a million creds for anyone with an old nuclear warhead they want to get rid of. But you've got to be quick – the offer expires in fifty-eight minutes time! What do you think of this special offer, Chip?'

'Well Candy, I almost wish I had an old nuclear warhead lying around my conapt, I could do with the extra creds! Now, here's sport with that funny, funny guy, Alan Partrid – '

Tommy 'Gun' Topolinni laughed as he switched off the tri-D monitor in the Don's office. 'Y'hear dat, Don? Dey's offerin' us a million creds to hand in da nuke!'

The new Don didn't find the broadcast so amusing. 'Dis ain't no joke, Tony. I've got a good mind ta launch da nuke now – den we'll see who's laughin', huh?'

'Take da money, kid, it's a good deal!'

The new Don spun round to see who was talking and gasped. His father was standing in the doorway. 'Pa! You escaped!' The young ape loped over and hugged his father warmly. When the embrace was over, Don Uggi III walked into the centre of the room.

'I didn't escape – dey let me go,' he explained.

'Dat's amazin' – and we didn't even hafta fire da nuke!' gasped Tommy. 'Hey, now we's can use it again. What should we ask for dis time? I vote for more power!'

The old Don slapped him across the face. 'Shaddup! Dis ain't no democracy!' He turned to the door and shouted for Brighton to come in. 'Dis here is Judge

Brighton, and he's a good kid. He's gonna give us a million creds in exchange for da nuke.'

His son was puzzled. 'But why do we wanna make a deal with da skinfaces, Papa? We's the power here in da Jungle.'

'Boy, ain't ya been payin' attention?' asked the Don angrily. 'We got our asses kicked by dose lousy dames, we lost half our lieutenants and if we don't give up the nuke, my guess is da Judges will nuke da whole Jungle before they let us use our bomb. Dat right, kid?'

Brighton nodded reluctantly. The old Don loped over to his desk and slipped back into his chair, taking command of the situation. 'But me, I got us a plan. We's gonna start a whole new Ape Nation – in da Congo!'

Dredd held the info-wafer in his gauntlet-clad hand and stared at it. He had been unable to contact Hershey to tell her about the Prometheus Project – she was out, no doubt organising the delegation for the meeting with McGruder at midnight. Dredd's discovery about the continued secret research on the robo-judges would be a valuable weapon in gathering more senior Judges to their side.

A siren wailed throughout the sector house and Symes burst through the door into Dredd's office.

'It's started! Something's trying to burst through the doors down in the motorpool!'

'On my way,' responded Dredd, leaping from his chair as Symes rushed out again. But before leaving his office, Dredd paused for a second to slot the info-wafer into one of the pouches on the utility belt around his waist. If the identity of the Prometheus Project's leader was correct, Dredd wasn't sure who he could trust anymore . . .

FIFTEEN

Kill! Kill! Kill!

Situations of seemingly certain death can bring out the
best and worst in a Judge. At all times, a Judge should
remain calm, ready for any eventually. When it comes to
dispensing Justice on the streets on Mega-City One,
expecting the unexpected comes naturally to a good Judge.
But death, like all inevitabilities, is always a shock.'

Extract from *Dredd's Comportment*
Volume One, 2116 edition

'Sweet Jovus, it's trying to punch through the walls!'
Judge Jimmy Hopper had been assigned to the motorpool
beneath the Sector House 66 for more than ten years, but
he had never seen anything like this. He had lowered the
blast-proof metal doors just a few minutes before when
Brighton had left with the ape gang leader. Now those
same doors were being beaten out of shape by an unseen
assailant.

Hopper took another look at the security scan image of
the ramp outside the door, leading up to ground level. It
was dark outside now but the attacker was invisible, not
even casting a shadow under the spotlights illuminating
the rampway. The seasoned Judge switched the tri-D
monitor's setting to infra-red, and could just see the faint
outline of something lashing at the metal doors before it.

Another mighty blow, and another, and another. The
motorpool resounded to the sound of metal tearing and
shredding, almost as if the doors were screaming. Hopper
stepped back a few paces and levelled his Lawgiver pistol

at the doors, bracing himself for reinforced metal to give way. He had an ugly feeling in the pit of his stomach that a Lawgiver would be as effective against this creature as a munce pie.

Suddenly half a dozen Judges burst through the door behind him and took up positions around the room, all with weapons drawn. Another three had gone to one side and were assembling an array of tubes and power units. Hopper noticed Symes on his immediate left and shouted a question over the cacophony of blows against the motorpool doors.

'What's that?' He jerked his head towards the trio in the corner.

'Sonic blaster the Teks have been working on,' Symes shouted back. 'They think it might take a chunk off that thing outside.'

'I haven't heard them do any testing today,' bellowed Hopper. With the motorpool directly above the Tek labs, the room frequently shook with the sounds and vibrations generated by testing below.

'This is the test!' replied Symes grimly.

'Terrif,' mumbled Hopper.

Then the noise and the blows against the doors stopped.

slice through the metal like paper and you're inside. the smell hits you harder than any of the bullets, the scent of fresh meat and blood and fear. it exhilarates and excites, urging you on. you kill and kill and kill, gorging yourself on sweet, sticky red treats, until you can eat no more. then you wait for the real prey . . .

Dredd was running down a flight of stairs, headed for the motorpool, when the voice crackled over his helmet-com. He paused to listen.

'Where's the info-wafer, Dredd?'

'What info-wafer? Who is this?'

'Don't insult my intelligence, Dredd, you haven't got the time to be playing games. You know who I am; you know what I've been doing in my spare time and you know all about the Prometheus Project. I know you've got an info-wafer with all the data about the project – it's probably in your possession right now. This is a scrambled channel, so only you and I can hear this conversation. Now where's the info-wafer?'

'I've already made a dozen copies,' bluffed Dredd. 'They're already on their way to Chief Judge McGruder and – '

'Impossible. The technology to dupe info transferred by psionic modem doesn't exist yet, because I haven't invented it. Besides, you're hardly on speaking terms with the Chief Judge at the moment, from what I hear. So let's cut the crud, shall we? Where's the wafer?'

'I haven't got it, it's – '

'You just won't learn, will you? And now you're going to have to suffer for your stubbornness. Go to the motorpool – you'll see what I mean.'

Dredd sprinted down the remaining stairs and along the corridor, bursting through the half-open doorway to find himself standing in a pool of blood. Around him were the bodies of ten Judges, torn apart, savagely, callously murdered. Beyond them, stood the shredded motorpool doors, smashed inwards, jags of metal hanging at awkward angles.

Dredd spun round to hear the door close and lock behind him. The door and the walls around it seemed to shimmer and then the creature dropped its chameleon defences, making itself fully visible to Dredd, advancing towards him . . .

'That's right – my beautiful creature is in there with you,' snarled the voice in Dredd's ear. 'And only I can control it. Now – where's the wafer, or do I let the beast feast on your brains before I come and take the wafer away from your dead body myself? Hmmm?'

Dredd threw his Lawgiver to the ground and glanced wildly about the motorpool while he talked in his helmet-com. 'Okay, I've put my weapon down. Now what?'

His eyes lit on the sonic cannon, discarded during the slaughter. A green light winked on its side, indicating readiness for firing. Dredd began edging sideways towards it. The creature shuffled after him, teeth gleaming from inside its open mouth, a long drip of saliva hanging from the jawline, breath hot and fetid assaulting Dredd's nostrils.

'Now place the wafer on the ground in front of you.'

Dredd began reaching into a pouch on his utility belt.

'No tricks!' spat the voice in his ear.

'No tricks,' replied Dredd soothingly. He flipped open one of the pouches and produced the wafer, holding it up in front of the creature's face for it to focus on. (His other hand slipped into another pouch behind his back and gently slid a small object from inside.)

'Good,' smiled the voice. 'Now put the wafer on the floor in front of you.'

Dredd began to bend over, as if placing the wafer on the floor. The creature's head bowed forwards, following his movements. In a flash Dredd flung the frag-grenade into the creature's open jaws and flung himself to one side. A second later the grenade exploded and the creature screamed in agony . . .

you scream as the biofeedback surges through your body, pain upon pain lancing across your nervous system. but you live and the pain drives you on, just makes the killing urge the stronger, knowing your revenge will now be all the sweeter . . .

Dredd looked up and gasped as the smoke cleared. The creature was still standing, now with a gaping hole in its lower jaw but still standing. It focused on the fallen Judge again and began stomping towards him.

Dredd rolled over and grabbed at the sonic cannon. His fingers swiped at thin air . . .

* * *

you're nearly upon the prey now, you leap . . .

Dredd grabbed at the side of the sonic cannon again and nabbed it this time, pulling it closer to him and swinging the barrel round to face the creature that was almost upon him . . .

you open your mouth, ready to bite down on the juicy warm flesh . . .

Dredd jammed the cannon into the creature's mouth and stabbed the firing button. Seconds seemed like hours as the power built up . . .

you bite at metal instead, chomping down on it, desperate to reach the new meat beyond . . .

Then the cannon screamed . . .

The leader of the Prometheus Project tore the goggles off as the sonic cannon fired, desperate to avoid the deadly biofeedback from the sonic cannon. He knew the creature was dead. No matter, he could create a new one, a better one. But he had to have that wafer. He ran down the ramp towards the motorpool.

Dredd opened his eyes and winced. His whole body was bruised and bloody, mostly from the brutal recoil of the sonic cannon against his body. The creature – or what was left of it – was spread across the motorpool walls, floor and ceiling. Dredd coughed and tried to pull himself up into a sitting position against the wall behind him.

'Still alive? How irritating.'

This time the voice came not from Dredd's helmet-com, but from the doorway. A single figure stepped through the shredded main entrance and stood in the centre of the motorpool, light glinting on the frames on his glasses.

'Flint!' spat Dredd venomously.

'At your service,' replied the Tek-Judge, bowing mockingly, but always keeping Dredd covered with a Lawgiver. Flint looked around at the carnage. 'Such a waste. If you'd just given me the info-wafer when I asked, these good Judges would still be alive.'

'Spare me the self-righteousness, punk. Your monstrosity killed them, not me.'

'And you killed it – not very civil,' scolded Flint, mockingly. His face broke into a smile as he saw the forgotten wafer on the floor, lost in Dredd's struggle to reach the sonic cannon. The Tek-Judge reached down and retrieved the precious item, always maintaining his aim at Dredd.

'One question – why kill Kozwall? I know the other slayings were just field tests, it's on the info-wafer, but why Kozwall? You must have known it would lead back to this sector house.'

'True, but I knew I could muddy the waters when the investigation got too close – as I indeed did to you,' smirked Flint. 'As for Kozwall, that was a case of nerves – he was getting too close to discover the nature of my secret research and my superior told me I couldn't reveal my results yet.'

'What superior? Who?' demanded Dredd.

Flint just shook his head. 'Now that would be telling . . .' He was interrupted by the sound of footfalls and hammering against the door leading to the rest of the sector house. 'Looks like I won't have time to fully enjoy killing you myself after all, how sad.'

Flint altered the setting on his Lawgiver and pointed it at Dredd again. 'So here's a little something to remember me by instead,' he announced and fired.

Seconds later the Judges burst into the motorpool, to find Dredd the only one still alive. He lay against one wall, bleeding from a fresh wound in his shoulder, surrounded by carnage.

'Nobody touches anything!' he ordered, pulling himself to his feet. 'I'm going after Flint, he's behind all this.'

'Flint? But you can't go anywhere – what about your wounds?' called out Med-Judge Parris.

'They'll keep,' grimaced Dredd, climbing onto a Lawmaster and gunning the engine into life before roaring out of the motorpool and up the ramp to sked-level.

Ahead of him Flint was running back towards the artificial park three blocks away, back to the drop-ship. Hearing the sound of a Lawmaster approaching, he pulled the slave relay unit from its waist-strap and activated the remote control. 'Seek and destroy – total destruction!' he shouted into the com-unit, before smiling to himself. Even Magnus didn't know about the latest developments on the project . . .

On the drop-ship a hatchway burst open and a shape dropped to the ground, shimmering slightly against the background.

'You just won't give up, will you ?' Flint's voice hissed into Dredd's ears above the roar of the Lawmaster. 'Well, here's something to think about. That bullet I fired into you, it's a homing device. Right now another of my beauties is homing in on you – and there's nothing you can do about it!'

'Spare me the melodrama, creep,' barked back Dredd. Ahead an indistinct shape was running towards him – another of the monsters. The stern-faced Judge activated the voice-response unit of his bike's on-board computer weapons system. 'Cyclops laser!'

A large circle on the front wheel guard of his Lawmaster glowed red, then orange, then white before a laser beam shot out of its centre. The beam caught the oncoming creature square in the chest and threw it backwards. But the monster got up and started running at Dredd again.

'Silicon skin is refracting the beam,' snarled Dredd. 'Bike cannon!' Now twin barrels mounted either side of the front wheel spat round after round at the advancing creature, but these barely slowed it.

'Need to put this thing down,' muttered Dredd. He

thought for a second then began accelerating towards the monster, riding harder and faster towards it. The Lawmaster and monster were on a collision course. At the last possible moment, Dredd flung himself off the bike, curling his body into a tight ball so it rolled along the ground.

The Lawmaster flung itself into the creature, tearing a motorcycle-sized hole in its chest, wheels skidding on the scaly flesh, pinning the monster to the ground. But still the creature's arms and legs and tail and tentacles thrashed about.

Dredd smashed into a rockcrete wall, the impact forcing the breath from his body. He lay there for a few seconds, recovering his wind before looking up at the thrashing mess of metal and monster. The Judge activated his helmet-com.

'Dredd to bike – initiate auto-destruct sequence, sixty seconds to detonation,' he growled, using the wall to pull himself upright.

'Confirm auto-destruct sequence?' asked the bike computer.

'Are-Why-Bee-Zero-One-Alpha,' replied Dredd, already staggering away in the direction from where the creature had come. Logically, that should lead him to Flint and the info-wafer.

'Auto-destruct sequence acknowledged. Auto-destruct in sixty seconds, fifty-nine seconds . . .'

Flint was just climbing into the drop-ship when the night sky was lit up by the Lawmaster exploding. Could Dredd have survived the new prototype's attack? The Tek-Judge shook his head. It wasn't possible, surely. The homing target was as good as a bullet in the head for ensuring the terminal nature of Dredd's existence.

No matter, thought Flint. Even if Dredd did survive, he didn't have a future in the department if what Flint had been told was correct . . . With the info-wafer back in his hands, he could just wait for Dredd to tumble and then reveal his results to the rest of the division. Soon, he would get the recognition he truly deserved.

Flint was so busy congratulating himself as he piloted the drop-ship's take-off, he didn't notice the shadow of someone or something slipping back into the ship through the still-open hatchway.

Dredd lent back against the bulkhead and pulled his boot knife out of its sheath. He unclasped his badge and pulled the main fastener of his bodysuit down to his waist. Painfully, he slipped both shoulders out of the top half of the uniform, revealing a chest half covered in scar tissue from more wounds than he could remember anymore.

Dredd slipped off a gauntlet and stuck it between his teeth as something to bite down on. Then he plunged the knife deep into his injured shoulder, blood spurting from the wound down his chest and onto the floor. He dug and probed around in the wound, finally pulling the knife away, a small bullet-shaped object coming out with it.

The granite-jawed Judge pulled some magni-heal pads from one of his pouches and quickly, methodically applied a field dressing to the shoulder wound. He had already lost a lot of blood and needed to staunch the flow quickly. That done, Dredd pulled his uniform back up and reattached his badge, now speckled with his own blood. He put the boot knife back in its sheath and clasped the homing device in one hand. Lawgiver drawn and ready, he began moving through the drop-ship.

At one point Dredd was just drawing level with a caged enclosure when a set of talons materialised in the air, swiping down at him. He ducked, sprawling to the floor, rapidly scrabbling away from the cage. Another monster! How many prototypes did Flint have at his service?

Dredd made a thorough search of the drop-ship and found two more such enclosures, but both were empty – they had obviously caged the creatures he'd already faced. The Judge returned to the surviving monster's cage and drew a frag grenade from his belt. Pre-setting the timer carefully, he rolled it towards the cage before making his way forwards to the cockpit for a final confrontation with the devious Tek-Judge Flint.

The leader of the Prometheus Project whistled a merry melody quite tunelessly, until he was rudely interrupted by a voice from the hatchway.

'Don't give up the day job.'

Flint whirled round to find himself staring down the barrel of a Lawgiver. 'Dredd!'

'Your killing schemes are almost as bad as your whistling.'

'What happened to the prototype?'

Dredd just shook his head. Through the cockpit window he could see they were just flying into the airspace above the forbidden fall-out zone as the lights of the city disappeared to be replaced by darkness below.

'Returning to base, are we?'

'Yes, I'm going to – '

His words were cut short by an explosion. Immediately red lights began flashing across the drop-ship's control panels. 'Warning! Engine function and stabilisers impaired! Warning!' announced the on-board computer helpfully.

'What have you done?' demanded Flint.

Dredd held up the homing device in his spare hand. 'I've just released your remaining prototype. Right now it's charging up here, searching for this.'

'Are you crazy?! It'll tear us apart trying to get at that device!'

'But I thought you said you could control your creations?' asked Dredd mockingly. His hand flashed out and grabbed Flint by the chin, dragging the Tek-Judge out of the pilot's chair. 'Perhaps, while you're eating your words, you can try swallowing this.'

With that Dredd forced Flint's mouth open and stuffed the homing device down his throat. The Tek-Judge choked on it but involuntarily swallowed, his eyes bulging as he realised what Dredd had done.

235

'No! You [cough] mustn't! It'll [cough, cough] kill me! You've got to help me – '

'You mean like you helped all those who've died for your hideous experiments, just so you could get some glory? Help yourself!' spat Dredd and turned away. He slipped into a side passage as the final prototype surged past him towards the cockpit. When he baled out of the rapidly descending drop-ship he could hear Flint screaming.

Flint was still alive as the prototype burrowed into his chest to claw out the homing device. The Tek-Judge looked mournfully at the info-wafer, housed safely in the bracket on the wall of the cockpit. Outside the window, the ground rushed up towards them . . .

Dredd dropped to the ground and rolled, adding a few more bruises to his night's tally. As he landed the night sky was like bright day for a moment as the drop-ship accelerated into the barren, radioactive ground and exploded in a massive fireball.

The Judge watched the flames fade away on the horizon before activating his helmet-com. 'Dredd to Control, can you receive me?' Silence. 'Dredd to Control, can you receive me?' More silence – the radioactivity was muffling the signal.

'Looks like I'm walking back,' grumbled Dredd.

In the wreckage of the drop-ship, the info-wafer melted away in the searing heat of the explosion. No trace of its data, or the creature spawned by that data remained. The Prometheus Project was over.

SIXTEEN

Mysteries and Mutiny

The Prometheus Project: This was allegedly a special initiative to create a new, controllable bio-weapon to be used in major conflicts. The deaths of more than a dozen Judges in an attack on Sector House 66 were blamed on the project by the acting sector chief at the time, Judge Joe Dredd. He claimed the project was run by Tek-Judge Phillip Flint, funded by the Tek-Division, and that three 'prototypes' were created.

These claims were rejected by the head of Tek Division, Judge Todd Greel. He stated the project was, in fact, the work of a single, unbalanced individual who died in mysterious circumstances. Greel led a special investigation into Dredd's allegations but could find no evidence to back them up or link the project with the so-called Sector 66 Slasher. The Greel Inquiry did find remnants of an animal of some kind at the scene of the sector house incident, but concluded that these remains failed to substantiate Dredd's claims.

In view of revelations in the immediate aftermath of the attack on Sector House 66, no further investigations were made into the matter.

> Extract from a confidential report about
> the Prometheus Project, 2116 AD

'Mechanismo is back and it's here to stay! It's midnight – you're watching tri-D 23. I'm Candy O'Hara – '

' – and I'm Chip Blake.' The smiling face of tri-D 23's top newscaster beamed out at the hover-cameras recording the bulletin. 'That's right! Shock statement from the

Chief Judge's office – as of midnight tonight, robo-judges will once again be patrolling our skedways! Candy?' He turned to look at his co-anchor, a woman with teeth so white the cameras had been fitted with a special filter to cut down on the glare from her gleaming dentures.

'Yes, Chip! The robots, now with redesigned bodyshell and upmoded armament, will initially be deployed in the city's major troublespots, tackling jobs considered too hot for normal Judges to handle!' Candy gave her hair a playful little toss, keeping the cameras on her for as long as possible before handing back to her partner and bitterest rival. Behind her a hologram showed library footage of the carnage caused by the first field tests of the original robo-judges. 'Chip?'

'Thanks, Candy. Tonight the Chief Judge's office stressed there is no possibility of a repetition of the violence and bloodshed which marred the introduction of the Mark I model. We go live to our Justice reporter, Russell Roberts, on the steps of the Grand Hall of Justice. Russell, can you hear us?' asked Chip rhetorically as he swivelled his chair to face a tri-D projection of Russell. A stern-faced visage appeared in the light beam.

'Yes, I can hear you Chip!' replied Russell, holding a hand up to one ear in the time-honoured fashion used by all reporters on-the-spot. In fact Russell had a transceiver surgically implanted in his inner ear so there was little chance he could fail to hear the question, but tri-D 23 liked its reporters to keep up the pretence. Market research showed the gesture to be popular among the demographically-identified sector of the audience the station was currently targeting.

'Russell, I understand you have heard some rumours about the Mechanismo programme, is this true? What information do you have for us at this time?'

'Well, Chip, I understand that certain high-ranking officers within the Justice Department strongly oppose the re-introduction of the robo-judges. A delegation of Senior Judges is believed to be meeting with Chief Judge

McGruder to discuss the Mechanismo programme at this moment, here at the Grand Hall of Justice, as I speak these words to you!'

Now Candy chipped in a question, determined not to be left out of events. 'Russell, I understand Chief Judge McGruder is due to fly out in the morning on a tour of the colony on Hestia, the tenth planet!'

'That's right Candy. The question on everyone's lips now is, who will she leave in charge? I understand that – '

'I'm sorry, Russell, that's all we've got time for!' interrupted Chip. 'Now, sports news! And Mega-City One's top farter, Randy 'Too-Loud' Langstrome, has blown out organisers of next month's invitational event in the Vatican City . . .

'Jovus, Dredd! You look like you've been in a war!' exclaimed Hershey. She and the rest of the delegation had been waiting impatiently for him to arrive in her private office, just down the corridor from the Chief Judge's chambers. Dredd was standing in the doorway, battered and bruised.

'Something like that,' he agreed, before explaining about the Prometheus Project, Flint and the prototypes.

'This is incredible!' gasped Hershey. 'If we can prove that Greel was linked to these experiments, there's no way McGruder can keep the robots on the streets!'

Dredd shook his head. 'We can't prove anything. There's barely enough left of the creature that attacked Sector House 66 to analyse, let alone draw any conclusions. All data on the project was destroyed along with Flint when the drop-ship crashed.'

'But what about the laboratory in the fall-out zone?' asked Hershey.

'I've already had it investigated,' interjected Niles of the SJS. 'Dredd called me and I sent in some Judges. Something was going on, but there's nothing to link it to Greel or McGruder.'

'Well, it doesn't matter. If we can get McGruder to listen to us, then we can force her to have a full inquiry into the project,' decided Hershey.

'That's a big if,' commented Dredd.

Extract from the personal journal of Judge Laverne Castillo:

Something very strange is going on tonight. McGruder's been keeping me outside her chambers in the anteroom, while she talks with Greel. There's someone else in there with them, but I didn't get a chance to see who. I've got time to scrawl these words because I've just seen the Chief Judge's new bodyguards – two robo-judges! They appeared just before midnight, metal giants of gleaming black, menacing, almost disturbing in their appearance. The creepiest touch has to be the fact they've been given names, as if to make them more human! How can you make a machine designed only for killing human?

Even more worryingly, the Chief Judge seems to be looking forward to this big meeting with Dredd and the others. They're coming to try and depose her and she's all smiles and jokes. It's almost as if she doesn't believe it'll happen, as if she's somehow above such trivialities.

Gotta sign off for now, Greel's just relayed an order from the Chief Judge – it's time to bring in the delegation. The meeting is about to begin . . .

'So how do you feel?' Kevin Brighton was visiting Lynn Miller at the med-unit. He didn't like to admit it, but he had a fondness for his superior officer. He was glad she had survived the explosion at Bet Lynch.

'Like a building fell on me,' joked Miller and started laughing, her smile turned into a wince of pain as torn muscles across her stomach cried out in agony. 'Grud, don't make me laugh!' Once the pain had subsided, she was able to speak again. 'How are things in 66?'

'Getting back to normal – whatever that is,' grinned Brighton, ever the optimist. 'With the She Devils gone and the ape gangs buying their own country in the Congo

Development Area, things are gonna be pretty quiet for a while.'

'I doubt it. Some new gang will want to muscle in on the empty turf, you better watch out for that.'

Brighton nodded. 'How long till you'll be back on the block?'

'Two, three days. The robo-docs say the magni-heal pads are doing their job well.'

'Oh, good.' Brighton felt awkward making small-talk, it wasn't something that came naturally to a Street Judge. 'Nice hair colour!'

'Grud, I'd forgotten about that – you should have seen the outfit I was wearing!' recalled Miller. 'I wonder if they'll let me – '

She was interrupted as another Judge burst into the room.

'Have you heard? The meeting with McGruder has just broken up. Dredd's just been arrested! Apparently he's pleaded guilty to perjury, trying to pervert the course of justice and destruction of Department property – McGruder's taking him to Titan today!' gasped the Judge before running out of the room again.

'Holy Stomm!' exclaimed Brighton. 'Hey, wait! What happened – ?' But the messenger was already gone, so he turned back to Miller. 'I forgot to tell you – they've just put a new series of robo-judges on the streets! Do you think Dredd's arrest is something to do with that?'

Miller shook her head. 'Who knows? Grud, if Dredd can go bad, what hope have the rest of us got?'

Brighton had thought of something else. 'You better get well quick. We're going to need a new sector chief for 66!'

'Shock news this hour! Judge Joe Dredd is under arrest! I'm Chip Blake and you're watching tri-D 23! Candy?'

'That's right, Chip. The top story in the news is that Dredd – the city's best-known figure of Law enforcement

241

– earlier today confessed to falsifying evidence on the controversial Mechanismo Programme! Chip?'

'Thanks, Candy. Dredd is on board the spaceship Justice 4, which is due to leave for the tenth planet, Hestia, in just under an hour's time. It is understood Chief Judge McGruder is carrying out an official visit to Hestia but the final destination for the flight is the Judicial penal colony on Titan! A sad end for the city's most feared and revered Lawman!

'We'll be bringing you three reports on this dramatic development within the ranks of the Justice Department, beginning with this overview of the career of the man they called Dredd . . .'

Extract from the personal journal of Judge Laverne Castillo:

I've just got time to write a few words and pack a bag quickly – we fly out for Hestia on Justice 4 in less than an hour. I've been on guard duty, watching over Dredd since his arrest at the meeting with McGruder last night. He hasn't said a word to me since it happened, just sits in a cell beneath the Grand Hall of Justice staring straight ahead of himself. Grud knows what he's thinking about; that face tells you nothing.

The only time he spoke was when Hershey came down to visit him. She arrived about two hours after Dredd's arrest. She didn't have any authorisation to see him, but I let her in anyway. Somehow I feel I let her and Dredd down: I should have warned them what McGruder and Greel had planned.

But then again, Dredd pleaded guilty to the charges, so he must have done something wrong, mustn't he? I left them alone to talk (after making Hershey swear on her Judge's oath not to try anything stupid) while I stood outside and kept watch for anyone coming to check on the prisoner. 'The prisoner' – hardly the words you'd expect to hear describing Judge Dredd. It's all just so strange. If Dredd can break the Law, if the greatest Judge this city has ever produced can be corrupted, what chance have I got, a screw-up with a history of making mistakes? How can I believe in myself if I can't believe in the Law –

and for a lot of Judges, Dredd is the Law. Or at least, he was.

Right now, I just don't know what to believe in.

'How are they treating you? Is everything okay?' asked Hershey but got silence in return from the prisoner. 'Jovus, Dredd, at least speak to me!'

'About what?'

'About this! About this madness! You're under arrest, McGruder's off her rocker and she's leaving Greel in charge of the city while you're gone! He'll have a robo-judge on every corner by the time Justice 4 returns! Don't you care about that, about what happens to yourself?'

'I violated the code, now I've got to pay for that.'

'Well, what about the city? You can't tell me you don't care about the city, you've saved it often enough!' demanded Hershey, raising her voice to try and get through to Dredd.

But he just shook his head. 'It's too late.'

Hershey tried another approach. 'Look, we can get you out of here. I've got dozens of Judges who would die for you, who are willing to – '

'No!'

Hershey turned away, frustration contorting her face. She took a minute to compose herself before speaking again. 'Y'know, this all seems sadly familiar. I remember when I was a final-year Cadet and Cal took over. You were arrested then and going to be sent to Titan, but you escaped and came back to the city to clear your name. Without you, Cal would never have been defeated.'

'That was different,' muttered Dredd.

'Why?'

'I was innocent; Cal framed me for murder. This time, I committed the crime of which I'm accused. Drop it, Hershey. I'm going to Titan to serve my sentence and that's it.'

'But surely there's something we can do?' she persisted, but Dredd had fallen silent again. He wouldn't speak again and after a few minutes, Hershey left, thanking Castillo as she departed.

SJS Judge Eliphas smiled as the news of Dredd's arrest filtered through from the Grand Hall of Justice. So McGruder had got him at last.

'I always knew there was something crooked about Dredd,' muttered Eliphas, as he increased the intensity of the electric shocks being pumped into his prisoner. The unfortunate interrogation subject screamed and screamed and screamed, but to no avail. 'Nobody's that clean.'

Eliphas looked down at his victim. 'Now, let's get started again, shall we? We have evidence linking you to corruption, perjury . . .'

EPILOGUE

From *The Justice Years*, by former Chief Judge McGruder:

The mission to Hestia was a disaster. The colonists had no need for the Mechanismo robo-judge units we were trying to sell them. Indeed, the units began to behave erratically, not following our commands. The trip was cut short and we planned to leave atmosphere and return to Earth, stopping only to drop off the captive Dredd at Titan.

But the flight never left Hestia's stratosphere. Justice 4 was sabotaged (by a Mechanismo unit trying to kill us, it was later discovered) and crash-landed in the Wilderlands of Hestia, thousands of klicks from the nearest help. We were badly concussed and in danger of dying.

It was only the courage and determination of Joe Dredd (whom we put in charge before losing consciousness) and a few of the other Judges – including Laverne Castillo – that saved us from death and another attack by the robo-judge assassin. The survivors of the crash were rescued and we have since made a full recovery.

Ironically, the near-disaster was probably the best thing that could have happened to us. It proved, once and for all, that Dredd was right about the robo-judges, they could not be trusted with human lives. Upon our return to Mega-City One, Dredd was given a full pardon and the Mechanismo programme was shut down forever, all units disassembled.

We resigned, leaving Hershey, Shenker and Niles jointly in charge until a new Chief Judge can be elected. We wonder whom they will vote in as our successor?

'How does it feel to be back on patrol?'

Castillo smiled. 'Strange. I still haven't gotten use to it. After the ordeal on Hestia, it's a relief to be back on familiar territory.'

Psi Judge Karyn nodded. 'I said you'd make it and I was right.' The pair were sitting atop their Lawmaster motorcycles in a watching bay, a bustling overzoom spread out below them.

'You were, thank Grud.' Castillo glanced down at the time display on her bike computer. 'Look, I've gotta go. I'm on patrol with Dredd today.'

'Old Stony Face! Good luck – you'll need it.'

'Thanks.' Castillo gunned her accelerator and pulled out into the ever-flowing stream of traffic. She sent Karyn a final message on her helmet-com.

'See you on the streets!'